LICENSE
TO LIE

LICENSE
TO LIE

Terry Ambrose

Oak Tree Press   Taylorville, IL

Oak Tree Press books may be purchased for educational, business or sales promotional purposes. Contact Publisher for quantity discounts

First Edition, January 2013

ISBN 978-1-61009-051-3
LCCN 2012953601

To my loving wife Kathy. Thank you for your emotional support, your help as my in-house editor, and your love. This one's for you.

Author's Note

I wanted *License to Lie* to feature two main characters, a con artist and a criminologist. Roxy Tanner's world is all about money and taking advantage of others. Skip Cosgrove has dedicated his life to helping others find justice.

If you've read my McKenna Mystery *Photo Finish*, you may see a resemblance between Roxy and the con artist in that book. The resemblance is not accidental and you may even catch references to events you recognize from Roxy's past.

License to Lie lets two characters who look at the world very differently tell the story of how a kidnapping and a $5 million con forced them to wonder, what would happen if you could never trust a soul...even your own?

Terry Ambrose
December 2012

CHAPTER ONE

She said, "I'll probably die with my secret."

I was eight years old when I discovered how badly I wanted to live—and how easy it would be to die. I've lived with that lesson for twenty years. Despite all the cons and scams I've pulled, despite all the lies I've told during those years, I've never revealed that one simple truth. I'll probably die with my secret. Given the life I've chosen, maybe sooner than I'd like.

My mouse hovered over the bank balance number on my computer monitor. I wet my lips and suppressed a giggle. I exaggerated each syllable as I mouthed, "Four mil-lion eight hundred thirty-seven thousand two hundred ninety-eight dollars."

I winked at the monitor. "And fifteen cents."

Rustling noises from the other room drifted in. My secretary getting settled.

"One last investor." The words came out as no more than a breath. Soft as the silk of my favorite blouse.

I nudged the number with my mouse as though I could bump the dollar amount up by sheer force of will. It didn't matter.

I had that last investor on the hook. In about 15 minutes, he'd park himself in the chair opposite my desk. Closing the deal would be easy. A pretty smile. Chitchat like I was interested. Flirt as though I cared. I'd learned a lot in the past twenty years. Especially about how to bury pain.

CHAPTER TWO

He said, "There's plenty of blame to go around."

Skip Cosgrove wore patterned board shorts and a weathered two-tone, blue and gray jacket to cut the chill of Carlsbad's damp morning fog and sea breeze. At lifeguard station 36, he spotted the outline of the Encina Power Plant tower, a spire that rose into the gray mist until it vanished. Skip checked his watch. 7:30 a.m. Calm surf. Few intrepid souls dared brave the dark water's chill on this particular morning.

"Why don't you give them something good today?" he asked the ocean.

The sea gave him no answer. He knew it wouldn't *speak* to him, but he liked talking to it—or her. "Sailors have always thought of you as a woman. Are you?"

Tentacles of ocean laced with kelp erased Skip's footsteps from the sand as he strode along the beach.

"Maybe they're right." He continued, "You can be temperamental."

Another small wave washed across his bare feet. Each morning, those first few splashes felt icy. But after a few, the skin and nerves numbed. "You can't chase me away that easily."

Skip continued his morning routine. He surveyed the swells breaking no more than fifty feet away. One benefit of being self-employed, he thought, no clocks to punch. No one to tell him he couldn't do this. He watched the water. "Not even you."

His cell phone chimed in its holster. Shit. Already? "Cosgrove."

"Skip, can you meet me at nine? Got a client with a missing kid."

"This morning?"

"I know, it's less than two hours, but Paul Nordoff went missing last night and his parents are freaking out."

A large wave washed in, putting Skip calf deep in sixty-two degree water. He shivered. Okay, *that* felt cold. "Wally, you know I hate missing-kid cases. What was that name again?"

"You heard me, Nordoff. The mother's in hysterics, the father blames her for not paying attention to his kid. I need you to probe her brain, find out what she knows. You know, do your thing, man."

Skip pressed the cell phone to his ear and backed up as another large swell rolled in. Wally, always making it sound so easy. Skip was a contract criminologist who also practiced forensic hypnosis. His business was split about half-and-half. Sometimes, he worked for the cops, the rest of the time, for private parties. Lately, business had been slow. He should take Wally's case, but he couldn't guarantee results—he might not find the kid. Wally knew that, but he was a high-profile, overpriced attorney and when his clients asked for something, he made sure they got it. Skip shrugged off his reluctance. If these people had Wally as their attorney, they had bucks. Big bucks.

"There's plenty of blame to go around, isn't there?" said Skip.

"No."

"What's that mean?"

"Like I said, it's complicated."

"Fine. The usual fee?"

"Of course. You'll do it?"

Shit. He felt his blood pressure rising. He needed the cash. And staying in Wally's good graces was crucial to his business. "Yeah. Where do I go?"

He got the address, then disconnected. He could now see the power plant belching steam into the marine layer, almost as though the escaping vapors were the source of the fog hanging low in the sky. Thanks to Wally, he didn't have time to go all the way to his normal turnaround spot. So much for being his own boss.

On the walk back, he contemplated Wally's case. Why did they always blame the mother? Why couldn't the husband bear some of the responsibility for the missing kid? Where had he been? Had he done something to make the kid run away?

Skip hurried back to his ground-floor condo. He rinsed and dried his feet, then entered through the sliding glass door to the living room. It only took a few steps to cross the room. In the kitchen, he poured himself a cup of coffee. He checked his e-mail—three pieces of spam, two ads, and nothing else. He deleted them all and headed for the shower.

Missing-kid cases. They were so depressing. If he got lucky and found the kid, it often uncovered more problems. Hot water pelted his face. The sting became almost unbearable as he muttered into the water, "I hate missing-kid cases."

CHAPTER THREE

She said, "Make the payoff worth the risk."

To normal people, my life wouldn't make much sense. Normal people don't grow up intending to prey on others. They don't strive to become criminals. Deep down I don't think I ever wanted to be a bad person, but to some of us, as the saying goes, shit happens.

I pulled my first con on my mother when I was eight, so I was hardly what you might call a late bloomer. Just like anyone else starting a new job, I had to learn the ropes. Contingency planning. Backups. Game theory. Those were all foreign concepts to me back then. My plan seemed solid enough—sell the fake Rolex my mother tossed in the garbage for spending money. But things got complicated when Mom wanted the watch back. So my first great con almost landed me in the worst possible jam an eight-year-old tomboy could imagine herself in—a princess costume for Halloween.

If only a stranger hadn't taught me how much worse things could get. And no shrink—or any amount of therapy—ever got me past that memory.

I was sitting at the kitchen table enjoying my after-school snack of chocolate chip cookies and milk when Mom stormed across the room, almost ripped the lid off the garbage can, and threw something in. She whirled and faced me.

I froze, a half-eaten cookie in my mouth. My mouth went dry. Had I done something wrong?

"Goddamn piece of shit! It's not even a real Rolex." She left the way she came in—with a red face and steam practically coming out her ears.

At first, I felt relieved because Mom was mad at whatever she'd thrown away, not me. Then, my kid-curiosity kicked in. I was still a bit confused by this whole "goddamn piece of shit" stuff that cropped up every once in a while. Mom and Dad didn't say it that much, but when they did it always seemed to apply to something different. As my stomach settled down, I realized that it would be easy for me to see for myself what a goddamn piece of shit was. How cool, I had an undercover caper. Just like a real spy. I put my half-eaten cookie back on the plate, slipped off my chair, and tiptoed across the room.

I lifted the garbage can lid and peeked in. Oh, gross! Peach slime everywhere. Mom had been canning *again*. But there! Halfway down. In between the peach pits! It was the watch Mom had picked up when my parents made their last trip "south of the border." That was their big, fancy code for Mexico. Why parents used big, fancy code words seemed stupid to me but, more importantly, I now knew what a "goddamn piece of shit" was.

It was the watch. So how had it turned bad? She'd bragged about that watch to all her friends for weeks now. She'd gotten a steal. It was a Rolex. It had real diamonds—a girl's best friend according to Mom. It had a perpetual date thingy that was supposed to tell Mom what she couldn't seem to remember—what day it was. And she'd just *thrown it away*?

I stole a glance at the door. No Mom. Parents think kids are stupid, but the reality is that kids know their parents better than parents know their kids. That means we have the advantage. Our codes are better, too. We keep them simple and quick and use them for important stuff—like when a grownup is around.

Mom would be back in a couple of minutes so I reached in and plucked out the watch. I held it out in front of me. "Yuck," I scrunched up my nose. "You need a bath," I muttered as I slipped over to the sink. "We don't want to get slimy junk on Mom's floor. Or me!" I rinsed off my new possession.

"I'll put you in my tree house," I said. The tree house would be safe. I kept it locked to keep out intruders—like Mom and Dad.

Was the watch broke? I checked the time on the watch against the clock on the wall. They both said 3:27. So what was Mom's problem? I dried off the watch with a dishtowel and shoved it in the front pocket of my jeans.

I made it back to the table just before I heard Mom's footsteps. Right on time, I thought. I took a bite of my cookie and let the sweet mix of sugar and chocolate fill my mouth. Mom marched past me toward the trash. I tried to say something, but crumbs caught in my throat. Mom stood over the can, glaring at it. Suddenly, the cookie didn't taste so good.

Today, I look a lot like my mom did back then. I'm 5'6", have a slim build, long blonde hair, and a nose that everyone refers to as cute. In my book, noses are a big waste. They drip and run, expel germs when we sneeze, and nobody, I mean nobody, has one that looks *that* good. Still, I probably wound up with one of the better ones given how easy it seems to keep men focused on my face while I get them to empty their wallets.

Most people in my business would justifiably scream slander and call one of their attorneys if someone referred to them as a con artist, but the world of investments is full of people better at separating their clients from their money than investing it. The trick is making unsuspecting clients think someone else blew their bundle, not the investor.

I swallowed hard to clear my throat. It amazed me how that single incident had shaped my life. I remembered how Mom opened the trash lid and peered inside as if it were happening before my eyes today.

Mom got a funny look on her face, then glanced in my direction. "Roxy, did you see that watch I just threw away?"

Maybe it was the cookies—all of a sudden they seemed really dry. Like I'd just gotten a mouthful of sand. I gulped down some milk. The scratching in my throat wouldn't go away. Did Mom know how much I hated these types of choices? I could lie and tell her I hadn't seen it—in which case she'd get all cranky when she emptied all that slimy peach junk from the can—holy moly. I was busted. Mom would never trust me again.

"Are you okay, honey?"

Uh, no. I'd only told one lie that I could remember—it wasn't even a good one—and I'd gotten caught. I'd pinky-sworn with Teddy, my favorite bear, to never lie again unless it was really, really big. You know, like an emergency or something. I wasn't about to break that promise when my odds of getting caught were so high. I didn't want to give up my new watch either.

"Mmmm, why?" Lame, but the best I could do on the spot. Mom probably wanted it back and I'd be out a watch.

"I wanted to spit on it."

Wow, she was ticked off. "Mom, why do you hate the watch so much?"

She brushed back the bangs from her face. "Well, honey, it's because someone took advantage of me. He told me the watch was a real Rolex that he found on the street. He said he was selling it to raise food money for his family." Mom lowered her voice and whispered, "And a real Rolex costs thousands, I got this for a few hundred bucks. Besides, I think he stole it and if the police found out I bought it ..." Her eyes shown with fire as her voice trailed off. She glared at the garbage can. "Bastard!" Her face went red. "Sorry, honey. That guy *lied* to me."

What should I do? Grownups call me precocious—I had to go look that one up. It took a long time because I had to find Mom's dictionary, which she'd taken to stashing in her closet. My other problem was that I didn't know how to spell the word. That meant I had to go through almost all the words starting with a P. Once I knew what the word meant, I abused it for about a week until Mom and Dad offered me a deal—no more word, no dishes for one night.

My bargaining skills weren't very good back then, so I took the deal.

I swallowed hard. "You could go to jail because of the watch?"

She forced a smile. "Probably not, honey."

I recognized that fake smile. The last thing I wanted was for her to go to jail. Sure, she said she wasn't worried about it. So why would she look at all those slimy peach pits and peels and whatever else that was in that can? That meant—she *had to* get rid of the watch.

I pulled it from my pocket and held it out, doing my best to be strong for Mom. I felt like I needed a good excuse for digging into the garbage, so I said, "Here it is. When I saw what it was, I thought how perfect it would be for my princess costume at Halloween." I had no intention of spending Halloween in a stupid princess costume, but Mom had been after me for years to give up Darth Vader. Technically, I guess this was a lie, but I think Teddy would agree this was an emergency. We'd have a long talk later to sort this whole thing out.

I knew I was in trouble when she got all teary. Jeez, Mom.

"Oh, Roxy, you're going to be a princess at Halloween?"

Uh—*no*. This wasn't going right. Now what? "I was gonna surprise you."

She tilted her head to one side and got that big mushy-eyed look she always got when I did something really good. I squirmed in my seat as she crossed the room. Even the safety pin I used to pin the key for my tree house lock onto my jeans dug into my skin. I was trapped and sure that she was going to smother me in kisses—and take the watch away.

She wrapped her arms around me like an octopus. "I'm so happy you want to be a princess. I was a princess when I was your age! Oh, you know what, you keep that watch. It's a fake—a piece of costume jewelry—you use it for your costume. That seems perfect to me."

She left the room, that silly smile still on her face. With her out of the way, I started thinking about what I'd done. *A princess costume?*

I mumbled, "Teddy, we need to talk."

But I didn't need to talk. I knew what I needed to do. Ditch the Rolex. Maybe Mom was happy letting me have it, but what if it really was stolen? Even if it was a fake, I had to get rid of the evidence so the cops couldn't—would they take her away?

Maybe the watch fit Mom's wrist, but it was huge in my hands. What was I gonna do? No way I could let the cops come after her. I turned the watch over in my hands again. It gleamed in the sunshine streaming through the window. It was so pretty. And hot. The stupid watch could send Mom to jail. But I could stop that.

Two days later, I put on a pair of raggedy jeans and a T-shirt and rode my bike the few blocks to downtown. Using my best woe-is-me attitude, I approached a man in a fancy suit about two blocks from the courthouse...

I straightened up in my chair and wiped a tear from my cheek. That man ruined my life. My hatred for him drove me to where I am today. My mantra became simple. If you're going to take chances, make the payoff worth the risk. That's part of the reason I go after clients with lots of money. If I'm going to do jail time, something I've never done, or have some goon beat the crap out of me—got saved on that one thanks to a "superhero" who, I guarantee, didn't regret his efforts—I might as well get paid for it. My payoff today? A quarter of a million bucks.

My "clients" were the greedy people. A shrink would probably tell me they were symbols for the man I wanted to kill. Every time I took them for money, I was getting revenge. They were money-grubbing bastards with no scruples and would eventually get what they deserved—a big fat zero.

I wiped away another tear as it dribbled down my cheek. The money couldn't make the pain, the terror I'd felt as a child, go away. I could never play Pin the Tail on the Donkey or any of those other childhood games where you get blindfolded—not after that man. I leaned back and put a couple of drops in each eye to clear the red. Whenever the memories came back, this little bottle became my drug of choice. No red eyes—no suspicion that something might be wrong.

I mentally shoved the memories away. In about ten minutes, Sonny Panaman would walk through the door and put me over my goal. He was going to hand over a quarter of a million from his trust fund for me to invest. Maybe it wouldn't erase the past, but it sure as hell would secure my future.

CHAPTER FOUR

He said, "What are you hiding?"

Skip pulled into the Nordoffs' driveway just before 9:00 a.m. Wisps of fog hung low in the sky like a fleet of ghostly Chinese junks descending on a waiting harbor. He recognized Wally's black Lexus in the brick-lined circular drive, which occupied a space adjacent to the front entrance of the house. Skip knew from walking the beach that the homes in this area were as close together as a string of birds on their favorite power line.

Skip parked his Porsche behind the Lexus. He'd barely gotten out of the car when the Nordoff's front door opened. Wally. Typical. One briefing coming up. The other man glanced over his shoulder before closing the door and shrugged as if trying to shake off a chill. The tension in his voice—though he seemed to be trying to mask it—filled the air about them. "'87 Porsche 911. Mint condition. Full leather. You just keep that looking so pristine."

"If it wasn't for my Uncle Fred, I'd be driving some beater."

Wally raised an eyebrow. "Every time I see it, I get jealous. If you ever want to sell, let me know. How much was your take in your uncle's estate, anyway?"

Skip ignored the question. He knew Wally wasn't interested in how much money he'd gotten from the estate though he did seem to be fascinated by the Porsche—or perhaps just the idea of owning the Porsche—which had become Skip's most prized possession. "My uncle was the only owner and I'm going to maintain that tradition. I'm keeping it until one of us dies."

"You or the car?"

"Me or the car." Skip waited. The discussion had become a ritual.

A prelude to his briefing. And during that briefing, Skip always wondered how far the lawyer would go for a client.

Wally's eyes defocused as he seemed to ponder a dark secret or dilemma. "Let's talk for a minute."

Skip had never seen Wally so distracted. "Big, huh?"

"Powder keg. The guy wants you to hypnotize the wife and ask her what happened to the kid. The wife says she doesn't want anything to do with that. You gotta break the logjam, buddy."

Skip leaned his head forward, then from side to side to loosen his neck muscles. Whether he trusted Wally or not, the two had become friends. And Wally knew the delicate balance Skip had to maintain to get results. "I can't do anything if she doesn't want to be hypnotized."

Wally waved his hands in front of his chest. "I know, I know. But maybe you could talk her into it. Full-on sales job."

"I don't—"

"Bullshit. You can be the most persuasive son of a bitch I've ever met—when you want to be. We need to see if she really wants to find the kid. This whole situation's bizarre. Let's go."

Skip grabbed Wally's arm. "What's the deal with the kid?"

"Paul Nordoff. Eleven years old, diagnosed with one of those designer disorders the docs like so much. Whatever happened to kids just being kids?" Wally turned and strode toward the house.

Skip caught up to Wally just inside the front door. "Holy shit, this entry's almost as big as my living room."

His friend glanced around the room, then shrugged. "Yeah. Place is huge."

"What happened here?" Skip pointed to a hole in the drywall just a few feet inside the doorway.

"Herman tells me they had a couch delivered yesterday and the delivery guys lost control. You know how those guys are. They don't give a crap about anything."

Skip nodded as if he knew about movers or delivery guys. The last time he'd bought furniture, it hadn't been new and he'd borrowed a friend and a pickup to schlep the furniture. The rich could afford delivery charges. People like Skip schlepped.

They made their way through the living room. The floors, a dark hardwood, gleamed. The lowest part of the ceiling, a corner where a ficus tree filled the space with greenery, was about ten feet high; the rest was probably thirteen. The back wall of the house faced the beach and was lined with windows that stretched from the floor to about a foot below the ceiling.

As he passed an overstuffed black leather couch, Skip pointed at it. "That the couch?"

Wally's eyebrows knitted together.

"The one that got delivered yesterday. Is that the couch?"

"Didn't ask, man. Don't know." Wally turned away and continued out onto the back deck.

Skip nodded and muttered under his breath. "Of course." How far *would* Wally go? Envy encroached on Skip's thoughts as the panoramic ocean view unfolded before him. The fleet of ghostly fog ships was dissipating as the sun took control of the day. Before long, only a handful of the largest would remain to ride air currents back out to sea. At dusk, the fleet would return in full force.

Skip had seen these homes from the beach. He'd never been in one and didn't know much about multimillion-dollar beach houses on the coast, other than they seemed to have decks on every floor. Visitors entered the Nordoffs' house as he had, on the street level. He guessed that all of the bedrooms were on lower floors with equally impressive ocean views.

A man in a blue polo shirt with a small insignia on the left breast and freshly pressed khaki slacks stood on the deck. He was short and stocky and his hairline had retreated halfway back on his scalp. A shock of graying chest hair peeked through the open slit of the polo shirt. He wore leather deck shoes. No socks.

Wally made the introductions. "Herman Nordoff, this is Skip Cosgrove. Skip, Herman."

Nordoff glared at him. The man had an intensity he had seldom seen. Skip extended his hand, which Nordoff gripped with equal ferocity. He held Nordoff's gaze as he returned the pressure of the man's grip—a grip that telegraphed a wealth of information in two heartbeats—vice-like hold, no up-and-down movement, just solid pressure.

Skip knew immediately that Nordoff was a controller, the kind of man who bent everyone to his will. In a dog pack, he'd be the alpha dog or would die trying. He was willing to use his strength to overpower and crush those around him. He probably worked out, was disciplined, and didn't take crap from anyone. Skip glanced at Wally for a split second and got a nod in return. It was the reason he and Wally *had* become friends. Instant understanding. He held Nordoff's gaze until the other man relaxed his grip.

"Can tell a lot about a man from his handshake," Nordoff said.

"Indeed." Skip's hand throbbed. It wasn't anything he wouldn't get over in a few minutes, but he wasn't about to let Nordoff see even temporary discomfort. "Nice to meet you, Herman."

Nordoff's cheek twitched and his jaw tightened almost imperceptibly.

Skip read the body language. He catalogued the response. He analyzed Nordoff's reaction with the detached demeanor of the seasoned investigator—a question forming in his mind. He kept the question to himself, but it hung in the air between them. *What are you hiding, Herman Nordoff?*

CHAPTER FIVE

She said, "Goddamn piece of shit."

Sonny Panaman. He'd been on my hit list for months. My intent was to convince him that his "investment" would get a guaranteed return of ten percent with likely returns in the neighborhood of fifty. I had two things going for me. One, Sonny had never earned a dollar in his life—he was filthy rich thanks to daddy's good fortune. Second, my investment advice was exactly what he wanted to hear.

A movement to my right caught my attention. My secretary, who detests the term and prefers to be called "Office Manager," leaned against the doorjamb. Stella Robbins has been with me since nearly the beginning of this operation. She has the sweet exterior of a southern belle, the work ethic of the chronically unemployed, and the business acumen of the doorjamb she was using as a back support.

"Hey, Stella, is he here?"

"You look deep in thought."

I shook my head. I'd go back to sharing secrets with my teddy bear before I'd trust Stella with anything other than my lunch order. Stella had been unemployed when I found her and would likely have stayed that way for the rest of her natural life—which, by the way, may be the only thing about Stella that is still natural. I've paid her well enough that she's had a boob job and a tummy tuck and she's got plans for liposuction in places that, even if you paid me, I'd refuse. She's also had her hair dyed, her brows lasered and God knows what else. I'd have been saving the cash for a rainy day. In Stella's case, she saw these expenses as an investment in her quest for the perfect husband. Rich.

I set my jaw. "What's up?"

"Your mom's on hold."

Stella was wearing a navy twisted-mini-dress and matching plat-forms. I must confess that I have a huge weakness when it comes to expensive evening wear, but for work I try to keep my clothing expenses in the "practical" arena.

Stella must have caught me eying the dress. She glanced down. "Think Sonny will like it?"

A catty little calculator began running in my head and told me that the skin-to-material ratio was somewhere in the 60-40 range. Damn, she looked good. Standing, the hemline was just below her ass. Sitting, she'd just better not sneeze. "If that doesn't get Sonny worked up, he's gay." I picked up the phone. "Hey, what's up?"

"It's your father, Roxy. He's been out drinking again."

I checked the time. It was *nine freaking thirty in the morning*. The news helped confirm my worst fears. If anyone was smart enough to figure out my business plan, it was my dad. He ran a title company until about a year ago. That's when he retired and started asking me questions. I'd been able to deflect his Q&A for a while, but eventually he'd grown suspicious despite my continual recitation of the mantra, "No, Dad, I wouldn't do anything illegal. It's a complicated business plan." Lately, I'd become concerned that he'd figured things out.

I asked, "Where is he now?"

There was a long pause. "I don't know. He spent two hours on the computer this morning and got into a hideous mood. When I asked what was bothering him, he got all pissy. Then he pulled out his flask—"

"He what? I thought you got rid of that. I thought—"

"He told me he'd thrown it away! Men and their stupid little props."

"When did this start?"

"He's been doing it a lot lately."

"Mom, how long? How long has this been going on?"

"Maybe two months."

I closed my eyes to block out the world. Shit. That was the last time he'd asked me about the business. The fact that my parents would be disgraced when I disappeared with five million in other people's money weighed heavily on me, but some things just couldn't be helped.

Stella was back at the door flanked by Sonny Panaman. Sonny stood within breathing distance of Stella, who leaned slightly in his direction. She might be dumb, but the girl had her Masters in Flirtation.

Stella turned on the charm. "Sonny's here." She turned and put her hand on his chest. "Lunch, then?"

He smiled sheepishly and nodded. His eyes popped as he watched Stella sway away. I wondered how much she'd "invested" in the dress.

"Mom, I've got to go. I've got a client right now, but I'll call you back once we're done. Sit tight." I cradled the phone and gestured toward one of the chairs in front of my solid oak desk, which, like everything else in this office except me, of course, was rented. Even the artwork on the walls fit that category. Good replicas, but fakes, nonetheless. And easy to forget when I walked out the door that last time. I stood to greet Sonny.

The beauty of being a woman in this business is that men expect to be swindled by other men, not a blonde in a short skirt and high heels. The plan, simple as it was, involved a real-life venture capital offering from the East Coast. Working in the shadows of a real offering gave my company credibility.

In the past few months we'd taken in just under five million bucks. A substantial retirement fund, true, but my goal was a minimum of five million. You never know when that last little bit might come in handy. I figured that with Sonny's contribution, I could even give Stella a little bonus on my way out the door.

We shook hands and Sonny whispered, "Sorry about that, I kinda got roped into lunch."

"Hey, it's not a problem for me. If you two like each other, just invite me to the wedding." Not that I'd be around for it. My plans included a quick exit to a warm beach in the Caribbean.

I'd quickly learned that acting like his big sister seemed to put me on the right path with Sonny. I'd gotten tired of the drill almost immediately, but had to keep up the charade—for now. Time for some chitchat about his parents. "So, how are Mom and Dad?"

He raised his right hand and held it out flat, fingers splayed, then rocked his hand from side to side. "Mom's busy arranging some big society thing, Dad's busy making money and playing golf. They see each other for meals." He laughed. "When it suits them, which isn't this week."

"I hear you on that one. Raising parents can be a trial." I wasn't about to go into my troubles. Not with Sonny. Not with anyone for that matter. I held eye contact. "My grandma wants a family barbecue for her 75th. Everyone is going to be there—cousins, uncles, aunts—it'll get really obnoxious. We call grandma Crazy Lacy because she likes to wear miniskirts and go clubbing with her sixty-something boyfriend."

Sonny's eyes lit up. "Sounds like fun. More than this society thing."

I nodded. "My grandma's fun." And she was, but her name wasn't Lacy and she didn't go clubbing, though the boyfriend part was close to true.

"You ever go with her?"

"What?" It took me a second to realize what he was asking. I shook my head. "No."

"What do you like to do? In your off time, I mean?"

Oh my God! Was he hitting on me? This SOB had just been tugging on his pants over Stella and now he was *working me*? For some reason, I couldn't bring myself to flirt with this worm. "I'm kind of a homebody—very boring. Anyway, let's get this wrapped up, shall we? You brought the check?"

Sonny loosened his collar. My people-radar went off. That wasn't a good gesture.

"Uh, not exactly," he said.

I forced a smile. "What's 'not exactly,' Sonny? Is there a problem?" After all the time I'd spent working this son of a bitch, making nice like his big sister, he'd better not flake out on me.

He shook his head. "Dad kind of, uh, well, he—"

"He locked down your trust account."

There went the finger in the collar again. "Uh, yeah. He thinks I've been spending too much money lately."

It was all I could do to keep from smacking him on the side of the head. "I thought we talked about this early on. You were going to start investing and slow down on the spending. You knew your dad was watching. Why did—"

"It just happened!" He glanced over his shoulder and whispered. "I, um, bought a new car."

A river of anger raged through my head. I'd spent hours with Sonny, prepping him, coaxing him, explaining the value of investments, especially those with a high return. I didn't want to know, but I had to ask. "What kind?"

His face brightened as though he'd just gotten a new toy at Christmas. "Maserati Quattroporte Sport GT S. Roxy, it's *so* sweet. 440 horsepower. It'll do over 170—"

"How much?" This idiot had spent *my money* on a goddamn car?

Sonny grimaced. "How much? You mean, how much did it cost?"

"How much did you spend, Sonny?" I felt like his mother. I'd practically spilled blood to keep this from happening. I knew why his dad had locked down the trust fund. Greedy little bastard. In my family, he'd have had to get a *job*.

"Around a hundred and fifty. You want to go for a ride?" He raised his eyebrows a couple of times and gave me a flirtatious smile. "I could pick you up for dinner."

My anger began to subside as another emotion crept in—irritation. Sonny was like a mosquito buzzing your ear in the middle of the night. "You just made lunch plans with my secretary."

"It's just lunch," he whispered. "Besides, I told you, I got roped into that. She, like, threw herself at me."

I'm a helluva poker player and had learned a long time ago that taking someone's money hurt them far worse than any amount of bitching and moaning. I never insult people unless I've got a reason or they've relegated themselves to the "worthless, never again" category, which was where Sonny belonged. I wanted to swat this little mosquito. He couldn't write a check big enough to make him worth the effort. "No dinner, Sonny. You need to get it together. Your dad's right, you're out of control."

I stood and held out my hand. Punching him in the nose struck me as the more appropriate action, but I wasn't an eight-year-old tomboy anymore.

Sonny rose from his chair, a weird, confused look on his face. Apparently, he'd never been kicked out of an office.

I shook his hand. "Call me when you get it together and Dad releases your trust fund. Maybe I'll be able to get you into this deal then."

He held out his hand, his grip was limp and damp. "Uh, Roxy—"

"Sorry, Sonny, but now I have to start making some calls. I've got to find a new client who's got $250,000."

"What about my dad?"

I'd considered going after Bruno Panaman in the beginning, but the guy was a brilliant businessman. Sonny had been an easy mark because his business acumen was on a par with Stella's and he suffered from a "you've got to believe" syndrome. Not so with the old man. Selling him would be like walking a tightrope, not a task I was sure I wanted to tackle.

"What about him?"

Sonny winked. "I've already talked to him. He's willing to consider an investment."

I eyed him. "You told your dad about this."

"Well, yeah. He always likes to know how I'm spending money."

"And you didn't tell him about the car?"

He squinted at me like a scolded child. "Guess that's where I got into trouble. But he's interested. At least, I think he is."

Thanks to Sonny, I was starting over. I had a couple of referrals, but this might be worth checking out. "Find out when I can meet with him."

Sonny nodded. He stuck both hands in his pockets and got his weasel-faced look that said he was going to ask a question. "I guess dinner's out?"

My glare gave him his answer. He nodded and made his way out the door, then waved at Stella as he left. A few seconds later she was at my door.

"What'd you do to him?"

I shook my head. "It's not what I did. He spent the money he was going to invest on a new car."

Stella's smile went into overdrive. "Really?"

I suddenly realized who I was talking to. Stella's financial investments involved doctors and surgical procedures. I waved her away. "I've got to make some calls."

Stella nodded, did an about face and returned to her desk with a dreamy look on her face. They were a pair, a perfect pair. With me pissed at him, I hoped Sonny would stay focused on Stella. And that he'd help me get his dad to invest. Otherwise, I'd be calling Sonny what he should be called, a goddamn piece of shit.

CHAPTER SIX

He said, "That attitude will get you nowhere."

Nordoff's anger seemed to envelop the deck in a dark shroud of tension. A movement to Skip's right distracted him before he could decide if he should walk away or tough this one out.

"This is my wife, Mariane," said Nordoff.

Mariane Nordoff was small, blonde, and had a pasty-white complexion. She winced as she stood. Her shoulder length hair was disheveled, her pale gray eyes dull. She cradled her right forearm, which was in a cast, then lowered it to her side as she approached. She extended her left hand in greeting. Her handshake was the opposite of Nordoff's. Instead of firm, hers was limp. Rather than hard, hers felt lifeless. It all seemed to match her worried appearance. "Mr. Cosgrove," she said.

Skip placed his other hand over hers and squeezed gently. "I'm sorry about your son. Call me Skip, please."

She nodded, "I'm worried about him."

Skip noticed the creases lining her temples deepen. He wondered if the redness in her eyes was from lack of sleep—or crying? Mariane Nordoff didn't look like the kind of woman who was used to hard times. She lived in a well-to-do neighborhood and probably socialized with others who also had money. Other than those few little worry lines, her skin was smooth. Her clothing, though impeccably tasteful, was not ostentatious. No, Skip surmised that life had been good to Mariane Nordoff—at least until now.

"Skip, the Nordoffs want you to help find their son," said Wally. "When they got up this morning, Paul's room was empty. Bed hadn't been slept in. We think he snuck out last night."

It was the hesitation in Wally's voice that made Skip suspicious. "Have you reported this to the police?"

Nordoff's eyes darted upward. "I don't see why we need the police in this." His words came out fast and in a short burst. "That's why you're here."

Skip glanced again at the cast on Mariane Nordoff's arm. He realized now that her ashen complexion might be due to physical pain in addition to the emotional strain she was under. And what about the other warning signs? That faint bruise on the left side of her neck— was it on the way in or out? That damage to the drywall in the entryway. Had there been a couch delivered yesterday or was Mariane Nordoff the victim of domestic abuse? Skip stared straight into Nordoff's eyes. "Why don't you want the police involved?"

Nordoff held Skip's gaze. "That's my business. Not yours."

"If you want me to help find your son, it's absolutely my business."

Nordoff turned to Wally. "Look, you said he'd cooperate. Find me someone else." He started to turn away.

His wife reached out and took her husband's arm. "Herman? Please? I'm sure Mr. Cosgrove will be discreet. We have to find Paul."

As Skip watched the interaction, he immediately recognized the communication disconnect between Nordoff and his wife. Nordoff thought of things in images. He spoke fast. His words conveyed the pictures in his mind. She, on the other hand, was more in touch with her feelings. She spoke slowly and wanted harmony. Rapport would be her primary concern. Nordoff wasn't bothered by trivial details like other peoples' emotions.

Nordoff glared at his wife. His face reddened and Skip could almost feel the anger boiling beneath Nordoff's skin.

"Herman, he's the best," said Wally. "He'll find Paul."

Mariane faced Skip, her eyes brimmed with moisture. "Please, Mr. Cosgrove, you have to help us."

"I don't take cases where I don't have access to all the information." Inwardly, Skip knew he'd take the case anyway—for her sake. He knew what would happen to this frail woman if he didn't. To be sure, he'd check the public records. That would be easy enough. If Nordoff had abused his wife in the past, there would be a record. He could find that information with just a little digging.

Wally's jaw muscles tensed. "Skip, look, the Nordoffs have their reasons for not wanting to involve the police. It's not something we can discuss. Those reasons have no bearing on Paul's disappearance." He repeated his recommendation to Nordoff. "He is the best."

Nordoff balled his fists and glared at Skip with fury.

Skip wasn't about to let himself be intimidated by a client who hadn't even hired him. "Herman, that attitude will get you nowhere. Wally, I don't know that this is a good fit. I'm sympathetic, but if Mr. Nordoff is going to stonewall me, I won't be able to do my job. I want to know what I'm not being told." He pointed at Mariane Nordoff's neck. "I want to know where those bruises came from. And what's the real story with the hole in the wall in the front entry?"

Mariane Nordoff raised her hand to the bruise on her neck.

Wally's face paled to the color of the sand on the beach three stories below. Beads of perspiration formed on his forehead. "I assure you, there's no relation."

"You see, there's the problem," said Skip. "I'm not sure you know, Wally. I don't think you'd ask. That's what I don't like about attorneys. They don't care about the truth. But that's what drives me. Maybe it's all innocent. Or maybe there's some dirty little secret that caused the boy to run away. I won't work for clients who have secrets."

Nordoff turned away and gripped the deck railing, his back to Skip.

Mariane Nordoff moved closer. The worry lines on her face deepened. She wiped at her cheek, though there was no tear there. "Paul is ... troubled. He's only eleven. He's run away before, but always ended up staying overnight with some friends who live a few blocks away. We always knew where he was because they'd call us."

Skip noticed that Nordoff now faced them. Nordoff watched his wife with narrowed eyes and his arms crossed over his chest. Wally backed away a couple of feet and licked his lips as if wondering what to do next.

Skip reached out and laid a hand on Mariane Nordoff's shoulder. "Go on."

She took a deep breath. "Paul was in a fight yesterday at school with a couple of other boys. Herman left work early and met with the principal. He picked up Paul and brought him home, then made him go to his room. Herman had to go back to work for a couple of hours. Mr. Cosgrove, Herman's never laid a hand on me or Paul. It was Paul who broke my arm, not Herman. And it was Paul who put these bruises on my neck the last time he ran away. Mr. Cosgrove, he tried to strangle me."

CHAPTER SEVEN

She said, "We're screwed."

I should have squashed the worm when I had the chance. Now Sonny's dallying was going to cost me more time. I'd been meeting with him almost every week for a couple of months and, in the end, what had he done? He'd blown the money on a car. With his track record, I'd probably hear from him about a meeting with his dad when hell froze over. So when Stella poked her head into my office, her news was the last thing I expected.

"Sonny's on the phone for you. He sounds pretty upbeat."

What had he done, bought another car on the way home? "Sonny?"

"Hey, Roxy. My dad's agreed to meet with you this afternoon. Would 3:00 p.m. work for you?"

I was so shocked that Sonny had actually done something other than act like a spoiled playboy that I didn't know what to say. "Sure." Why I thanked him after that can only be attributed to Mom's obsession with turning me into a little lady when I was still hanging out in my treehouse. I failed Ethics, but at least I passed Manners.

If Sonny's recommendation got me in the door and helped me convince his dad to invest, I'd be grateful—so grateful that I might *not* mention it since the elder Panaman would be pissed at Sonny once he learned he'd been fleeced.

At lunch, I made a quick trip to one of my favorite haunts for an outdoor lunch of fish tacos. The restaurant is in a mostly residential section of Carlsbad on Harding Street, but the ambience always gets me. I'm a sucker for outdoor dining and this place has a patio enclosed by a white-washed pony wall out front and is filled with colorful umbrella tables. The food is also good, so I keep going back. Today, because of this afternoon's meeting with Bruno Panaman, I opted for takeout back at my desk where I could rehearse my presentation. I had the material down cold, but thankfully the tacos were still warm—okay, lukewarm—by the time I got to them. When I finished lunch, it was time to deal with the next most pressing issue, my dad.

I dialed the house.

"Richard?"

"No, Mom. It's me."

I could envision her biting her upper lip. "Sorry—"

"I'm on my way. We'll find him, Mom. I'm sure of it." Was I really?

I hopped in my pukey beige Corolla and drove to the house. For now, this nondescript, but reliable, vehicle helped me keep a low profile. Once I pulled the plug on this scam and walked away with the five mil, I might want to treat myself to a new car. More likely, it would be a sunny beach where my bikini would be purely optional and reserved for dress-up occasions only.

My parents live in the hills up behind Carlsbad. Their street is reminiscent of the town when things were more rural. No sidewalks, still some big trees, mostly older homes. The house, which is on the west side of the street, has distant ocean views from the back yard. It has three bedrooms, two baths, and a killer back patio with an arbor that's ideal for sitting out at sunset on a summer afternoon. The kitchen faces the street, and that's where I spotted Mom. She was in cleaning mode, which is where she ends up when the worry bug bites. Unfortunately, I hadn't inherited the cleaning gene. Still, I have to admit I've gotten pretty good at picking a maid service. Mom calls that an extravagance. I call it hygiene-survival skills.

Mom gave me a halfhearted wave as I got out of the car and met me at the front door. She wrapped me in her arms and we both held the tight embrace, perhaps to help us remember that we were in this together. I was surprised at how alone I felt when she let go.

"Have you heard anything?" she said.

I opened my mouth, but couldn't bring myself to say the word. I shook my head instead.

We walked, arm-in-arm, back to the living room. As expected, the place was spotless. Mom had been busy. She sat on one end of the couch and patted the empty space next to her. "Where could he be, Roxy?"

"Have you tried his cell?"

"He left it here."

Dad never went anywhere without his cell phone. "Where's he been hanging out lately?"

She shook her head. "You know your father. He doesn't 'hang out.' He's become addicted to that damn computer ever since he sold the business."

Dad had started with a local title company in LA right out of college. The detail work had been right up his alley and he went from clerk to title examiner to vice president in a short period of time. A few years later, he left LA to start his own company in Carlsbad. He recently sold the company to one of the behemoths that now dominate the field, but would never say how much he'd gotten. To top it off, retirement hadn't agreed with him. Boredom had prevailed and that's how he'd started poking around my business dealings.

"You said he got really upset this morning and started drinking after he spent a couple of hours on the computer. Have you got any idea what he was working on?"

Mom stared out the patio door. No response. Atypical behavior for my mom. She probably would have made a helluva con artist herself, but she had the honest gene—another one that seemed to have eluded my DNA. At times, I wondered if these were my real parents.

"Mom. Do you know what he was working on?"

"Roxy—how much money do you have?"

"What? That's a pretty personal question. Why?"

Mom's eyes brimmed with tears and her face grew red with worry. "Your father didn't want me to say anything."

Crap. Did she *know*? "About?"

"Don't worry about it."

"About *what*, Mom?" When had she changed? She'd always been able to say what was on her mind. Why couldn't she just spit it out?

"I may need to borrow some money. Things have been tight lately."

"What? What happened to the money from the business? Dad must have gotten a lot from that."

Mom shook her head. "Between the business debt, taxes, and a few other things, there wasn't much left—maybe two hundred thousand. Your dad put a lot into a stock he heard about from a friend and that went down. He bought more, thinking it was going back up. Then he started borrowing to buy even more of the stock. It just kept going down. We owe more than all of that stupid stock is worth.

We're broke, Roxy. And now I think he's left me."

Thunder pounded in my ears so loud I couldn't think. How many of my friends had seen their parents divorce? The split family was the new American standard. I'd never believed it could happen to me. To them. Over *money*? I managed a weak smile. "That can't be right. You and Dad—you'd never—"

Mom burst into tears and leaned into me. Her body shook as her sobs took hold. "He's found ... a way ... out. He's ... gone."

I put my arms around her shoulders and held her close. Was I trying to reassure her—or myself? The pressure of tears built behind my eyes. The roaring in my ears continued. This couldn't be happening. Mom's shoulders shook and mine grew damp where her tears soaked into my linen blouse. A lone tear traced its way down my cheek, but I didn't wipe it away, I just held onto Mom.

"He wouldn't. Not Daddy."

"He's been unhappy for so long. He's been so—so preoccupied. Maybe there's someone else. Maybe he's been e-mailing another woman. Maybe he's—"

"Shhh." She would have rambled on, but I put my finger to her lips. We rocked back and forth. Together we let the tears flow and clung to each other for the one bit of comfort we both had, the other's touch. Finally, I summoned the nerve to test my voice. I swallowed first. "Do you, um, want me to take a look at his computer? If there's something there—if he had been e-mailing someone—or checking out web sites or something, it would be there."

Mom pulled away. She wiped her cheeks and nodded. "I'm sorry to burden you with this. You've probably got some big business deal going on or something. You've been so busy lately."

Shit. Bruno Panaman. How long had I been here? I glanced at my watch. It was nearly two and I had just over an hour to get to Bruno's home. And now I probably looked like puffy-faced raccoon. I let out a deep sigh. "I forgot about that. There's this meeting in Encinitas. I've got to get cleaned up—I might have to change tops."

We both laughed. Mom winced and rubbed my wet shoulder. "I'm sorry about that. I've ruined your blouse. I'll buy you a new one."

"Don't worry about it. I'm sure the dry cleaner can take care of it."

Mom's eyebrows went up. "You dry clean a linen blouse? Why don't you just wash it?"

I knew better than to mention cleaning issues of any sort to the expert. "It keeps it looking crisper." I took her shoulders. "If I'm going to look at Dad's computer, I need to get on it."

Her lower jaw went tight as she nodded. She understood the gentle reprimand—no cleaning talk. We needed to focus.

"I might need his password," I said.

Mom shook her head from side-to-side and grimaced. She swallowed, "I don't—"

"It's okay." I gave her a reassuring smile and stood. "You want to wait out back?"

Without a word, Mom opened the patio screen door and stepped outside. I went down the hall to Dad's office. I jiggled the mouse, hoping that the machine hadn't locked itself. The display came alive and my worst fear confronted me—a password screen.

I stared at the blank field and felt my hopes sink. We were screwed. My opportunity to see if Dad had been investigating my business or starting an affair with another woman or researching ways to escape was blocked by some stupid code known only to my father. And what super-secret little code would he use?

I searched the desk for a scrap of paper. Nothing under the paperweight. No scrap of paper with a password in the desk drawers. I slumped back into his desk chair. My dad knew better than to write down that type of information and leave it near the computer. He knew better than to use a birthday or a dog's name or anything else so easily guessed. Screw it. I had to try.

I clicked in the password field, typed "TannerTitle" and hit the Enter key. The system sneered at me with its invalid password message.

I tried it without capitals and got the same result.

I tried "Richard." Nothing.

"Evelyn." Same.

I tried my name, pet names, dates, and after ten minutes, threw my hands up in exasperation.

Shit. Mom, my only hope, had already told me she didn't know Dad's password.

I muttered, "We're screwed."

CHAPTER EIGHT

He said, "We'll find out soon enough."

Skip let out a breath that felt stale and dirty. He wished he could start the entire conversation over. He couldn't. He prided himself on his ability to read people and situations accurately. Body language, eye movements, tone of voice, and changes in skin color or breathing patterns were all clues he employed to get at the truth when the other person's words might not tell the full story. There was only one thing he could do.

"Herman, I apologize for jumping to conclusions," he said.

Nordoff's eyes defocused as he stared off into space for a few seconds. He waved away the apology. "You helped me to see something I didn't before."

Nordoff's politeness only made things worse. Herman Nordoff wasn't an abuser. And Paul hadn't seen an argument and run. Paul was just a little boy with big problems and parents who hadn't gotten him the help he needed. He never should have misread this domestic situation.

This family needed help from a professional, but first someone had to find Paul. Skip made his decision. "I'll help you find Paul. Once he's back, you've got to get him in for counseling. Kids just don't try to strangle their parents."

Mariane nodded.

Herman Nordoff's brow wrinkled. "You said it was a mugger."

"I'm sorry! I thought I was protecting Paul. I didn't want him to have to go through that, too."

Skip felt himself narrowing his gaze on Mariane. "Clinical depression?"

She turned her glance aside, which gave Skip a moment to do a quick assessment of her skin color, breathing, and listlessness—he pressed further. "Did you go through treatment?"

She cradled the cast in her left arm. "I'm on medication. Forever. I never dreamt Paul would have to go through that."

Skip's mind raced as he tried to process this new part of the equation. He shot a glance at Wally. The lawyer had known someone was lying, just not who. Skip had assumed that because Nordoff was gruff and strong, he was the problem. But Mariane's appearance—her complexion, her demeanor—and the fact that she'd lied to her husband had thrown everyone off the trail.

He had questions about Mariane's condition. And about Paul's behavior. But one question in particular bothered him most. "Herman, why don't you want the police involved?"

Herman glanced at his wife, who mouthed the words, "Tell him."

Nordoff stared at the deck flooring as he spoke. "When Mariane told me she'd been mugged, I insisted that we file a police report. The officer who took the report appeared to think Mariane was making the whole thing up and that rankled me." He winced, then glanced at Skip. "I laid into him. He practically accused me of having broken her arm."

The cop had made the same assumption he had. Nordoff had a lot of anger burning inside. The easiest conclusion was also the most obvious. "So things got out of hand."

Nordoff glanced down. "I owe him an apology."

Skip turned his attention to Mariane. "Were you also trying to protect Paul from some sort of criminal prosecution?"

She pressed her hand to her lips. Tears brimmed again. "Yes." The word came out in a hoarse whisper.

"He needs help," said Skip. "Not jail. I need to see his room."

Skip spent over an hour scouring Paul's bedroom while Herman Nordoff paced out on the deck and his wife fretted in the living room. Periodically, Skip heard their footsteps from the stairwell. Moments later, they'd appear in the hallway and remind him of where they each waited. Skip would acknowledge their presence with a wave of his hand, but otherwise ignore them until they left.

At the end of his search, he'd put together an impossibly short list of helpful information—eleven years old, troubled by something deep, he liked sports, he played soccer after school, and his phone had text messages from two friends who sent back sympathetic replies indicating that they, too, had parent issues.

Unfortunately, neither Mariane nor Herman knew these friends or how to find them. Skip considered sending a text message asking for help. But what good would that do? The friends would warn Paul that his parents were searching for him. Parents weren't included in the trust network, so that option was out. There had to be another way.

Skip stared at Paul's calendar. Soccer practices were at three. He went to Paul's closet. "Mariane!" he bellowed. He began rummaging through the closet again, this time realizing that he wasn't looking for what was here, but what was not.

Mariane appeared at the door. "Did you find something?"

"What does Paul wear for soccer?"

"A jersey, shorts, shin guards. Why?"

"Where does he keep them?"

Her face flushed. She made an expansive gesture with her left arm. "Where do eleven-year-old boys keep anything, Mr. Cosgrove? Wherever it lands. If it wasn't for mothers, you wouldn't be able to stand, let alone sit, in a child's room."

Didn't she realize how much more he might have learned if the room had been in its normal state? "Where's his soccer stuff?"

Her face went blank. Then, she glanced around and gazed at Skip. "I was so upset when I came in here. I don't know. I just started putting things away. I don't remember seeing it. Why? Is that important?"

"Look at his calendar. See how he's circled each practice and game. Soccer is important to him. Top of his list, I'd say, because I don't know many kids who mark events on calendars. He's tracking his attendance. Last week's game isn't circled. Did he go last week?"

She shook her head and tears brimmed in her eyes again. A few seconds later, she said, "Oh, God. I kept him home. He'd been acting out and I kept him here as punishment. He was so upset, but I never thought he'd just vanish."

Skip pointed at the bruise on her neck. "That's when that happened?"

She nodded.

"Mariane, your son is eleven. He's focused on the here and now. If he missed a game and was upset about it, he wouldn't want to miss another. That's probably his therapy, his way to cope. He just might be going to soccer practice this afternoon."

Her hands fluttered in the air. "I can't believe he'd run away just so he could go to a stupid soccer practice. It's just a game."

Skip pointed to a poster on the wall for the LA Galaxy. He pulled a piece of paper from the printer. "Look at this, it's information about a soccer camp in LA. Your son is crazy about that 'stupid game.' If you want to get through to him, learn about soccer."

Mariane plopped down onto the bed and hunched over the paper Skip handed her. Her lower lip quivered as she read. When she'd finished, she held the paper to her chest. "Mr. Cosgrove, if you get him back, I'll see that he gets into this camp."

"The first step is to find him. He should be there this afternoon. I'll talk to the school and the police and let them know what's going on. And, by the way, I'm going to give you the website address for a GPS locating service. If he runs away again, you'll be able to find him in seconds. If he has his phone with him, that is."

Mariane stared at the floor as if lost in thought.

Skip grimaced. "It won't work if he doesn't have it with him."

"Herman and I should go with you."

"You need to keep some distance. If he sees you, he might run. He doesn't know me. With the right introduction from the coach, I can get close enough to talk him down. We're only a few minutes from the field. I'll call you when I want you to come get him."

By 2:00 p.m., Skip had been to the Carlsbad Police and spoken to the sergeant in Family Services, explained Paul's problems, advised her that Paul had run away, and made arrangements for a quick response should something go wrong at the soccer field. He'd also been to the school and spoken to the principal and the soccer coach. The coach had been reluctant, but under pressure from the principal and Skip, had agreed to perform the introductions.

Later, when Paul walked onto the field, the coach got an uneasy look on his face. Skip kept his tone level with the coach. "What's the problem?"

"I don't know. This doesn't feel right. I don't want to mess up the practice. You know what I mean?"

"Afterwards. We can do it after the practice. Will that work?"

The coach shifted position. "Yeah. That'll work."

"You still seem hesitant."

"It'll be fine."

Skip walked away wondering what was bothering the coach. What could possibly be the problem with getting Paul back home?

A short while later, the practice was in full swing and Skip stood on the sidelines with the parents of other kids. At first, most of the observers were silent, with the exception of Skip, who cheered the kids on. Initially, the players, including Paul, gave him a strange look when he let out a cheer, as though wondering who this crazy guy was who rooted for everyone on the team. But soon, as more parents got in the mood, the players responded to the growing cheering section.

The practice was almost over when Skip noticed a blue Ford Focus zip into the parking lot and squeeze into a spot at the far end. The driver, a man wearing a red T-shirt and jeans, got out of his car and put the strap from his camera around his neck. The man rushed toward the field. Skip figured the guy for a parent who had lots of money to spend on photography equipment, but little time for his kid's practice.

The man trotted to where the coach stood, said a few words, and began snapping pictures. Skip turned his attention back to the game. Paul had received a pass from one of his teammates. He dribbled the ball forward. An opposing player tried to block his path. Paul feinted left, but went right. He slipped past the player, made his kick and scored. Skip let out a whoop along with several of the parents. He suppressed a laugh as Paul's teammates gathered around and congratulated him with their eleven-year-old versions of chest and fist bumps.

The coach blew his whistle and Skip realized that practice was over. It was time to go to work. The self-doubts kicked in. Would he be able to talk a scared little boy into going back home willingly?

"Soon enough," he said to himself. "We'll find out soon enough."

CHAPTER NINE

She said, "Holy Mother of God! Payday."

Late afternoon shadows deepened as the time for my appointment with Bruno Panaman neared. With the gray of morning long gone, the sky had turned what *seemed* like a bright cerulean blue, punctuated only by an occasional smudge of fog. In reality, the moisture-laden air dulled the blue and the smudgy punctuation marks were more prominent than I cared to admit. It was a typical Southern California hazy imitation of clean air with visibility limited to a few miles.

I twisted my driver's mirror to check my face and winced. Little drops of oil beaded up on my nose. A man could ignore something like that on *his* nose, but not a woman making a sales pitch. I wasn't about to let Bruno Panaman compare my nose to an oil spill.

I pulled out a little packet of Palladio Rice Paper from my purse, tore off a piece, and dabbed with the matte side, then with the powdered side. I stuffed the used piece into a little trash bag and the rest of the packet back into my purse, checked my teeth for any leftover fish-taco particles, fluffed up my hair, then got out of the car. The air was almost still, the temperature hovered in the mid seventies, which gave the air outside the car a refreshing feel. Everything was great—except, of course, for the fact that my dad had gone on a bender and I was wearing goddamn panty hose. I'd thrown on a pair at Mom and Dad's as a precaution. With Sonny, I hadn't needed to worry about bare legs. He was of the generation that accepted the look in the business world. But Bruno was one generation back and probably had definite ideas about women's business attire. And whether they should even be in business. Since I wanted a quarter of a million of his money, it would be best to play it safe and wear the damn nylons.

The Panaman residence hogged the premier spot on a hilltop with a panoramic view of the Pacific. The neighborhood was not much different than my parents' place in many ways. The homes had been built back in the 70s and 80s. From the outside, they appeared modest, probably three or four bedrooms. The yards, well-manicured palettes of tropical foliage, included palms of various varieties, hibiscus, camellias, and ornamentals with leaves nearly the size of the hood on my car.

The house was painted an off-white with blue and gray trim and accents. Stone veneer covered the lower half of the walls. The stone also formed a walkway that curved around and hugged one side of the house. The front door was a highly polished dark wood, which I guessed was mahogany or some variety of rosewood.

I once dated a landscaper. What time he didn't spend trying to turn me into an arborist or some other plant scientist-guru, he spent ranting about politics. The only thing I got out of that short relationship was a hundred-dollar dinner bill and a firm resolve to never date another loser who wouldn't look me in the eye.

After I skipped, there'd be no expensive dinners, no more thousand-dollar cocktail dresses, and no falling for someone else's get-rich-quick schemes.

My finger was just inches from the bell when the door opened. I jumped. "Sonny! You surprised me."

He did his usual quick x-ray scan of my body. His eyes widened when he got to the legs. "You look sensational."

Given that my skirt was only a couple of inches above the knee, I considered that quite a compliment. Stella hadn't gotten a "sensational" rating this morning, but she had gotten the big eyes. "Thanks. Where's your dad?"

He motioned behind him with his head.

It suddenly occurred to me that Sonny might not have set up an appointment with his dad at all. This could all be a ruse to get me inside the family lair. I quickly dismissed the concern. I had a black belt in tongue-lashing and a red in karate. If I couldn't talk Sonny down with words, I could always put him in the hospital for a month with injuries he'd remember for a long time. "Fabulous! Let's go see him."

Sonny closed the door behind me. It didn't escape my attention that he'd tossed on an extra splash of cologne. He smelled more like a Macy's perfume-testing refugee than a seducer of women. He paused momentarily as he slipped past. If he was expecting me to melt at his feet and beg him to take me to bed, he was sorely mistaken. The overpowering scent might *put* me in bed, but it would be alone with a couple of painkillers for the headache, not begging for his undivided attention. His smile fell when I shifted my briefcase so that I held it between us with both hands.

To his credit, Sonny seemed to recognize the signal. "He's out back. Dad likes to watch the ocean in the afternoon."

How nice for your dad, I thought, mine's out drinking away his sorrows. The house furnishings were generally older generation—lots of leather, dark colors, massive furniture. The patio, however, was a knockout, complete with a redwood arbor covered by a mountain of San Diego Red bougainvillea. Three clusters of Queen Palms surrounded a waterfall that stood nearly as tall as me. Koi swam in circles in the pool at the base of the palms. One did a quick flip out of the water. Others did the fish equivalent of someone pacing as they waited for dinner.

Bruno rose from his chair at a glass-topped patio table. He was a fireplug of a man, short and squatty, with arms that stuck out slightly to the sides, and stubby legs. My immediate reaction was that Sonny, with his roguish good looks and height, must be adopted. While Sonny had the bright white smile of a Hollywood leading man, Bruno's reminded me more of the guy chosen to play the swarthy villain.

I shook hands with Bruno. "Good afternoon, Mr. Panaman. I'm Roxy Tanner. Sonny's told me a lot about you." Okay, trite, but it was better than asking him to write a check on the spot.

Bruno bowed at the waist. "Miss Tanner. I've heard about you, also. My son tells me you have quite an investment opportunity. Lovely day, isn't it?"

While Bruno lacked a bit in the looks department, he'd gotten a full double scoop from the suave ice cream bucket. His handshake had been gentle, yet reassuring. His voice was melodic. And that little bow. Wow, hadn't seen that one since I'd had the flu and spent three days watching old movie reruns. "You have a beautiful home." I made an expansive gesture to take in our surroundings. "This back yard is stunning. And your view is spectacular. Your landscaper did a fantastic job."

"It has been a work in progress." He pointed to a spot just off the patio about twenty feet away. "Next week, they install an *outdoor kitchen*. Can you believe it? When I was young, we thought we were rich when we bought a little hibachi. Now, everyone grills and we must have elaborate kitchens in our back yards."

Bruno and I laughed while Sonny stood to one side with lines of impatience etched on his face. What a difference in generations, I thought. Sonny just wanted instant gratification—hop in the sack and hump away. Bruno enjoyed the process—the flowers, the drinks, dinner and seduction. I gave Bruno my best winning smile. "My father has been talking about doing the same thing. You two could compare recipes."

Bruno smiled. "If he is as delightful as his daughter, it would be my pleasure. Perhaps two old dogs could teach each other new tricks." He pulled out a chair and motioned for me to sit. He glanced at Sonny, "Bring Miss Tanner—" He turned to me. "An iced tea?"

"That would be wonderful. Thank you."

Sonny wandered away, presumably to find the indoor kitchen, where he'd probably rummage through the fridge trying to differentiate between the iced tea and the apple juice.

"So, Miss Tanner, tell me about this investment opportunity," said Bruno.

I set my briefcase on the table and extracted a set of brochures and financial statements. "Let me begin by saying that this isn't one of those once-in-a-lifetime opportunities. You could certainly get returns of this nature elsewhere if you looked hard enough. And there's an element of risk here that you won't see with more traditional investments." There, he'd gotten the disclaimer—you could get screwed by someone else just as easily, but if you're a greedy bastard, you'll go for this.

I continued. "However, I must say that we are on the cutting edge with this technology. What I've done is to secure a small block of venture capital with a firm that will be moving their wave-to-energy technology to production. The principals of the firm intend to take the company public within two years. At that time, the investors will be repaid. The returns here could be quite handsome."

Sonny appeared bearing a bamboo tray containing three glasses of iced tea and an assortment of cheeses and crackers. He bent forward and extended the tray. I nodded and took a glass. Bruno followed suit, then Sonny took up a position at the table. He arranged the cheese and crackers so we could each easily reach the goodies.

"Wow! I had no idea you were so domesticated," I said.

Sonny grabbed a piece of cheese with his fingers and slapped it on a cracker. He leaned back in his chair and puffed up his chest. "Yeah, I'm a man full of surprises."

I smiled, though what I really wanted to do was roll my eyes and say, "Who helped you?"

Bruno's voice remained soft, yet conveyed impatience. "We have smoothed out many aspects of Sonny's behavior, however, we have not yet tackled humility."

Sonny snorted, then smiled. "Cheese? Cracker?"

"Thank you." I speared a piece of cheese with one of the toothpicks that Sonny had ignored and placed it on a cracker. I placed the cracker on a small plate that Sonny had also ignored and put that in front of me, then took a sip of my iced tea. "This is really good!"

Bruno nodded. "It's a sun tea. We brew it fresh each day once the weather turns nice. It's a tradition we carry over from our less fortunate days."

I took another sip. "Excellent." I handed my primary sales brochure to Bruno. "As you can see from this prospectus, the block of venture capital that we're guaranteeing is just a small part of what the company needs. This is, in a sense, venture capital for the little guy."

He took the brochure from my hand. He pulled a pair of reading glasses from his breast pocket and slipped them on. Bruno smiled at me. "Can't read a thing without them." His eyes flicked over the page. "Why are you doing this?"

The sun slipped below the arbor. Not long and we'd be baking in the direct rays. "I have several reasons. First, I've worked for a couple of different venture capital firms. I saw the returns their clients received and was taken aback. My last boss taught me everything about the business, so when a couple of my old college friends came to me looking for a way to get venture capital to bring their invention to market, I decided it was time to move off on my own. Are you familiar with the wave-to-energy technology concept?"

Bruno continued to inspect the brochure. He shook his head absently. "No, what is it?"

Excellent. We were already off into the technology. That was a good sign and meant he was interested. The sun's rays were crawling up my legs, making my nylons feel like wet sandpaper. "You're probably aware that the oceans cover more than seventy percent of the Earth's surface. And, whenever you go to the beach, you see firsthand how powerful waves can be. Wave2E's technology takes that energy and converts it to electric power."

"And how much money did you need? Sonny said something about $250,000."

"I've secured a minimum twenty-five percent stake in the company launch. My portfolio includes one last block of $250,000, but if you wanted to invest more, we have the ability to go up to thirty percent," and, I thought, if you're that greedy, I'll be happy to take your extra money.

Bruno gazed at me over the brochure. "I've heard about this type of thing being done. This technology—this turning waves into electricity—it's fascinating."

To the side, I saw Sonny's eyes light up. He, too, could see where this was going. Bruno was hooked. I doubled back to the technology issue. "The concept of using wave energy is actually pretty simple. You use a device to capture the wave movement, that movement creates mechanical energy, which can then be used to turn a turbine. The turbines convert the mechanical power into electrical power. The obstacle has always been the unpredictability of the wave energy."

"Hurricanes?" said Bruno.

I nodded. "That's part of it. But think about this. On land, there are places where it seems that the wind blows constantly. Right over in the Coachella Valley, for instance, they have the windmill farms because the wind blows through the pass nearly all the time—or so it seems. Wave2E's concept is to site their wave farms in similar locales in the ocean—where the waves are more consistent. For instance, one competitor has put tide-powered turbines in New York City's East River. Portugal has a project that should supply more than 1,500 homes with electricity."

Bruno nodded. Sonny beamed. I took a breather and grabbed my glass of iced tea. Bring it on, Bruno. I'm ready for any questions you've got.

He picked up the brochure again and opened it. "I've spoken to my banker. And to my investment manager. I certainly have the necessary cash."

I was in full sun now and was starting to feel as though I'd just gotten out of the shower. Where the hell was the breeze? Screw it. Bruno was about to write me a check and I wasn't about to break the mood just because my bra felt like a wet rubber band scraping against my skin.

He went on. "If I wrote you a check today for, say $300,000, you'd get me into this fund?"

Holy Mother of God! Payday. "You must feel pretty comfortable with this then? I guess Sonny did fill you in." Speaking of which, the little urchin was practically drooling on himself.

Bruno nodded. "I'm quite comfortable with my decision."

"Yes, I could get you in. Let me get the disclosure form."

He tossed the brochure onto the table. "Normally, Sonny has no head for business at all."

"Pop!" Sonny's protest went unnoticed by the elder Panaman.

"In this case, I'd say he's outdone himself. This is the worst recommendation he's ever made. Thank you, Miss Tanner, but you won't be seeing any money from me."

CHAPTER TEN

He said, "Don't get your hopes up."

It was time. Soccer practice had finished. The coach had been briefed. The cops were not far away in case they were needed. And Skip felt ready. He felt good. Confident. He'd prepared for any contingency. He dialed the Nordoff's number. "Herman? I'm about to meet with Paul. You and Mariane should head on over here."

"We're on our way." The relief in Nordoff's voice was obvious. *"Thank you."*

Skip watched Paul and his coach as they approached. The coach glanced in Skip's direction, then over his shoulder. Skip examined him more closely. Stress lines furrowed his brow. Another glance in both directions. Skip didn't recall the coach appearing so nervous in their previous conversation. Something's wrong, he thought. To Nordoff, he said, "Don't get your hopes up. Not yet, anyway."

Skip disconnected the call with a hurried good-bye, unwilling to let Paul know why he was here until he had established rapport with the boy. Paul and his coach were about twenty feet away and the man with the camera, the one who had arrived late, was taking photos of everyone. The guy reminded Skip of one of those amateur photographers who took thousands of photos and posted them on his web site for all his friends and family to view.

The coach held Paul's shoulder as he gestured at Skip. "Paul, I'd like you to meet Skip. He wanted to talk to you for a minute. I'll leave you two alone. Paul, I'll be right over there if you need me, okay?"

The boy nodded. His facial muscles were tense. His eyes darted in different directions. The boy was obviously on high alert for trouble.

"Paul, you played pretty good out there," Skip said.

The boy glanced at the ground. "Thanks. Who are you?"

"My name is Skip Cosgrove. I'm a friend who likes soccer. The Galaxy's my favorite team. Yours, too?"

Paul squinted at Skip, obviously torn between trusting based on the coach's introduction and fear of a stranger. Good for you, thought Skip, being leery of strangers will keep you safe for a while. "Let's just sit down, okay?"

Paul nodded and sat on the ground. He pulled his knees tight to his chest. Skip sat opposite him, cross-legged, purposefully maintaining distance between them. That couple of feet seemed to relax Paul, so Skip continued, "You must really like soccer. You've got some great moves. Have you thought of attending any camps?"

Paul's interest perked up for a second. "My mom said I couldn't."

"Parents don't always understand, do they?"

Paul rolled his eyes. "That's the truth. They made me miss last week's practice 'cause I got in a fight at school."

"What was the fight about?"

"Some kid called me a retard."

Paul's trust was building quickly so Skip leaned forward a few inches. "Why would he do that?"

"I didn't move out of the way when he tried to push me. He shot me in the face with a spit ball. So I hit him."

Skip noted that the boy had unconsciously relaxed his position and also sat with his legs crossed. Skip had established rapport, but had a huge chasm to cross. "Sounds like you were provoked." Skip knew he only had a few minutes left. "Is that why you hit your mom, too? You were provoked?"

Paul flinched and started to rise.

"It's okay," Skip said. "I'm not here to hurt you. I just want to talk."

In the distance, Skip noticed the man with the camera lining up kids and parents for shots. He had a few pose with the ball. Skip's pulse rate rose along with his suspicions. He couldn't watch the boy and the photographer—and the coach. The coach watched the photographer from a distance also. Skip desperately wanted to ask Paul if he knew the man, but didn't dare lose the rapport. He turned his attention back to Paul, who wiped at his cheek.

"I talked to your parents. They're very sorry about how things turned out and want you to come home."

The boy shook his head. He put a hand down on the ground. It appeared as though he might run.

Skip held up his hand and scooted forward. He could reach the boy now if it became necessary. "You don't want to run away again, do you? Wouldn't you rather be home? This whole thing is just a misunderstanding. Your mom didn't mean to hurt you by keeping you away from practice. She just didn't understand how important it was to be here. I get it. So does she—now."

Paul's tears flowed freely now. "I didn't mean to hurt her. I just got so mad when she said I couldn't come to practice."

Skip put a gentle hand on Paul's arm. The boy recoiled at the touch. Skip used his most soothing voice. "She understands now."

Paul shook his head. "She's so mad at me. I can't ever go home. My dad would kill me."

"Do you really think that?"

"Maybe." He stared off into space. "I dunno. Guess not."

Skip shifted position so that he sat cross-legged facing Paul. "You need a translator."

"Huh?"

Skip made little talking heads with his hands, speaking with one, then the other. "It's like your parents speak German and you speak Spanish."

Paul smiled. "That's so totally true." He glanced up into Skip's eyes. "Are you, like, the translator?"

Skip raised his right hand. "Guilty. I'm here to help you get back home safe and sound. And to stay that way once you get back." For the first time, Skip realized that the photographer had been taking shots of him and Paul and was moving closer. To his left, he saw the Nordoffs approaching. The coach's role and the reason for his nervousness suddenly made perfect sense. The photographer was from the press and the scene that was about to play out would be front page news if he didn't do something to stop it. He couldn't warn the Nordoffs away without alerting the photographer and he couldn't leave Paul.

He took hold of Paul's arm. "Paul, something is about to happen that I didn't anticipate. There's a man taking pictures. He's from the press."

The last thing this kid needed was notoriety. He wouldn't last a day in school with all the harassment he'd get from the other kids.

Skip continued. "Things are going to get ugly here in just a minute. That photographer is going to want to take pictures of you and your folks. I had no idea this was going to happen. We're going to need to do something to keep him away from you. I need you to be strong. Your parents want you home safe. You want to go home, right?"

Paul nodded. Tears streamed down his cheeks as he watched his parents move closer. His eyes widened and he glanced over his shoulder toward the photographer.

The man raised his camera to take a shot and Skip gripped Paul's arm. Paul faced Skip again. "Ignore him. I'll get rid of him. But I need you to get to your parents. Will you do that?"

The boy glanced around as if searching for an escape route.

He shook the boy's arm. "It's just a soccer play. I'm the decoy. You ready."

Paul nodded.

"Run to them, Paul. Right now!"

The boy was on his feet in a second and running full out to Mariane's arms. As she embraced her son, Skip said to himself, "I'll deal with the menace."

Skip surveyed the field while he strode toward the photographer, who was doing his best to nonchalantly close in on the reunion. Most of the other parents and the kids were gone. There were just a few left. In the parking lot, Skip spotted the coach jogging toward his car. He was the only other one who had known. That son of a bitch. He remembered how the photographer had first arrived. His first contact had been the coach. Of course, the coach had a working relationship with the press.

Skip clenched his fists as he inserted himself between the photographer and the Nordoffs. He ground out the words, "I know who tipped you off."

The photographer took a step backward. "This is, like, big news, man. C'mon, let me get my story."

Skip glared at the photographer. The last thing he intended to do was to let the Nordoff's quiet reunion become today's headline news.

CHAPTER ELEVEN

She said, "Everybody's a freaking specialist."

Talk about having your day go to shit. I'd been rejected by Bruno Panaman. I'd gone from being inches away from my goal to starting the race all over in two heartbeats. Setbacks don't usually bother me, but something about Bruno's brush off seemed especially cruel. He'd known from the beginning he wasn't going to do anything. At least, that's what I suspected. Apparently, I wasn't the only one who'd been surprised. If anything, Sonny had been more shocked than me. In fact, Sonny had been downright angry. Had Bruno met with me, lured me on, and *seduced* me just to be cruel? Or had he been teaching Sonny a lesson?

I suppose there was a certain perverse logic to Sonny being so upset, he'd been insulted *and* rejected. Me? I'd just had a bad first date and it pissed me off. The more I thought about it—and I did plenty of that—the more I realized where my anger was directed. Sonny. Again. He'd let me down. He'd wasted more of my time. Something I didn't have a lot of right now.

After the meeting, I'd driven back to my parents' house and found Mom making phone calls to all her friends. Eventually, after running out of phone numbers and friends to pester, we'd cried on each other's shoulders for a bit, then ordered a pizza. It was now 6:43 p.m. and we were watching the "local" news, which, in our case, meant San Diego. We'd already been through half a bottle of wine, a story about the City Council's latest faux pax, the weather, three commercials, and half the pizza.

The TV anchor said, "After the break, how a Carlsbad man brought a family together." The station cut to commercial.

"Mom, have you got any ideas where he might have gone?"

Mom's eyes were red and bleary. Her worry ran deep. There were no more tears though, she'd cried herself out. "We've been through everyone I can think of. Do you want to take another crack at his computer?"

"I'm locked out without his password. I've tried everything I can think of. Maybe it will come to me, but I'm at a loss right now. Tomorrow, we'll go into the bank and see if he's hit an ATM."

"Roxy ... maybe I should call the police."

"To what? Report a middle-aged man took a vacation?"

Mom winced. Inside, so did I. "I shouldn't have said that."

She stared out the patio slider at Dad's barbecue for a minute. Her voice cracked, "You're right. What would they do?"

"Look, tomorrow, I'll call the credit card companies also."

"Your dad always uses his credit card." She sniffled. "A couple of weeks ago, he was at Home Depot and there were two checkers waiting. Your father went to the self-serve checkout so he could charge some stupid little thing he bought for two dollars. That man frustrates me so much. Two dollars!"

Until we found him, I was sure that those types of memories would flood Mom's thoughts. The station's logo came on, the screen went black for a second, then the anchor was back on screen.

"This afternoon in Carlsbad ..."

I said, "Hey, this is about us!" We both leaned forward to watch really local news.

"... when a young boy ran away from home last night. Skip Cosgrove, a Carlsbad investigator, found the boy at his soccer practice. Mandy Ochoa is on the scene with Mr. Cosgrove."

The image of the on-scene reporter, which had been in a small segment of the screen, filled the picture. "Thanks, Crystal. I'm here with Skip Cosgrove, a local investigator, who was called in when eleven-year-old Paul Nordoff ran away last night. Paul's father, Herman Nordoff, is a local venture capitalist who has financed several large projects in San Diego County. We thought this story had special appeal because of how the boy was found."

The reporter turned to a hot-looking guy who stood just a little taller than her. He had short, dark hair that had a controlled, bed-head look. He was muscular, but not overly so. What caught my attention, though, were his eyes, which were intense as he focused on the camera. Anyone who got into a staring contest with this guy would definitely lose.

"Mr. Cosgrove, where did you find Paul so he could be reunited with his family?"

The hot guy on screen took a deep breath. He was either bored to tears with this interview or doing it under duress. "Soccer. He was at his soccer practice."

"And how did you know to find him there?"

"I was called in to locate Paul. I noticed he had a strong interest in soccer when I was going through his room. His practice game was today so I was able to find him and talk him down."

"Talk him down?"

"Lessen his anxiety. Reassure him that his parents loved him. Alleviate the usual fears that kids have."

The reporter did the typical reporter "uh-huh's" and nods and kept glancing at him instead of the camera. She smiled and made nice with the investigator guy—a little too nice, in fact. I had a sudden thought that she was *flirting* with this guy on camera. Hell, what did I care? He was hot, she wasn't bad herself. Let them do whatever, *off camera*. Get back to the story, the Nordoff kid.

Nordoff? I did a quick mental review of my investor list. It was epiphany time—the big "aha" moment. Nordoff was on my target investor list, I just hadn't had a connection or any other way of making a contact other than a cold call. Unfortunately, now would be a crappy time to call the guy for money.

The reporter said, "There was quite a scuffle after the game. Tell us about that."

The investigator guy grimaced. "Things got a little out of hand when a press photographer tried to get pictures. That was the last thing the Nordoffs wanted. They just wanted a quiet reunion with their son."

"That's actually why we're interviewing Mr. Cosgrove. The Nordoffs have refused comment. Mr. Nordoff, who seeks coverage for his business projects, has decided he wants no press interference with his family at this time. Is that correct, Skip?"

So now they were on a first-name basis. Whatever.

The investigator guy said, "That's right. The Nordoffs are only interested in helping their son return home to a safe environment. And that, I think we can all agree, would mean a normal environment without lots of outside influence."

Well said, I thought. This guy was smart as well as hot.

Mom said, "He's right."

"No kidding." I glanced away from the TV to my mom.

Mom smiled, "He's cute, too. Huh, Roxy?"

Shit, what did I have, "aroused" written in big red letters on my forehead? "I guess—if you like that sort." I turned back to the TV.

The reporter asked, "So Skip, what's the lesson here for other parents in San Diego?"

"Basically, it's that parents need to listen to their kids. Try to find out what they're interested in and make that their interest."

The reporter pressed her hand to her ear and gave a little nod. Obviously, someone had just given her new instructions and she was cutting the interview short. "Thanks Skip. There's a good lesson for all of us parents. Back to you, Crystal."

"Well, at least someone's got some good news," I said.

Mom stared off into space. What the hell was she thinking about? "Mom? Hey, more wine?"

She shook her head. "Maybe we should hire him."

"Who?"

"That investigator. What was his name? Cosgrove?"

I did a double take. *Oh, my God.* I flushed. She was still thinking about that Cosgrove guy. *No way.*

"You think he'd help us out?"

Oh, that's why she was thinking about him. "He probably only looks for missing kids. You know how people are. Everybody's a freaking specialist."

"I'm sure he does more than that. Besides, money's money."

"I thought you were broke."

Mom groaned. "Oh, that. I wonder how much he'd charge, though."

"If he's working for Nordoff, probably more than you've got." That's when it hit me, if he was working for Nordoff, he could be a way in. For Nordoff, a quarter of a million was nothing. "Mmmm— what did you have in mind?"

Mom muted the sound on the TV. "I was just thinking that maybe we need professional help. We've tried everything we can think of short of going to all the bars in town. Maybe we're missing something. He went to the Nordoff's place and noticed that the kid liked soccer and knew right where to find him. Maybe there's something here that we're missing. What do you think?"

"It makes sense. I suppose it's worth a try. We might be asking the wrong questions. Still, he probably charges a lot of money."

"I've still got a little cash in the bank. If it would get your father back, I'd spend it in a heartbeat."

My breath caught. Here I was getting five million from rich people and my own mother had barely enough money to hire an investigator. I cleared my throat. "Sure. I think it's a good idea."

"This has you upset, too. I can hear it in your voice. You always try to be so strong, but inside, you're just like me."

No. No, I *was* strong. I had to be. And then I was eight all over again. The man, my mark, is standing before me. He's wearing a dark suit that hangs on him like it's a size too large. His hair is shaggy over the ears, but he's carrying an expensive-looking briefcase. Mom always says that rich people try to look poor. He wasn't going to fool me that easily. "Hey mister, would you like to buy a Rolex? My mother wants me to sell it for food money. If you have fifty bucks, I'll let you have it."

He stares at me with keen, blue eyes. He nods and licks his lips.

There's something wrong with this guy. Maybe I made a mistake. Maybe he's not rich.

He smiles. It's a friendly smile that relaxes me a bit. "Sure kid. For a Rolex. Sure. My wallet's in the car."

"Roxy?"

It was Mom's voice that cut through the memories. "What?"

"You were far away. You've done that since you were little, but it always scares me. Is it the stress?"

Apparently she thought I'd been thinking about Dad. "I'm fine, Mom."

I stood and went to the kitchen, then tossed the rest of my wine down the drain. This stuff was making me soft. Get it together, Roxy. How could I have been so stupid? I'd been eight, not twenty-eight.

I turned around and started. "Mom! I didn't see you there."

"I didn't mean to sneak up on you. So what do you think about hiring that guy?"

"I told you. I think it's a good idea. I'll call him in the morning, it's probably too late now."

"But if we wait, that means your father's out there somewhere overnight." Tears brimmed in her eyes.

I put my hands on her shoulders and pulled her close. Mom was right, we couldn't wait. "Let's see if he's in the phone book."

"Maybe he can come over now."

I mentally calculated Cosgrove's rate at double overtime. Mom slipped away and opened the drawer where she kept the phone book along with a pad of paper, a pen, a flashlight, two candles, and a book of matches. I suppose if the power ever went out in the middle of the night and she wanted to call 9-1-1, the drawer contents would make sense. Right now, it seemed like overkill.

As she flipped through the phone book, I considered how I'd approach Skip Cosgrove. It was one thing to hire him to find my dad, totally different to use him to get money from Herman Nordoff.

CHAPTER TWELVE

He said, "He knew exactly what he was doing."

Skip found the address without difficulty and angled the Porsche into the driveway next to the beige Toyota as Miss Tanner had told him to do. He was dead tired and hadn't had dinner thanks to that damn TV interview, but after the way things blew up at the soccer field, handling the press for the Nordoffs was the least he could do. Herman had seemed extremely grateful and had told Skip to call him if he ever needed a favor. Often clients made such an offer, but seldom did they expect to fulfill their promises. To be honest, Skip doubted that he'd ever again have contact with Herman Nordoff.

The house the Tanners lived in looked like your basic rancher—single story, three bedrooms, two baths, and a two-car garage. But, unlike the others in this neighborhood dotted with a mishmash of architecture and money, someone was missing from this house. Skip shook his head in disbelief. Two missing people in one day. He made his way up the concrete path to the front door and rang the bell. The ring was the standard "ding-dong" and served as a reminder that this home was very different from the Nordoff's.

Skip judged the woman who greeted him to be in her late forties. She had on a blue flowered blouse, a navy scarf wrapped around her neck, and black slacks. The rims of her eyes were tinged with red and she wore no makeup. Skip wondered if she never wore the stuff or if she'd just washed her face to erase the day's tension.

"I'm Skip Cosgrove, you must be Miss Tanner?"

The woman shook her head and gave him a weak smile. "No, I'm Mrs. Tanner. Roxy is the one who called, she's my daughter. I'm Evelyn." She stepped to one side.

Skip entered and shook her hand as he said what everyone was expected to say in situations like this. "I'm sorry to hear about your husband."

"Thank you. I have a bad feeling about this. He's never disappeared before."

Skip caught how she averted her eyes when she said that and suspected she was lying. His next question was, why? He filed that one away for later and reassured her. "I'll do my best to find him."

"Thank you. Let's go meet Roxy." Evelyn led the way, Skip followed her into the living room where another woman, a much younger version of Evelyn, sat.

The similarities between the two women were striking. The younger woman's features were more defined and less rounded, but she had the same trim build, the same blonde hair, and the same blue eyes.

As the younger woman stood, he caught himself watching her closely. She was captivating, seductive, and something else—yes, dangerous. "Hi, I'm Skip."

"Roxy." She smiled. "That was nice work you did with the Nordoff kid. You handled the interview very well."

Skip felt himself flush. "It was supposed to be a quiet reunion. As luck would have it, the soccer team coach called a reporter so he could get favors in the future. You know, get better coverage when he needed it." Skip shook his head. "I got sold out by the kid's coach. It turns out he's up for a coaching job at a private school and thought having his name in the press would get him the inside track."

He realized that he was rambling. Shit. Why was he so nervous? He shook his head quickly. "Anyway, it ended well."

Roxy smiled at him. He recognized the move. It was what he'd do to calm a client.

"Please, sit," said Evelyn.

Skip took a chair to one side of the couch. Evelyn and Roxy took up seats on the couch itself. Skip noticed a subtle difference between the two women. Evelyn was tense and worried, Roxy seemed worried also, but almost calculating in the way she positioned herself. Skip pulled a notebook from his back pocket. He directed the question to Evelyn. "Um, so when did your husband disappear?"

"This morning. He started drinking and got really depressed. Then he went out and never came back."

"It's a little unusual to start a search for an adult when they've only been gone a few hours."

Roxy shifted position. "Skip, my father's been a homebody since he sold his business a while back. We think he's been getting closer to some sort of breakdown. We—Mom and I—are worried that maybe it's happened. My mom doesn't want to wait." Her voice took on a pleading tone. "What if something's happened to him already?"

Evelyn nodded and began to wring her hands.

Skip glanced around the room. The furnishings had been very nice at one time, but they were showing their age. There was no expensive artwork on the walls, no sculptures or other fancy stuff on the tables—this was a middle-class family caught in a bind. He'd made a nice profit today. He could work this one without the big fee. "I charge $100.00 per hour. I'll only charge you for time worked. Normally, there's a minimum retainer, but I'll waive that in this case."

Evelyn's back straightened. "I don't want charity, Mr. Cosgrove."

"Mom! A hundred an hour is hardly charity. Besides, you're stretched as it is."

Evelyn crossed her arms over her chest. "You're right, honey. I'm sorry, Mr. Cosgrove. I didn't mean to snap at you."

"No problem. This is a tense time. Let's get started. And please, call me Skip. I've been Mistered too many times today. What's his full name?"

"Richard Allen Tanner."

"Date of birth?"

"March 4, 1959."

"Do you have a picture?"

Evelyn nodded. "I can get you one."

"When was the last time you saw your husband?"

"This morning, maybe ten. No. About nine thirty."

"You said he was drinking. That early?"

Evelyn's face turned red and she licked her lips. "I guess you need to know this. He started about two months ago. He was working on some special project on his computer, but wouldn't discuss it with me. He thought I didn't notice. I guess I should have said something to him."

Skip had warning bells clanging in his head. Special project? Drinking for two months? Was Richard Tanner shifting into a pattern of alcoholism? Skip also noted that, for the first time, Roxy looked a bit uncomfortable. Could his disappearance have something to do with her? "Roxy, what can you tell me?"

"I didn't realize there was a problem until Mom called me this morning. I was at work. I'm just starting a new business."

"Oh, what kind?" It didn't really matter, but at least it was a polite way to handle the leading statement.

"Venture capital. We're funding an ocean-wave technology project for our first deal."

Whatever ocean-wave technology was, it didn't matter. He had a guy to find. "Let's take a look at his office. Maybe we'll find some clues there."

Evelyn led the way, followed by Skip, who was followed by Roxy. They started down a hallway and Evelyn turned into the first doorway on the left. Another open doorway on the right led to a bedroom that Skip guessed had once been Roxy's. At the end of the hall, a door stood ajar, a flickering half-light peeped out through the crack. Skip continued down the hall to the door.

Behind him, he heard Roxy. "What the hell?"

He felt Roxy grip his shoulder as he pushed the door open slightly. He glanced inside the room, then smiled at her. "Just curious."

"You think we're so stupid that we didn't check the bedroom?"

"Not at all. When you're looking for people, it helps to know where they came from." He held her gaze. "What they left behind."

He waited half a second for a reaction. When he didn't get one, he mentally catalogued that also. This woman *was* dangerous. He continued, "Seeing what a nice house and wife he abandoned makes this all the more curious."

Skip walked past Roxy, who stood with her jaw hanging slack. He found Evelyn in Richard's office, where she'd turned on the overhead track lighting. She motioned toward the chair at the desk. He sat and recalled this morning's mistakes all too clearly. "Have you moved anything?"

"I spent about a half hour in here earlier trying to find something," Roxy said. "I went through his drawers, everything. I can't find his computer password."

Skip glanced from mother to daughter, then back again. So alike, yet so different. He scanned the desk. "He has no notes about anything? No reminders?" Roxy shook her head. There was nothing. Not a single clue.

Skip opened the top desk drawer. Pencils. Pens. Postage stamps. Paper clips. How strange. He opened another drawer. He found an address book with only a few entries. "Do you know these people?"

Evelyn said, "Most are relatives that live elsewhere. We've called everyone local that's in that book. No one has seen Richard."

In a file drawer, he found lots of hanging file folders. Skip thumbed through the labels. "Was your husband in the title insurance business?"

Evelyn nodded. "He sold the business, but could never quite give it up. He always said he wanted to stay on top of things just in case he had to go back to work."

All of the folders were blue with one exception, a yellow folder labeled "O-W Tech." Skip pulled the folder and laid it on the desk. He noticed that Roxy's posture stiffened ever so slightly. He had warning bells—again.

"I guess Dad also liked to follow what I was doing in my business. I just found it this morning. I never realized he was so interested. I could have told him a lot more about it."

"Any significance to the color?"

Evelyn picked up the folder and ran her fingers over the face. "Richard always liked color coding. He said it made finding things easier."

Roxy's face remained impassive. "That's the only reason I can think of. My dad's pretty anal in that respect."

Skip flipped through magazine articles, white papers downloaded from the web, and brochures. Odd, he thought, how a man who was so interested in his daughter's business wouldn't talk to her about it—unless that had something to do with why he disappeared.

Skip glanced around. "Evelyn, neither of you has cleaned this room, right?"

Both women shook their heads. Evelyn spoke first. "I haven't dared to clean up in here for the past couple of months. Richard would have torn my head off. He's been very particular about this room."

Roxy laughed. "Don't look at me. I have a cleaning service."

The pictures hung neatly on the walls. There wasn't a speck of dust anywhere. The mouse was clean. Even the keys on the keyboard, which would normally have discolored with oil residue, were spotless. One thing was obvious—Richard Tanner was no ordinary drunk. And if these women hadn't cleaned up in here, Richard Tanner had.

Skip said, "Mrs. Tanner, he knew exactly what he was doing. He sterilized this room before he left it."

CHAPTER THIRTEEN

She said, "Gotcha, Skip Cosgrove."

As I watched Skip Cosgrove rummage around my dad's desk, I had a short panic attack. What if he found Dad's password? That would mean we'd find out what Dad had been researching. We'd learn what had been making him crazy. And I might be exposed.

For the briefest moment, I didn't want this guy to do anything. But that was stupid because I did want him to find my dad. I considered how I'd deflect the investigation if he hacked his way into the computer, then suppressed a smile. This professional was having no more luck than I had had earlier. He made a weird comment about the room being sterilized by my dad. To me, that would imply Dad wasn't drunk.

Mom's brow furrowed and she glanced at me, then back to Skip. "What's that mean?"

"He didn't want anyone following his trail," I said.

Skip nodded. "Exactly. People always leave a trace of what they've been working on. Here, there's nothing. Your husband wanted to make sure that if something happened to him, nobody could come in behind him and retrace his footsteps. You could probably hire a forensic computer expert to go through this, but that would be expensive and time consuming. I know a guy who could do it. He might do it as a favor, but I don't know if he'd be available. He's got a big deadline. On second thought, maybe we'd be better off just going back to the old way of doing things."

"What's that?" asked Mom.

"Legwork," he said. "I'll need to go wherever he would normally go and ask around. I'll need a picture and a list of places to visit."

This wasn't anything I couldn't do. In fact, that had been my next step—visit the places Dad would usually go—not that there were many. There was his Rotary lunch—a week away. There was the bar around the corner from the title company—he hadn't been there in months as far as I knew.

"He'd been going to Agua Hedionda a lot lately," said Mom.

"What?" I blurted. That was ridiculous. My dad, a nature guy? "When did he start visiting the lagoon?"

"Maybe a few weeks ago."

"Had he gone there recently—in the last few days?" asked Skip.

Mom shook her head. "No. Not in the last few days."

"Something's bothering your husband, Evelyn. If we knew what that something was, we might have better odds. I suspect we won't figure that out until we find him. The lagoon's out for now. He'll probably be going someplace where he can drink."

"Keller's," Mom said.

I nodded. "The bar near the title company—Dad always used to go there after work. We could go do that now."

"I prefer to work alone," Skip said. "Look, if he's running away from something that happened here, seeing either of you might trigger a flight response. I'll go down there myself."

No way was I letting this guy out of my sight. If he found Dad and they started talking, my business dealings might come up. I had to go. Besides, I needed more time to work him for access to Nordoff. "My dad and I were always very close. He wouldn't run from me."

Mom's jaw fell. "And he'd run away from *me*?"

Skip stood and put his hand on Mom's arm.

I know he was only consoling her, but seeing him touch her like that pissed me off. I felt like an idiot. Was this guy stirring some primal instinct in me? Jealousy? Fear that he'd move in on my mom? I cleared my throat. "It's probably got nothing to do with you. But he'll be expecting you to come looking for him. If he's trying to sort something out on his own, seeing you would tip him off. Skip and I can handle this without alerting him to what's going on. Right?"

Skip grimaced. Actually, he looked annoyed. "It would be better if—"

"I'd like Roxy to be there," Mom insisted. "Richard would do anything for her. As I think she would for him."

That comment sent a chill to my soul. Would I? What if he asked me to not steal the five million? I gave that thought a quick burial. No way, I wasn't going there.

Mom continued. "She should go with you."

He glared at me. "You have to agree to follow my directions."

Oh, big bully man, I'm scared. Careful, buddy, or I'll knock you on your ass—unless you've got a higher-degree belt than mine in karate. "Sure. You're the boss."

He stared at me for a few seconds, obviously unimpressed by my quick acquiescence.

"What? I said you're in charge. You want me to sign something?"

He hesitated. "Fine. Just listen when I tell you to do something, okay?"

Shit, you'd think he knew me or something.

"Listen to him, Roxy. He knows what he's doing."

Jeez. What was this, the We Know Roxy Society? "And I know my dad. I want him back as much as you do!"

Mom took two steps and embraced me. She leaned her head against my shoulder. "I'm sorry, honey. It's probably all my fault. I must've done something, I just don't know what. Find him and bring him home. We'll work it out."

I gripped her shoulders tightly. "We'll find him, don't worry." I just wished I could believe that. "So, where's a picture for Skip and me?"

Mom relaxed her grip and then turned away. "I'll be right back."

Skip looked me in the eye. It gave me a creepy feeling, like he could see inside me or something.

"Roxy, I'm serious. I think I should do this alone."

I held up my hand, palm facing him, fingers splayed. "Talk to the hand. I'm going along. Quit complaining."

"Just let me make the initial contact, okay?"

As long as you get to him first, buddy. "I've got no problem with that. You did good with the Nordoff kid, I'm sure you'll do fine here."

It was no more than ten minutes later that Skip and I were headed toward Keller's in my Toyota. We'd agreed to take my car since we could always put someone in the back seat." I decided to stick to the business pleasantries. "Business must be good, you drive a Porsche."

In the glow of the dash lights, I found myself glancing sideways to take in Skip's features. He had a strong jaw and well-defined nose, kind of ruggedly handsome—if you like that sort. Who was I kidding? I did. He seemed to take on a different appearance in every light. Maybe it was just that he was good at masking his feelings. Hard to read. Like me. Damned if that didn't concern me. The last thing I needed was to be around a guy I couldn't manipulate.

"I only take a few cases like this. Mostly, I like to work with people to help build their self-esteem and improve their communications." His voice was deep, almost melodic.

"Are you a shrink?"

He laughed. "No. I'm a criminologist. I'm also trained in clinical hypnosis. I started out in the police academy, but I was a square peg in a round hole. I quit that to do what I love doing most, helping people make themselves better."

Oh, brother. His was as big a racket as mine. "So you're not a PI?"

In the dimness, his five o'clock shadow dominated. He stared straight ahead, his eyes glassy in the reflected glow. "For the most part I stay out of crimes. Those guys deal with the criminal element. Me, I prefer finding people who didn't break the law. Every now and again the cops bring me in. So what's your business? You said venture capital?"

Was he probing or just making small talk? Be careful around this guy, I thought.

I tapped my brakes as we came down Tamarack, making sure to keep my speed at the limit—and my response generic. "This is my first big deal. I worked for a VC before, but didn't like some of the practices." Like not sharing the profits. We were approaching the I-5 on-ramp, so I flicked on my signal. "It's a fascinating field, just tough to get a start."

"Where'd you get all that money, if you don't mind my asking?"

"I'm just a broker. I put together the deal, other people have the money. But I will get a nice chunk of the profits from the deal." Like, everything, I thought as we merged onto the 5.

"I guess that's how another client of mine got started, small deals."

"Nordoff?"

"Yeah, Nordoff."

"Is he looking for any new deals right now? I was thinking of calling him since I have one slot left open on this one." I dared not look at Skip, sure that he was sizing me up.

"So you know Herman Nordoff?"

"Peripherally." In the most generic six-degrees sense. I know you, you know him.

"Hmmpf. I have no idea. He didn't discuss his business deals with the likes of me. That's way beyond my ken."

I slowed for the off-ramp to Carlsbad Village Blvd. So much for Round One. I'd work him a bit later. If I pushed further now, he'd get suspicious. This way, he'd be left wondering why I hadn't asked for an introduction or recommendation. "Keller's is down in the Village. We should be there in just a few minutes."

"Let's hope we find our man," said Skip.

I made the turn onto Carlsbad Village Blvd. "I have a good feeling about this." And I did. I was sure I'd already found mine. Gotcha, Skip Cosgrove.

CHAPTER FOURTEEN

He said, "We don't have time for niceties."

The Carlsbad night air had an uncharacteristic cold bite to it. Dampness clung to skin like a cold, soggy blanket, leaving behind a chill that crept through to the bone. Skip wanted nothing more than to find Richard Tanner, return him to Roxy and her mother, and get home to a cup of hot cider spiked with something strong enough to knock away the chill.

Keller's was located on Roosevelt just a short distance from Carlsbad Village Blvd. Roxy parked in a lot to the side of the building. She'd driven there almost as if on autopilot and Skip surmised that she was no stranger to this particular bar. As they walked toward the entrance, he asked the obvious question. "Been here a lot?"

"Dad used to bring me here and sit me on the barstool. He'd feed me pretzels and beer." She laughed. "The bartender never told me it was root."

Skip let her laughter warm him. In the streetlight, her golden hair shone. Her smile had a childlike quality to it that just made him want to laugh with her. He opened the door, resolving to get this done as soon as possible and to put this woman in his rearview mirror before she got to him. No sooner had the door closed behind them than his cell phone rang.

"Go ahead, he's not here anyway," Roxy said.

He nodded and punched the connect button on his cell. "Cosgrove."

"Herman Nordoff. What the hell happened with that interview?"

Skip backed out of the warm surroundings and into the damp chill of night. The last thing he needed was to piss off Herman Nordoff. "I don't understand. I thought you wanted me to handle that."

"I did. But you were supposed to keep them from calling."

In the distance, a car alarm went off. Skip said, "Who's calling you, Herman? Which channel?"

The car alarm ended.

"Hell if I know, someone named Worthington."

"That's not the reporter I talked to. It's probably another station that picked up the story and wants an interview. Give me the number and I'll handle them. If you get any more calls, tell them to call me."

Silence.

"Herman? You there?" Skip said.

"Do you know what time it is?"

"Just after eight. Why?"

"You should have been off the clock hours ago. I expected to get voicemail."

Skip chuckled and thought, *so you called me anyway?* To Nordoff, he said, "It's no problem. Just keep my number handy and have the news chasers call me."

Nordoff gave him the number, thanked him for following through, then said good-bye.

"I'll call you tomorrow to check on Paul. You may even want to turn off the phone until morning."

Silence on the line had Skip beginning to wonder if Nordoff had disconnected. Several seconds later, he heard, "Skip, if you need anything. You know, a favor sometime. Call me. I like to repay my debts and no amount of money can repay you for what you've done for us today. Thank you."

Skip blinked. It was the second time he'd made the offer. Apparently, he was serious, not just being polite. "You're welcome. I'll keep that in mind."

When he disconnected, Skip stood in silence for a moment. The night air didn't feel so cold now. Inside, in his heart, he felt just a bit warmer. And Herman Nordoff had a heart, too. He laughed. Who would've thought? He opened the door and did a quick search for Roxy.

The inside of Keller's had the typical pub atmosphere—lots of highly polished dark wood; a backlit bar lined with bottle after bottle of different gins, scotches, rums, and more; and a bartender wearing a Padres baseball cap. Skip spotted Roxy sitting alone at the bar.

She motioned with her head for him to join her. She raised her glass of wine in his direction. "You want something?"

He shook his head. "Not while I'm working. Did you ask the bartender if he's seen your dad?"

She took a sip from her glass. "Nice chardonnay. No, I thought you'd want the honors."

He sat on the stool next to her and planted his elbows on the lacquered countertop. The bartender, a tall, skinny man who looked old enough to be Roxy's father, approached. Skip wondered if the guy's Padres cap concealed a hairless scalp. The bartender tossed a white towel over his shoulder. "Hey, Hot Rox, how's the wine?"

Roxy smiled. "Superb, Tommy."

Skip raised an eyebrow and watched Roxy. "Hot ... Rocks?"

Tommy laughed and winked at Roxy. "Not like in a stone, man, like in short for Roxy. Girl's thought she was hot since she was twelve. Probably before that. She conned me out of a quarter for the jukebox first time I met her."

Roxy smiled and tipped her glass in Tommy's direction. "You remember that, huh?"

"How could I forget? I'd worked here maybe two days when you walked in alone." He turned to Skip. "She bets me a quarter that she can get five bucks from the next guy who walks in the door. I figured I had nothin' to lose, so I took the bet. It was her old man who walked in, but I didn't know him because I'd only been here a couple of days. She walks up to him and says, 'Hey, can I borrow five bucks?'"

Tommy took a sip of water from a glass he kept behind the bar. "The guy hands her a five, then parks himself at the bar. She sticks out her hand and says, 'Pay up.' When her old man caught on, he was gonna make her give back the quarter, but I told him I'd lost fair and square. Kid did what she said she was gonna do. Been calling her Hot Rox ever since."

Skip watched Roxy's face as she took another sip of her wine. The eyes, the smile—he could see how this guy had been suckered so easily. Even as a child, Roxy had surely been a tease. He turned to Tommy. "Lesson learned, I guess."

Tommy nodded. "Ain't never taken another bet with another customer since, especially this one."

Skip leaned forward. "Actually, we're here because her dad's missing."

Tommy shook his head. "Drunk maybe, not missing."

The surprise was evident in Roxy's voice. "He was here? Today?"

"Till maybe an hour or so ago."

"An *hour*?"

"Yeah, He left with some guy I ain't never seen before."

Skip glanced at Roxy. "At least it wasn't a woman."

Roxy added, "Thank God for small favors. Where'd they go?"

Tommy raised his hands in a gesture of futility. "Don't know, Rox."

Skip glanced around the bar. He quickly counted a dozen or so stools at the bar and maybe twice that many tables. The place was perhaps half filled. "You do a good business for a Tuesday."

Tommy said, "I know what you're thinking, buddy, but none of these people was here when Richard took off. There were a few in earlier, but they was just grabbing a sandwich after work, then heading out. Wish I'd have known Richard went AWOL, I could've called Evelyn. It probably wouldn't have mattered much. The guy he left with seemed to connect with him pretty good."

Skip asked, "Did he know this guy?"

"Dunno. Like I said, never seen the guy before. They just struck up a conversation like they was old buddies. No, wait—the guy introduced himself. I think he said something about having worked for Richard once. I was getting kinda busy then."

"He was one of my dad's employees?"

"I dunno, Rox. Your dad didn't seem to recognize him at first. 'Course, he was pretty wasted by then. I never seen him drink like that before. I was gonna take his keys, but the other guy said he'd drive."

"I didn't see his car out front or in the lot where he always parks," Roxy said.

"Can't help you there, either. I can't really see where people park."

Roxy nodded. "I know. Just seems funny that it wasn't there if someone else drove."

"Yeah, you're right. Bizarro," Tommy said.

"Was Richard upset about something?" Skip watched Tommy closely and saw a glance at Roxy. He caught a slight setting of the other man's jaw.

"Yeah, but I don't know what he was upset about. He didn't say."

But you just did, thought Skip. "You said they left about an hour ago?"

Tommy nodded. "Wish I knew where they went."

Roxy drained the last of her glass. "So do I. I'm going to use the ladies room before we go. Be right back."

Skip nodded, thankful that he'd have a moment alone with

Tommy. As she slipped away, Tommy watched her while Skip watched Tommy.

"Girl's hot, man," Tommy said. "You her boyfriend?"

"She and her mom hired me to find her dad. I don't have much time. You lied about not knowing what Richard was upset about. Did it have something to do with Roxy?"

The color drained from Tommy's face. He grabbed the towel he'd hung over his shoulder and began to wipe the bar. "I—I can't."

"Richard Tanner may be in some sort of trouble. If you know something, tell me. I won't tell Roxy. This is in confidence between you and me. You don't have time to think about it Tommy, she'll be back in a minute."

Tommy let out a deep breath. "Richard never said exactly what he was upset about, just that Roxy lied to him about something."

"That's it? Come on, there has to be more." Skip glanced in the direction of the restrooms, no Roxy yet.

Tommy grimaced and crossed his arms over his chest.

"Don't lock up on me, Tommy. We don't have time for niceties."

"Okay, okay. It has something to do with Roxy's business. She's got him totally screwed up. He kept saying something about a scam."

Skip saw movement down by the restrooms, but it wasn't Roxy. Another woman emerged. She held Skip's gaze as she sauntered to a table where she sat with two other women.

"Barracuda, man, be careful," Tommy said.

Skip ignored the comment. "Did the other guy know anything about this? Did they talk about it?"

Tommy stared off into space for a second. "You know, now that you mention it, he did seem to be asking a lot of questions about it. Sounded like there was a lot of money involved."

"How much?"

"Don't know. I never heard a number."

As far as Skip could tell, Tommy wasn't lying. He spotted another movement by the restrooms. This time it was Roxy. He had thirty seconds, at most. "The guy that Richard was with, did he look dangerous?"

"Dangerous, I don't know. Suspicious, oh yeah. Big time."

Roxy smiled and winked at Tommy as she approached. "Hey, you two look deep in conversation. What's up?"

Skip nodded in Tommy's direction. "We have irreconcilable differences. He's a Padres fan, I'm for the Dodgers."

Her smile dimmed for a fraction of a second, but he noticed the reaction. She knew he'd lied. At this point, it couldn't be helped. They'd reached an impasse. She'd lied to him. He'd done it to her. He should walk away from this case. And her. But he felt a responsibility to Evelyn Tanner. He'd promised her he'd find her husband and he wasn't about to be the one to tell her Richard wasn't coming home. He had to find Richard Tanner as quickly as possible. And that meant he had no choice but to lie to Roxy. If he didn't, he had a hunch that Richard Tanner might never get home alive.

CHAPTER FIFTEEN

She said, "He's been kidnapped?"

Men seem to think that women have bladders about the size of a
thimble. All we have to do is say, "I gotta go," and they immediately
assume the "call" is legit. Handled properly, that little ploy can be
used to keep a guy at bay, reel him in, or just stall for time. On a double date, it can be used to compare notes, catch up on girl talk, or
even make up an excuse to bail. In this case, I suspected that Skip
had something he wanted to say to Tommy, probably about me, so I
downed my wine and played the ladies-room card—not out of neces-
sity, but curiosity.

As I suspected, the two clammed up immediately upon my return.
That could only mean one thing—my suspicions had been correct.
Like it or not, I had to wait to learn what it was that Tommy told
Skip. Despite the fact that I'd prepared myself for a ruse, the fact that
Tommy hadn't piped up with the truth hurt. I tried not to let it show,
but I didn't quite pull it off. Skip was probably as good at reading
people as I suspected, which meant that he knew that I knew that ...
Whatever.

We said our good-byes to Tommy and went outside. I breathed in
the cool air. "So, are we hitting a few more bars?"

"I think so. Maybe we'll get—maybe that guy took him to another
bar."

Mentally, I bit my tongue and held back a statement of the obvious. *After what you just pulled, you're definitely not getting lucky
tonight.* I pointed to my left. "There's O'Sullivan's over one block,
Mas Fina is an easy walk, too—assuming you're not dead drunk. But I
doubt that he's gone to either of those."

"Why's that?"

"If my dad wanted food, he'd probably have stayed here. But you never know."

He nodded. "I agree. What the hell, let's try 'em."

Skip tried to make small talk as we walked, but my mind was elsewhere. Now that I knew my dad had found a drinking buddy from the old days, I wasn't worried about him. Maybe I could turn this encounter with Skip into something positive—like a contact with Herman Nordoff.

In short order, we'd learned that my dad hadn't been to either of the two, so we expanded the search to a larger geographic area. It was nearly eleven and I'd lost track of how many bars we'd been to when we stepped into the chill night air and I said, "I don't think we're going to find him."

Skip shoved his hands into his jacket pockets. "As much as I hate to say it, I think you're right. Once they got in a car to go somewhere, they could've gone anywhere. Two guys who are drunk, who knows what they might do?"

I'd been nine the last time Dad had pulled a stunt like this. Oh my God. I'd been a holy terror for almost six months. For six long months I'd made Mom and Dad's lives miserable. I'd acted out in almost every way possible. I jumped at the touch on my left arm and jerked it away.

Skip peered at me in the glow of the streetlamp. "Hey, you okay? You look like you just saw a ghost."

"I'm fine. Just—thinking about my dad." I smiled. "I'm sure he's off somewhere with this new friend knocking down who knows what kind of drinks. He'll probably come home in the morning, or more likely, afternoon, with his tail between his legs."

Skip held my gaze.

I watched condensation from my breath dissipate into the night. "Guess I ruined your record for the day, sorry about that."

"I don't—oh, you mean Nordoff. In a sense, that was a lucky break."

"Because the kid was so into soccer?"

"Yeah. This is harder."

"Herman Nordoff has to be pretty happy with you right now."

He hesitated and hunkered down into his jacket. "Let's stay focused on your dad, okay?"

I thought, Dad's perfectly fine. He's found a new buddy. Mom's right, the pressure of his bad choices has gotten to him. "So, what do you want to do, then? We can't hit every bar in San Diego County."

"We need to figure out who the guy was that he met."

I stared at him, felt my jaw hanging slack. "Right. Middle of the night and we're going to do employment checks. We'll just call every former employee and ask them if my dad is sleeping on the couch by any chance."

Skip glanced at his watch. "It is late, isn't it? You should've called your mom."

"I didn't want to tie up the line in case Dad called her."

"Let's go back. I don't think there's much more we can do to-night."

We were quiet as we returned to the car. The silence continued and grew in the car until it dominated the air. Skip seemed lost in thought and the lack of communication wasn't helping my cause any. Somehow, I needed to get him talking again, this time about Nordoff.

Ahead of us, at the end of the off-ramp and on the other side of Tamarack, the circular remnant of an old 76 gas station sign loomed atop a fifty-foot support. The station had closed, the property had been fenced off, and the sign had been bagged in some weird black material that, on foggy nights, gave the place a ghostly cast. The station was an eyesore and an eerie reminder of how fickle fate can be.

I pointed at the closed station. "You ever wonder why they went out of business?"

"Who knows?" Skip said. "It could have been they needed to re-place tanks. Or maybe it's just too small. Everyone wants bigger stations like that." He jerked his thumb toward the AM/PM on the corner with it's brightly lit new pumps and minimart.

"My dad's business was small, but they had a good reputation. Even so, he couldn't compete with the big boys. That's why he sold out."

"Everybody bitches about crappy service, but what do they do? Flock to the big box stores for the lowest price. Your dad made a smart decision."

"That's where people like Nordoff come in. They finance those big deals so everyone can abandon the small businesses."

Skip turned sideways in his seat so that he was half facing me. "You're kidding, right? I'm not sure I condone all of his projects, but Nordoff's done some that have brought big improvements to several less desirable neighborhoods."

The light turned green, so I made my turn onto Tamarack. "That's true. He's got some environmental projects going, too? Doesn't he?"

"Beats me. All I know is that I see his name in the paper now and then. He's gruff, but he was certainly worried about his kid."

I made my turn off of Tamarack. This conversation was getting me nowhere. One last try. "I'll bet they're going to take the kid someplace quiet for a while, just to get away."

As I pulled into the driveway, Skip said, "I doubt it, they just want to get back to a normal life. That's what your mom needs to do, keep things normal. Do you want me to continue working on this tomorrow?"

"Let's ask her. Lights are on. Come on in."

I led the way to the front door, surprised that Mom wasn't standing in front of the kitchen window keeping guard. The porch light brightened the entryway, but left the doorknob and lock in shadows. I fumbled with my key, all the time wondering why Mom wasn't already at the door.

Inside, I flipped on the hall light. I called out, "Mom?" I faced Skip. "Where could she be?"

Skip's forehead creased as he turned to me. "Think she's asleep?"

Not Mom. She wouldn't fall asleep until Dad came home or she worried herself into exhaustion and collapsed. I walked into the living room. The lights were on, but no Mom.

"Roxy," Skip said.

"What?" I saw him point down the hall. Had something happened to her? I made it to the hallway in three steps. That's when I saw the light coming from Dad's office. Don't tell me she's been in there all night, I thought.

I took a deep breath and prepared myself for another crying jag. At the doorway, I looked in. There she was, sitting, staring off into space, at his desk. "Mom! What are you doing?"

Skip slipped into the room behind me. I barely heard him, but sensed his presence. "Evelyn?" He knelt in front of her. "Evelyn? Can you hear me?"

She stared at him blankly. Had she had a stroke? What happened?

Skip pulled a piece of paper from between her fingers. Her gaze followed the paper as he held it out for both of us to read.

My eyes widened as I read.

My pulse quickened.

Skip muttered, "Shit."

My breath caught. I had to read the cryptic message again. I stared at Skip, then Mom, then Skip again. The words almost stuck in my throat. "He's been kidnapped?"

CHAPTER SIXTEEN

He said, "This isn't about money."

Skip stared at the note. Computer generated. Laser printer. Nothing unique. Probably the work of a professional.

He read the message again. It was the worst possible scenario. One he'd never considered given the circumstances—middle-class family, retired, no major assets.

But the message on the note was clear. "We have your husband. Have $5 million ready by noon or we will kill him. No police."

Kidnapping had never been a crime directed at just the rich, but *five million dollars*? Were these people insane? The Nordoffs had that kind of money, not the Tanners. This had to be a mistake.

Skip read the fear and concern for her husband's life in Evelyn's watery eyes. They were tinged in shades of red far darker than before. The worry lines ran deeper than they had just a few hours ago. It was almost as though she'd aged ten years since he'd last seen her. She asked the obvious, and the most desperate, question. "What am I going to do?"

Skip took in Roxy's features—eyes glistening, jaw set. "This has to be a joke. A sick, twisted, perverted ..." Roxy turned away; her voice cracked. "Who'd do this?"

"And why?" Skip said. "Neither of you have this kind of money. Do you?" He already knew Evelyn's answer. She'd as much as said she had little left. But Roxy, what did she have? He remembered what Tommy had said at the bar. Roxy could be involved in some sort of scam. Was this all some sort of elaborate plan to get to her?

Roxy stared across the room into the corner. She shook her head. "How did this arrive, Mom?"

Skip felt his brow furrow. Why had she dodged the question?

Evelyn picked up an envelope from the desktop. She held it out. "The doorbell rang. I don't know, maybe an hour ago? I thought it was you—maybe you forgot your key or something."

"The envelope was on the door?" said Skip.

She nodded.

Skip started to take the envelope from Evelyn, but stopped. If it had fingerprints, they didn't need to complicate the forensics processing. "There might be prints on that. We should use gloves."

Roxy grabbed the envelope from Evelyn. "That would only be if we went to the cops. And we can't do that."

Skip fought back the impulse to slap her hand, but it was already too late. He settled for examining the envelope over Roxy's shoulder. It was a standard business #10. White. Self-sealing. The message on the front of the envelope had apparently been generated by a laser printer also. It read, "URGENT! EVELYN TANNER."

This wasn't what he'd signed on for. He was supposed to find a missing husband, not conduct a kidnapping investigation. "Look, I'm sorry, but I'm not licensed for this type of work. You need a private investigator. Better yet, the police or FBI."

Evelyn let out a moan. She stared up at Skip with pleading eyes. "Please."

"I'm good at tracking people," Skip said. "I'm a good hypnotist. But I'm not a PI." And not trained to investigate cons, if this was one. If so, who was being conned? And for what purpose? Other than the few grand that he'd made this morning, he had no money. He remembered Roxy's questions about Nordoff. His instincts told him Evelyn was on the level, but what about her daughter? Was this some sort of plot to extract money from Nordoff? Impossible. Nordoff had no reason to become involved.

"Maybe that's what we need," Roxy said.

"Need? What, a PI?"

"No, a hypnotist. Mom, did you see anything when you went to the door? Maybe you saw someone or something that could help."

Evelyn's lower lip quivered as she seemed to try and recall the moment. "There was something, some movement."

Skip asked, "Was there a car running? A person? Anything?"

She shook her head. Her cheek twitched. "I don't know."

Roxy persisted. "You could hypnotize her, right? Maybe she'd remember the details."

Evelyn Tanner just looked so *sincere*. She was a middle-aged housewife, not a con artist. She had to be telling the truth, right? That left Roxy. He dismissed the thought. No matter what she was doing, she wouldn't kidnap her own father. Would she?

"So will you do it?" Roxy said.

He could hypnotize Evelyn, but why? If they didn't have the money and they weren't going to call the police, Richard Tanner was a dead man. "I doubt that anything she remembers is going to bring your dad back. You don't have the money. You've got to call the police. If they want me to hypnotize your mom, sure. As it stands, there's no reason to put her through that." He watched Roxy's face carefully as she processed this information.

"If Mom and I had more information, maybe we'd know how credible this is. We'd know whether to start scrambling for money or try to buy time or—or even bring in the cops."

"Mr. Cosgrove, if it would help find Richard? Please?"

Skip shook his head. "This isn't a good idea, we're wasting time."

Roxy put her hand on his arm. Her eyes looked like two pools ready to spill over. "What do you want? More money?"

"This isn't about money. The more time the cops have to deal with this—they have negotiators."

"I'm a negotiator. A damn good one, too."

"You're personally involved, Roxy. Your feelings would get in the way."

The first tear traced a crooked path down her right cheek. "You arrogant bastard! Look at my mother! This whole thing is killing her. You think we don't want to call the cops?"

Skip tried to interrupt. "I'm just saying—"

"And do you think the cops are going to do something in *twelve hours*. Wake up, Skip. This is a crisis. We don't have time for them to gear up. If we don't do something, my dad is going to be dead tomorrow. Assuming this note is for real."

Skip watched the tears stream down her cheeks. He felt a hand clutching his and looked down. Evelyn held his left hand in both of hers. He took a deep breath. "What do you mean, assuming this is for real?"

"You heard how drunk my dad was. What if this guy he ran into decided to create this hoax just to—I don't know, upset my mom? Other than the letter, we don't have any proof."

Evelyn croaked, "You think this could be a hoax?"

What the hell? This could be her *father's* scam? Skip shook his head. "Nobody gets that drunk."

"Then let's see what my mom remembers. What happened? Who delivered this?" She shook the envelope in her fist. "What have we got to lose? You're getting paid, why the hell can't you just go along and do what we want?"

"This may be a kidnapping, but I don't think it's about the money." He examined Roxy's face, then Evelyn's. He sighed. Maybe he could do some good. Maybe they could figure out what really happened. Assuming this wasn't a scam. His curiosity was killing him. Who was behind this? Roxy? Her dad? Was this a kidnapping? Or something else?

Skip made up his mind. "I suppose there's no harm in trying. Hoax or not, I still think we need the police. I could do an induction and we can see what your mom remembers. I have to warn you, though, this may not work."

"Why?" asked Evelyn.

How could he tell her that he suspected her daughter was somehow involved? How could he tell her that perhaps Roxy had something to do with Richard's kidnapping?

CHAPTER SEVENTEEN

She said, "I'll get these bastards if it's the last thing I ever do."

I watched, fascinated, as Skip sat Mom on the couch and began what he called his induction. My job was going to be to listen to Mom's descriptions and write them down. Skip had said to transcribe everything, no matter how insignificant it seemed. While I wasn't terribly confident that this would produce a meaningful result, it wasn't an option I could overlook. I'd learned a long time ago that whether you were talking about interior design or pulling a con, the details made the difference. I wasn't about to skip any details in trying to get my dad back.

Skip's voice was soothing and melodic as he spoke to Mom. "Evelyn, you're standing on the beach watching the ocean. See the waves slowly drifting in. Each wave is peaceful, relaxing, gentle."

Mom giggled nervously. "Does this really work?"

Skip said, "Close your eyes. You're beginning to relax. See the waves. See the blue of the ocean and how it welcomes you. Take a step toward the shore. Relax. Release your tension."

Mom's facial muscles began to relax. His voice was so—man, did my eyes want to close—so soothing.

"Take another step toward the water. Feel the warm sand beneath your feet. The sand is soft and warm. Soft and warm ... it feels like powder between your toes ... with each step you take toward the water, you feel more relaxed. Now feel the waves lapping at your toes."

Maybe I could put this guy on a CD and play his voice every night before I went to sleep? My face was beginning to feel relaxed, too. Mom looked like she was about to fall over.

"The water is at your knees. Your toes are relaxed. Your calves are relaxed. Your eyelids are heavy."

Boy, were they. I shook my head. This guy was *good*. What could I learn from him? Anything I could use? His reassurances were making Mom as pliable as a Gumby doll. That's what I needed in my business, more pliable clients. I'd have my five million in no time. My eyelids felt lead weights dragging them down. I needed coffee. I needed ... My head fell forward, snapping me back to consciousness.

Skip glanced in my direction.

I mouthed, "Sorry."

He continued without missing a beat. "You feel yourself floating in the water, Evelyn. Your eyelids are heavy ... heavy ... relaxed. You're drifting to sleep. Let your mind relax. You can open your eyes now and you'll remain asleep. You're going to remember what happened earlier tonight."

I blinked and rubbed my face with one hand. Circulation. Circulation. I needed to be awake for this. I wanted to learn from this guy. Maybe I could take him on my next call? No, then he'd know the scam.

"Evelyn, what happened when the note arrived?"

"I was sitting on the couch. I wasn't paying attention to much of anything, but there was this knock. I thought maybe Roxy had forgotten her key. I got up from the couch and went to the door and opened it. That's when the envelope fell down onto the ground."

"Was the envelope stuck in the door?"

"I think so."

"Did you see anyone?"

Mom cocked her head to one side and she looked up. "I'm not sure."

As I made my notes, I imagined the front yard, where Mom would have been standing at the door peering into the night. It was hard to picture it, but maybe the notes would help.

"Evelyn, you can see every detail in the yard just as it was when you opened that door. You're right there now. Do you see the yard? Your memory is crystal clear. Are you there?"

"Yes, I see it."

"Good. You're not frightened or worried. Just watch the scene as if it were a movie. As you see things happen, I want you to describe everything you see. Can you do that for me?"

"Yes."

"Go ahead, then. Take your time and describe everything."

It was like she was reliving the incident, which, I suppose, she was. At least, in her mind she was. I wrote furiously, doing my best to keep up.

"I hear a noise at the front of the yard. There's a shadow. A man, I think."

"What's he wearing?"

"Jeans and a dark shirt. It could be a sweater. He has on a hat and those funny shoes with the reflectors on the backs."

Skip nodded. "What kind of hat?"

"It has a bill in front, but nothing in back. I guess it's a baseball cap."

"That's good, Evelyn. Is there anything else you remember about him?"

"He's short and heavy, but he moves quickly."

"I want you to picture his face. Take a moment to picture him, his skin color, distinguishing features, anything you can remember."

"His face is in shadows. I can't make it out."

She blinked, hard.

"You're fine, Evelyn. Tell me what just happened."

"There was a flash."

"It's okay. Relax. Just watch his face while that flash occurs. Do you see anything else?"

"He has a bright tooth."

Skip leaned forward. "What?"

"He's got a tooth that kind of sparkles when the light hits it."

"You're doing great," Skip said. "Is he getting into a car?"

Mom's brow furrowed. "No, I think he's riding a motorcycle."

"Why do you think that?"

"I can hear it idling in the background. Now, it's starting up— going away—like he's making a turn in the street."

Other than the sound of the clock in the corner ticking, the room was silent. Skip looked like he was stumped. I sure as hell didn't know what to say, other than I was in awe. This was *amazing*.

Skip asked, "Evelyn, do you know this man? Have you ever seen him before?"

"No, I've never seen him before."

He turned to me. "Any questions you can think of?"

"Yeah, can you teach me to do that?"

He smiled and then turned away. "Evelyn, I'm going to count to three and tap you on the shoulder. When you feel the tap, you're going to wake up. You'll feel refreshed and will be able to remember everything you told me. You're also going to feel stronger, like you're able to handle the pressure of this situation. One. Two. Three." He reached out and gave Mom's shoulder a gentle tap.

Her eyes opened and she glanced around the room. "I remember it all. Oh my God. I remember what happened at the door!"

My cell phone began bleating. It was a new text message. "Who the hell is texting me at this hour?"

I pulled the phone from my purse and shut off the ringer.

Skip seemed to be ignoring me and my telephone tribulations. "Evelyn, how are you feeling? Are you relaxed?"

Mom glanced down at the floor, then from side to side. "I feel better. I don't know why. More secure."

"Good. That's what we want."

My cell vibrated in my hand. For crying out loud! I glanced down. Another message from someone I didn't know.

Skip asked, "Who is it?"

"I don't know. Probably a wrong number. About once a month, I get a text from some idiot who thinks I'm someone else."

"Always the same guy?"

"Oh, no. Stupidity and bad dialing skills are as contagious as the flu. With a little time and practice, anyone can learn them. Fortunately, it doesn't usually happen this late at night."

Skip looked at me, then Mom. "I still think we need to call the police."

My phone vibrated again. This was beginning to piss me off. "I have to get rid of this guy, otherwise he might be doing this all night." I pressed the key to check my messages. The first message appeared on my screen.

"5 mil or he ded by 12 pruf nxt"

"Jesus Christ! It's from the kidnapper. It says we have to have the five million or Dad's dead by noon tomorrow. He's sending proof."

Skip reached for my phone. "Let me see that."

"No!" I jerked away, my fingers working frantically to move to the next message.

My eyes widened as I stared at the image on my screen. It was Dad, bound and gagged. Someone held a copy of the North County Times with today's headline in front of him. My fingers began to shake and I dropped the phone. Skip picked it up and studied the photo. I curled up and clutched my knees to my chest. My God! They had him. They really had him. Until now, it had all seemed like a big mistake or a bad dream. Now it was real. And it was my fault. He'd been drinking because of my business, I was sure of it. He'd told someone about the five million and now they wanted it.

"Was there another message?"

My blood pounded in my ears. My breathing was fast and ragged. "What?"

"Get it together. Was there another message?"

"Hit the—never mind. Gimme that." I snatched the phone out of Skip's hands. I glanced at Mom, her serene exterior had cracked. The veins in her forehead stood out, her skin was flushed. That's exactly how I felt, too, as I brought up the next message.

"NO COPS R ELS."

"They say no cops."

Skip said, "They always say that. They're counting on you being too afraid to call in the authorities. You have to be strong. You have to call the cops."

My dad's kidnapping was on me. If it hadn't been for me, he'd be safe and nothing more than bored in his retirement. I'd done this. "I don't have to do *anything*." I shouted. I brought back the picture of my dad. "You see that! These people have my father. He's never hurt a fly. That's the man who raised me, taught me everything!" And what had I learned?

Skip put his hand on my arm. I shook it off. "Roxy, you have to think clearly," he said. "You have to look at this logically. How did they get your phone number? How did they know to text you?"

"Maybe my dad—"

"Could be. Or it could be someone who knows you. But that's not the big question. We need to stay focused. Be logical. How can we get him back safely? That's our goal."

"Logic? Screw logic. You see that!" I pointed at the cell phone image. "They hurt him. They hurt *her*." I pointed at Mom. "I'll tell you one thing, I'll get these bastards if it's the last thing I ever do!"

CHAPTER EIGHTEEN

He said, "Salud! Loser."

Skip saw the frustration and anger in Roxy's eyes and the fear in Evelyn's. To both, he said, "I understand how you feel."

Roxy glared at him. "The system is screwed up."

Skip nodded. "I've been there. I had days where everything seemed that way."

"Yeah, I'm sure you've had bad days like this."

The bite in Roxy's tone made Skip wince. "I graduated from the University of California at Irvine with a degree in Criminology. The criminal mind fascinated me. Ever since I was little, I had dreams of joining law enforcement. You know—typical kid stuff like put the bad guys away and clean up the world. When I got out of school, I realized that I'd basically ignored the career counseling. I was the classic kid who thought he knew more than the experts. Why should I ask them for help?"

"What's this got to do with my dad?"

"I never made it into law enforcement. My career—no, my life—took a left turn when a car accident with a drunk put me in physical therapy for three months. I spent six months seeing a shrink. Even after six months of therapy, the psychological scars weren't healing. My life was headed down the toilet—really gruesome for a kid of twenty-two—I was getting worse, not better. I was halfway down the path to becoming an addict. That's when my psychologist recommended hypnotherapy. Sounds trite. But it changed my life."

"How nice," said Roxy. "Now that we know all about you, I guess you can leave since you're not willing to help us."

He glanced at Evelyn. "She's pretty impulsive, isn't she?"

"God yes. I thought she'd be the death of me when she was growing up."

Roxy glared at both of them. "You two can sit here and have a nice chat about me and sip tea or something. I've got to find my dad."

Skip kept his voice level, but stern. "*Sit down.*"

He was surprised when she actually did. The fire in her eyes flared, but she stayed put.

Skip continued. "I said my life changed. I wanted to be in law enforcement. I wanted to help clean up the streets. I still do. Yes, I've been arguing to bring in the cops because, in my mind, it's the safest thing to do. Roxy, these people know something. Either that or they're incredibly stupid and grabbed the wrong guy. Since they texted you and sent you a photo of your dad, I tend to think they're not that stupid. Which leads me back to they know something. Kidnappers don't do this unless their goal is within reach. So tell me, what do they know?"

"Why?" Roxy's face was flushed.

He saw her anger rising. Was there anything he could say to appease her?

"You're just going to go to the police. You're just going to do what your little criminal justice courses told you to do."

This woman—how did she know what it took to push every single hot button he had? The last thing they needed was to fight among themselves—but doing anything on their own without the police could put all of them in danger. And he knew better than to play vigilante. "I'm sorry, but I can't be a part of this. I'm not licensed or trained for criminal investigation."

"Then get the hell out! Mom and I have work to do."

"Mr. Cosgrove, thank you for what you've done so far." Evelyn grimaced and stared off into the corner.

Skip realized she was thinking of a way to dismiss him. He'd quit jobs before, but he hadn't been fired in a long time.

"I understand. I wouldn't stay if I didn't have to," she said.

Her matter-of-fact discharge hurt more than Roxy's anger. Anger he could deal with, being irrelevant was like a knife in his gut. He was caught between two opposing forces. Legally, he couldn't stay. Emotionally, he couldn't leave. He couldn't stand the thought of failing. "Thank you. Good luck, both of you." Skip stood and walked toward the front door.

Evelyn followed him. At the door, she delivered the deepest cut of all. "Send me a bill for your time."

Skip's stomach churned as the door slipped shut behind him. He stared at it, feeling like he was being locked out of a room because he wasn't old enough to see what was going on. Logic told him those feelings didn't matter. He should dismiss them. What mattered was doing things within the law. He stared at the door for a few more seconds, then turned and went to his car.

He glanced back to the front of the house. Evelyn had turned off the porch light already. Or had it been Roxy, sending a signal? *You're fired.*

Though there was a streetlight just a short distance away, the tree near the street cast the front yard in darkness. Loneliness washed over him. He'd failed. He told himself that it wasn't his fault, that he'd been caught in the undertow and sucked under by someone else's actions. The pep talk didn't help.

His gaze followed a line from the front of the house to the street. Evelyn had seen the man running away. What if he'd left something behind? Skip pulled a flashlight from the trunk. He traced the path from house to street, going slowly and examining the ground carefully.

He stood in the spot where he guessed the motorcycle had been parked. In the darkness, he saw nothing. Who was he kidding? Even if the person who had delivered the envelope had dropped something, what good would it do? Forensic science was good, but it took time.

He walked back to the Porsche, returned the flashlight to its cubby hole, got in the car, and fired up the engine. He sat for another minute thinking about Roxy and her mother before he backed out of the driveway and drove home.

At his condo, Skip parked the car and then went for a walk on the beach. He left his shoes and socks by the front door and rolled up his pants. The sand, like the air, felt cold and damp. Overhead, the moon's glow cast white reflections off the ocean's surface. His eyes slowly adjusted until he could make out shadows along the shore— clumps of seaweed that had washed up formed an endless line of sentries along the waterline.

A small wave splashed his feet. Tonight, even the chill of the water felt hostile. The ocean, which he normally longed to be near, seemed to be telling him—no, ordering him—to leave. Go away. You're a loser.

The sand and water continued to suck away the heat from his feet until his calves felt numb. When the feeling extended up to his knees, he turned around and headed home. He was shivering by the time he got inside, a cold numbness flowing like sludge through his veins.

He glanced at the clock. It was nearly two in the morning. He poured himself a shot of tequila, downed that, then had another. On his third, he offered up a toast, "Salud! Loser." The golden liquid went down easy. Too easy. He recalled the months after the accident. At least then he'd had a goal. He'd had people who hadn't given up on him—unlike what he'd done with the Tanners. He downed another shot of tequila, turned off the lights, and crawled under a blanket on the couch.

The tequila would numb his thoughts, he hoped. But it didn't. Instead, his feelings of failure intensified. He found the remote for the TV and flicked it on. He channel surfed until exhaustion took hold. The TV blurred. He muttered, "This is a chick thing. Isn't this what they do when they get upset? Maybe I need a bucket of ice cream."

He fell asleep on the couch, muttering to himself about women, ice cream, and how, with hundreds or thousands or millions of TV channels available, there was nothing to watch.

CHAPTER NINETEEN

She said, "Tell me where he keeps his gun."

At seven o'clock when I awoke, I realized how dark my mood had become. I hadn't slept well and a sense of gloom permeated my thoughts. I glanced outside. How appropriate, I thought. The morning sky was still a dull and monotonous gray—another of those half-lit, foggy-mornings we know so well. Today's marine layer hung nearly a thousand feet up in the sky. It would take a few hours, but the blanket covering the coast would burn off. Eventually. Maybe.

Skip was right about one thing. Whatever else I did, whatever the cost, I needed to remain focused on getting my dad back.

I had about $50,000 in my bank accounts. Mom had said she could raise another $50,000 by tapping the one source Dad hadn't maxed out, their line of credit on the house. If I hit my credit card for a cash advance, I could probably get another $20,000. That gave us $120,000 toward the ransom. It also meant my mother would lose the house in foreclosure within a few months. I grimaced. Well, so much for squeaking by. They wouldn't have to worry about that anymore. Adding a new loan payment would tip the scales in the wrong direction.

I took a quick shower to wake up, foregoing the usual leg shaving and tedious prep work we women have to go through. I bought coffee on my way to the office at one of my usual haunts—perhaps I was looking for some sense of normalcy in this whole crazy situation.

It was almost eight when I got in and discovered that the office door was still locked. Stella. Up to her old tricks. Until recently, she'd always shown up late. For a couple of weeks now, she'd been coming in early claiming that she had work to do. I didn't question her, but it led me to believe she might be looking for another job. The girl really was as dumb as a post if she thought she'd make this kind of money elsewhere.

At my desk, I punched the button to fire up my computer. While the machine went through its cycle to come alive, I paced in front of my desk. The boot-up process took forever this morning, but the second time I checked, the machine was ready for a password. I typed that in and began to pace again. Damn it! Where was Stella? What was I going to do about the money? I needed almost $4.9 million. That just didn't grow on trees. Unless that tree was my business clients' money.

I logged into my business account. The current balance had gone up just a bit thanks to the pittance in interest I was getting. The balance was now $4,838,002. Combining our $120,000 with that would give us $4,958,002—about $42,000 short. What would the kidnappers do? Was I willing to sacrifice everything to save my dad? I already knew that answer.

It was time to call Mom and if by some miracle Dad was home, I wouldn't need to do this. If he wasn't, I was going to be broke, a felon, and on the run for the rest of my life with nothing to show for it. I sat in the chair behind my desk and sipped my coffee while I stared off into space. Everything. Daddy, you're about to cost me everything. My head throbbed, but I had no tears left. I was dried out. Worn out. But I'd do it. I'd sacrifice it all just to get him back. I owed him that.

I dialed the house. The phone rang twice before Mom picked up. "Hello?" Her voice sounded weak and old.

"Did Dad come home?" I didn't have to ask, I already knew the answer.

"No, honey. Maybe we should call the police."

"I have the money. Well, I don't have it in hand, but I have access to it. They don't want cops. Neither do I."

"How did you—"

"Don't ask," I warned. "All you need to know is that I have almost all of it. You need to get the $50,000 from your line of credit." My cell phone beeped. It was another text message.

"Do U hv mny?"

"I have to go, Mom. I just got a text from the kidnappers. Call the bank. Tell them you're going to need that $50,000 today."

"But—"

"Call you back in a minute." I disconnected. My mouth went dry.

It was one thing to think about giving up everything, another to commit to it. I'd really do this?

I started typing a reply. "Hv mst. 42K shrt. OK?" My finger paused over the send key. I closed my eyes and sent the message.

I frittered away the next five minutes, worrying about how I could come up with more money. How could I have told them we didn't have it all? Now they were going to kill my dad.

My cell bleeped. Another message.

"OK. Snd dlvry nstrutsns 1 hr."

Tears welled in my eyes. They'd gone for it. In an hour they'd tell me how to get the money to them. I had to work fast. Given the banking laws and restrictions on large withdrawals of cash, I was certain these guys would be using an offshore account. Once that money was wired to the account, it was gone. There would be no duffel bag, no bicycles riding through the park picking up a satchel, none of that Hollywood stuff. This was real. I wouldn't send the money until I had Dad safe and secure, but how would I negotiate that? I didn't know.

I locked the door behind me on the way out. I got in the car and hit the speed dial key for Mom. It's illegal to use a cell phone while driving in California without a hands-free device. But everyone else does it and this was an emergency. The line was busy. Goddammit! Get off the phone. Shit, I'd told her to call the bank. I tossed the phone onto the passenger's seat and drove like hell.

As I pulled into the driveway, I spotted Mom perched at the front window. No sooner had I reached for the doorknob when she wrenched the front door open. "Roxy!" She threw her arms around me.

I squeezed my eyes shut and held on tight. Oh, God, to be eight again with no worries. No cares. Before that horrible man. Before ... My cheek felt wet. I didn't think I had any tears left—guess I was wrong about that, too. "Mom. I had a message from the kidnappers. They say they'll take the amount I have. It's not quite five million, but it's close enough."

"How did you get that much money?"

I glared at her. "I told you, don't ask. You don't want to know."

She wrapped me in her embrace again, this time even tighter. "I can't lose you, too."

I pushed her away.

She crossed her arms over her chest and began to rock back and forth. She sobbed, "I can't. Don't make me choose between you and your father!"

"You don't have to. It's done." The pressure in my head was killing me. After today, I'd never see her again. This time, I grabbed her and pulled her close. "I'm sorry, Mom. I'm sorry for everything I've done." I set my jaw and pushed her away again. My eyes were wet, I probably looked like hell, but we had a lot to do.

Her lower lip trembled and her breath came out in ragged bursts. "This can't be happening."

"It is. Did you call the bank?"

She nodded. "They wanted wire instructions. Where do you want the money sent?"

"I don't know yet. I'll be getting a text message in about ..." I glanced at the clock on the wall. "... in about twenty minutes."

"They said noon."

"That was the deadline. This is just to send me wiring instructions."

"You're going to *wire* the money? Like they do in those movies where it goes to an account where only the bad guy can get to it?"

"I'm assuming that's what they'll want. We could never get that much cash in one day. Any idiot knows that."

Mom shrugged. "I didn't. I just assumed—I guess I was being stupid."

"Not stupid, Mom, just naive."

"When did you become the expert on this kind of thing?" She stared at me, the outside corner of her left eye crinkling just a bit.

"I need one more thing."

"What can I do?"

"I need something of Dad's."

"Sure, what?"

"Tell me where he keeps his gun."

CHAPTER TWENTY

He said, "This is a kidnapping."

Skip sat on a boulder the size of a small car watching the swells roll into the jetty. Each tidal surge approached in a lazy march through the narrowing channel. The funnel effect compressed the waves as they pressed on through into Agua Hedionda Lagoon. Further inland from where Skip sat, the tidal surges settled into a steady current that controlled the wetland area and reinforced nature's delicate balance.

The waves seemed to mirror his anger with Roxy Tanner, his emotional ebb and flow perfectly synchronized with the channel's pulse. He'd been here since before the first light of day and the steady rhythm hadn't yet washed away his anger and frustration. He just couldn't seem to release it. Yesterday morning at this time, he'd been walking the beach and wondering if he wanted to take on Wally's high-paying client. Today, he sat here like a moron wondering why he wasn't helping a woman who couldn't pay him, had lied to him, but needed his help desperately even though she didn't realize it.

Another wave surged through. Skip's anger boiled. She *manipulated* me. She *lied*. She—she was the most exasperating woman he'd ever met. And the first to get under his skin. He remembered the way she'd flashed that smile in the bar last night when she returned from the restroom. She knew he was lying to her, but she'd let it go. That's because *she's* a liar! He watched another wave's rise and fall. Damn her.

The clouds smothered the coast with their gray. It seemed a perfect beginning for a perfectly screwed-up day. In the distance, he spotted surfers making their way into the water with their boards.

Maybe he should get his. No. He just wanted to be angry. He just wanted to curse her. Maybe then he could start to put her out of his mind.

In the distance, he watched a surfer misjudge an approaching wave. He paddled to gain momentum. He got his knees under him, then slowly started to raise himself to a standing position. He never made it. The wave slammed into his body, his board shot from under his feet almost immediately and he tumbled into the surf. The board hit the end of its tether and jerked back toward the surfer, nearly hitting him in the head. "Serves you right—amateur." Skip mumbled. "You were over your head."

He let out an exasperated explosion of air. "I suppose that means I deserve what I got last night." He turned his attention away from the surfers toward a pair of women walking. As they crossed the bridge over the channel, the one closest to Skip motioned with her hands. It was like watching a mime act. Did her words match her animated gestures? Who knew? Just like he'd never know what happened to Richard Tanner. Unless he saw the story on the news.

He rubbed his face with his hands. His lips tasted salty. How long had he been here? He checked the clock on his phone. Nearly two hours. What was he going to do? Spend the whole day moping around? Let her ruin his life, too? He wondered if he should call Evelyn. She didn't deserve this. He considered throwing the phone in the jetty, then jumping in after it. Oh Jesus, was he screwed up or what? "Come on, Skip, get over it. She's just a page in your book." A page he'd subconsciously savored last night, but wanted to forget today.

His back ached as he stood and balanced himself on the boulder. He traversed the rocks cautiously, aware that one moment's inattention could trigger a fall and weeks of painful recovery. Back on the sand, he followed the shore, closing his eyes when there was no one else around and letting the crashing of waves massage his senses. Hopeless romance, he thought. Not me. He picked up a handful of wet sand and compressed it into a tight ball. He weighed it, stared at it, and then compressed it again in his hands. "Roxy Tanner, I'm letting you go. You'll have nothing more on me. No more hold." He reared back and threw the ball into the ocean. As the ball approached the apex of its arc, it disintegrated.

He closed his eyes and drew in a deep breath of salty air. When he opened his eyes, he snickered. "They're right. It doesn't work." As the next wave rolled in, he let it wash over his feet and ankles, then bent over and rinsed the sand from his hands in the chill water. He wiped his forehead and cheeks with his cold fingers and palms and tasted the salt again. Getting her out of his head was hopeless—getting over her, impossible. He let out a tired sigh with the realization that the old trite saying was true. Only time would heal this wound.

His phone rang as he approached the condo. He checked the display. Evelyn Tanner. His pulse quickened. Should he answer? He swallowed hard. He had to. "Cosgrove."

"Skip, this is Evelyn. We still need your help. Roxy says she has the ransom together. She's on her way. Skip, I can't lose her. Can you come over here?"

Her voice was choked. He could visualize the tears on her cheeks, the red around her eyelids, and the little blotchy patch of white on her forehead where her emotions played out. "Evelyn, I don't know that I can—I mean, should, interfere. Roxy was very clear last night."

"You *can't* let her do this."

I can't? Was she nuts? He doubted that he could stop Roxy from stepping in front of a bus if that's what she wanted to do. He mustered his best compassionate tone. "Why would that be?"

"Because, I can't lose both her and my husband. Please, I'll do anything. *Anything.*"

Skip's eyes watered. He rubbed the back of his neck, which felt hot despite the fog's clingy cold.

Her voice was in his ear again. "Please. What's your price?"

He massaged his forehead. He had a killer headache building. He'd like to think it was the tequila and lack of sleep, but deep down he knew the real reason. It was because Evelyn was right. He couldn't walk away. He was in free fall. He had no lifeline, no parachute, and no safety net. And he had no way to stop. "I'll be there in under an hour. I'll try. Save your money for the ransom, Evelyn. Bye."

He disconnected, jogged into the condo, grabbed some coffee and went to the bathroom. He popped two aspirin and got in the shower. The hot water spray pounded his face. He let the pelting continue as his mind wrestled with Evelyn's news. *Roxy had the five million?* Tommy must have been right. Roxy was running a scam. The water's pounding eventually numbed his face and sent the tequila's aftereffects into remission. He should call Evelyn back and dump this case, but knew he couldn't do that. No, there was another option.

As he dried off, he decided that it was time to take up Herman Nordoff on his offer. He pulled on a pair of khaki pants, a blue "Porsche" T-shirt, and grabbed his jacket. He dialed Nordoff's number.

"Herman Nordoff."

"Herman, Skip Cosgrove. Guess it didn't take much time for me to think up a favor."

"You name it. I meant what I said."

"I'm involved in another case. The problem is, I have a client who claims to have a lot of money and I need to be sure she really does."

There was a moment of silence. "Your fee went up?"

"No. It's for a ransom. This is a kidnapping."

"Oh. What do you want to know?"

"Roxanne Tanner. She runs a venture capital firm. I need to know what assets she has."

Nordoff whistled. "You can pick 'em, Skip. That's a helluva favor. But I can do it. It'll take some time."

"I don't have much. Maybe a few hours."

"That should be enough. I'll call you when I've got something."

Ten minutes later, he was driving to the Tanner residence in silence, wondering how in the world he'd fallen for Roxy Tanner. Everything was wrong about her. *Everything*. Then why couldn't he get her out of his mind?

CHAPTER TWENTY-ONE

She said, "He's a dead man."

Mom and I had argued about Dad's gun, but in the end, she realized that my argument about not being able to trust kidnappers and needing protection was true. That was my argument to her. If she knew what my true intentions were, she'd never have shown me his hiding spot.

Mom opened Dad's side of the closet and pointed to the top shelf. "It's up there."

"The blue box?"

She nodded. "I told your father I never wanted it near me. So he put it out of my reach."

I had to stand on my tiptoes, but was able to finger the box out and catch it as it fell from the shelf. It was heavier than I'd expected and nearly went crashing to the floor. "He doesn't keep it loaded, does he?"

"He said he wouldn't. He *promised*."

We took the box into the kitchen, where I placed it on the counter. I lifted the lid and found myself staring at a black case and a box of ammunition. Cold fear shot through my veins. Was I really going to do this? Kill someone? "Did—did he ever—practice with this?" Thank goodness I didn't say shoot someone, though that's what I wanted to ask.

Mom's voice was solemn. "He went to the firing range several times a year. He said if he ever needed it, he wanted to feel confident. He wanted a reliable gun if he ever—you know. Roxy, have you ever fired one of these?"

"Sure." Technically, I hadn't lied. The truth was that I'd fired a gun twice at a firing range and came close once in Hawaii. "I went out with this guy who was all NRA. He rode a bike. He wore leather jackets. He even looked like George Clooney. He took me to a firing range both times we went out."

"You dated a guy who looked like George Clooney? And you let him get away?"

"He got pissed because I could shoot better than him. He had lousy eyesight and a bad case of the shakes from too much drinking. When we met, I thought, 'This guy's hot!' Then I wised up and figured out he was a loser."

We both laughed nervously. Mom and I had never talked about my dating habits before. Most of the guys I'd dated had "Loser" stamped on their foreheads, which wasn't a record that made me proud. I guess I just had bad taste in men. I said, "It's the only way to save Dad."

"Call the police, Roxy. I don't want you to do this."

"The guy who did this, he's a dead man."

What little color there was in Mom's face drained away. "You said you wanted protection."

"It's the only way this will be settled. Otherwise, we'll always wonder if—or when—he might strike again."

Didn't Mom get that? Didn't she understand what criminals were capable of? I sure as hell knew. Firsthand. I knew what I was capable of. I knew others who would do far worse things than I'd ever thought to do. Besides, as soon as the cops started sniffing around my business, I'd be in jail for a very long time. I'd rather live in self-imposed exile on a beach than have to deal with prison politics. In fact, I'd rather be dead than have to deal with prison politics. No matter what happened, I'd never be able to help them again. I needed nothing less than a permanent solution.

The box of ammunition indicated that the bullets were a 9x19 caliber. I checked the owner's manual for the gun, it was a Glock 17. "Dad wasn't kidding that he wanted reliability."

"That's what he said. I don't know anything about guns."

And I didn't know a whole lot more. *Just enough to be dangerous* fit my skill set level. And with one of these I could be just that. I heard a car door in the driveway and glanced out the kitchen window. "What the hell is *he* doing here?"

Mom dropped her gaze to the floor. Her lower lip quivered. "I called him."

"You *what*? *Why*?"

She bit at her lip. "Because we need him. Especially—now."

"Mother!" I shoved the ammunition back in the box and closed the lid. "Don't you dare say anything about this. Not a word!"

I didn't wait for her answer, but marched to the front door. I jerked it open just as Skip was about to ring the bell. I didn't even look at his face before I shouted, "We don't need you! Go away!"

The second the words were out of my mouth, I felt awful. He looked like a puppy that had been kicked for the first time. Despite the rejection painted on his face, he held my gaze. Shit, he was either tough as nails or as needy as a newborn.

I said, "I'm sorry. That was rude. Still, you're off the case. I'm handling this. Thank you, good-bye."

He reached out and put his hand against the door as I started to close it in his face. "No. I'm not leaving."

For once in my life, I was speechless. My tongue traced a path inside my lips as I tried to think of something to say. He wasn't acting mad, not angry, just so damned matter-of-fact. *No. I'm not leaving.* Who the hell says that? Behind me, I heard Mom.

"Roxy, let Skip in. He's here at my request."

I glared at her and saw my own resolution staring me in the face. My bravado fizzled. I had only enough energy to fight one war, if that. My resistance was tanking and I was five all over again, learning my manners with company. I stepped back and opened the door wide. "Come in."

"You look tired," Skip said.

"Didn't sleep much."

"Me either. Let's get your dad back, okay? Then, if you want, I'll leave you alone."

My heart pounded frantically with enough force to send a message across any distance. He probably couldn't hear it, but I could. Its message—at least to me—was clear. *This man will bring you down.* Skip walked past me without a second look and headed straight for my mom. I felt a little surge of jealousy. He was being nice to her, but I got the business tone. They hugged.

"How are you holding up?" he said.

She gave him a weak smile. I knew that meant she wasn't doing well, but her words were quite different. "Not too bad. Thank you for coming so quickly."

"It's okay. I want to help." He glanced at me. "What's up?"

He obviously caught my quick glance at the blue box with the gun because he immediately went to it and lifted the lid, "Please don't tell me you've got the cash in here."

His face went white as he saw what was in the box.

"Insurance." I said.

"Against *what*?" He said as he read the box of cartridges and then the imprint on the case for the gun.

"Losing my money and my dad. I want to be sure we don't get double-crossed."

"Glock 17. Sweet." He pulled a little key thingy from the bottom of the handle and stuffed it in his pocket.

"You know the gun, I'm impressed."

"Still have mine from my days in the police academy."

"That's right. You said you wanted to be a cop."

He probably thought I hadn't noticed that he'd pocketed that little key from the gun, but only a blind man could have missed it. Maybe he hadn't wanted me to miss it. "What was that you stuck in your pocket?"

"The lock for the gun. Your dad was smart and bought a lock. I have the key. The gun's useless unless you want to use it as a club. Here." He extended the weapon in my direction.

"Give me the key! I need it."

"I think I'll hang onto it so you don't hurt yourself."

All right, wise guy. You want to play games? Two can play. I rushed forward and began pounding my fists on his chest. It felt like a good imitation of the classic female in distress move to me. He seemed almost amused by it. Little did he know that I could just have easily broken his arm and flipped him onto the floor, then taken the key from him.

He gripped both my wrists and held them tight, my face inches from his. His hold was firm and strong. It didn't hurt. In fact, it almost felt—good. His grip made my back stiffen. For an instant I didn't want him to release me, then I regained my composure. "Let go."

He smiled and, with that damnable confidence, said, "Are you done?"

An overpowering desire to break the hold and hit him where it would really hurt came over me, but I shook the feeling. Why deck him when all I needed would be a quick distraction? I glanced down. "Yes."

A fraction of a second—the briefest moment of inattention on his part—and the key would be mine. I hadn't practiced that particular talent in a while, but it would be no problem. I'd learned to pick-pocket when I was twelve.

CHAPTER TWENTY-TWO

He said, "Tell him it's me, not you."

For the first time in his life, Skip knew what an overloaded electrical circuit felt like. Every conceivable emotion seemed to course through his veins as he held onto Roxy's wrists. He'd pocketed the safety key to Richard Tanner's Glock 17 for two reasons. First, he'd dropped his .357 Sig into the trunk before leaving the condo and saw no sense in using the lighter caliber weapon when he had the Sig at the ready. Second, he wanted to prevent Roxy from doing anything that would make her predicament even worse.

But now that he supposedly had her locked in his control, he realized that he'd done it for a third reason—to provoke exactly this type of response. But what sent him into complete overload was the "Little Miss Helpless" routine. It was a practiced response to an aggressive situation. He'd felt the almost instinctive move she'd started to make to break his hold when he'd gripped her wrists—then she'd stopped and done that demur little glance to the floor. That glance had sent him into free fall again. He began to wonder if the real reason he wouldn't give her the key wasn't that he couldn't trust her, but that he couldn't trust himself.

When the standoff had finally played out, they discussed their options. The more they discussed things rationally, the closer he came to returning the key. She'd used a gun before. The situation was dangerous. He could give her the key with instructions to keep it in her pocket. But he kept coming to the same conclusion. He couldn't trust her.

She'd already lied to him several times. She'd pumped him for information about Nordoff. And now she'd played him again.

It was 10:45 a.m. when Roxy's phone vibrated and let out a high-pitched, squeaky war cry, "Banzai!"

Skip snorted. "You planning on going to war?"

"I had nothing better to do at four this morning. It seemed quite appropriate to me."

The corner of his mouth curled up in a smile of recognition. "I went for a walk on the beach."

Roxy's fingers darted over the screen of her phone. "At four?" A second later, "It's from him. He's giving me an account to wire the money to."

"We're not sending anything until we have your dad back."

"That's what I'm telling him." Here, read this. She stood next to him.

Skip's pulse raced when her hip bumped against his shoulder. He shifted position as he took the phone.

"Sorry," she said, then walked away.

He read her text, "Hv $, mst hv xchng 2 snd, meet where?"

He turned and saw her sitting at a dining-room chair, staring off into space. "That's good. Proactive, I like it."

"Go ahead and send it, if you know how."

He sent the message. "You're not the only one with a smart-phone." He connected to the GPS tracking web site he'd told the Nordoffs about.

"What are you doing? Give me that!"

"I'm downloading an app I recommend to parents to help them track their kids."

"Why the hell would you do that?" She tried to take the phone from him, but he twisted away from her. "Whatever. Mom! We're going to have to leave in a few minutes."

Evelyn came into the room. Skip felt his heart sink. She had a dazed look that telegraphed sheer exhaustion. Her face was chalky and she clasped her arms in front of her.

"I think I fell asleep on the couch." She rubbed her eyes. "I didn't sleep much last night."

Skip tried to console her. "No need to explain. We understand."

He glanced at Roxy. She nodded and winked. He felt his pulse jump. What was it about this woman that he found so damned desirable? If he could understand that, maybe he could regain his control.

Roxy approached her mother and took her into her arms. "We'll be back later. We're bringing Dad home, safe and sound. You just remember that, okay?"

Skip wanted to caution her not to get her mother's hopes up, but the words caught in his throat. There'd be time enough for Evelyn to grieve if their plan didn't work. She'd have the rest of her life. Why not give her just a few moments solace? "That's right," he chimed in.

As if on cue, Roxy's phone screamed, "Banzai!"

She read the message silently, then said, "We're supposed to meet him in thirty minutes on the bridge over the jetty on Carlsbad Blvd."

Skip blinked. "What? Why there?" That was the spot where he'd spent the morning watching the ocean.

Roxy handed him the phone. "Make sure I got it right."

He read the message. "Shit. He's not going to hand off your dad there. He's making sure we don't have any cops. We're going to be chasing our tails for a while."

"Not us, me. He'll run if he sees more than one of us."

"Then I'll go. Text him back, tell him it's me, not you."

Evelyn added, "Please, honey. I couldn't bear that."

Roxy shook her head. "No. I have to do this."

He recognized the signs. Her resolve was an obvious, impenetrable shield. He knew it would do no good to caution her. Her eyes had glazed over. Her lower lip pulsed with anticipation. She had an adrenaline rush he couldn't overcome or compete with. He couldn't stop her. He knew it.

He capitulated. "Do you want the gun? And the key?"

Roxy smiled. She held up Richard Tanner's Glock 17 safety-lock key. "This?"

Skip swatted at his pocket. He jammed his hand down deep. His jaw fell as he stared at her. "What the hell?"

She winked at him. "I have a very light touch. Don't I, Mom?"

Evelyn shook her head and let out a nervous laugh. "Skip, my daughter has been incorrigible since she was seven."

Roxy corrected her. "Eight. I was eight when I grabbed the Rolex."

Evelyn gazed at her daughter with admiration. "I never thought I'd say this, honey, but I'm glad you were so difficult. It might just save your father's life."

CHAPTER TWENTY-THREE

She said, "I'm being kidnapped by Bush and Nixon."

As I stood on the bridge over Agua Hedionda Lagoon, my knees felt weak. My stomach churned. If possible, I was even more scared than when I'd been thrown into the trunk of that man's car. Maybe it was because there were two lives on the line this time.

Walkers ignored me as they passed. Beneath the bridge, seawater surged through the channel to feed the lagoon. Groups of people walked, talked, and laughed. I, on the other hand, was alone. My only comfort—and it wasn't much—was that Skip watched me from a parking spot further down Carlsbad Blvd.

It made sense that the kidnapper would have me come to this location, then send me somewhere else to make sure I was alone. Skip and I had agreed that this might happen several times before I made personal contact with him. At least I could see Skip from here. He looked like any other guy taking in the ocean scenery—but so many things could go wrong.

My phone rang. Okay, I told myself, be strong. "Yes."

"Go to the other side of the street. Now!"

The caller disconnected. The urgency in his voice drove me into immediate action. If he could see me, he knew that there was no traffic at this moment. I surveyed the area. No suspicious looking people in any direction. Shit. I hopped the barrier and dashed across the street. As I stood on the center divider, I watched cars approaching from the south. Traffic behind me cut off any hopes of retreat. As soon as I reached the other side of the street, my phone rang again.

"*What?*"

"Head towards town. Stand under the lamppost with the No Parking sign at the end of the bridge. You have thirty seconds." The caller disconnected again.

He *was* watching. He also needed phone etiquette lessons. I spotted the lamppost. At least, I hoped I had the right one. That's when I realized I'd used up half my time searching for the damn thing. Now I had to run to get there. To the north, a laughing couple pushed a stroller in my direction. To the south, runners and walkers did their thing. *Where was this guy?*

I ran toward the spot and had to squeeze past the couple with the stroller. I'd just made it to the lamppost when a white Ford Focus pulled to the side of the road. I peered about wild-eyed. The closest person was a runner halfway back on the bridge. The couple with the stroller had their backs to me and neither would be willing to jeopardize their child for a stranger. And neither would I. A gun pointed at me from inside the car. The person holding the gun wore a Richard Nixon mask.

"Get in!"

I hesitated. The voice sounded familiar.

The driver pulled the slide on the gun and pointed it at me. "Now!"

I opened the door and swallowed hard as I sat in the passenger's seat. This wasn't how it was supposed to work. Skip was on the other side of a divided road, he could never follow me. He'd have to drive the opposite direction just to turn around. As I pulled the door shut, I realized that there was someone in the back seat.

I felt a gun jammed into my ribs by the person in the back. "Give me that purse."

I handed my purse over my shoulder and saw that the backseat passenger wore a George W. Bush mask.

Bush ordered, "Sunglasses."

I took off my Donna Karan sunglasses and set them in my lap. Nixon grabbed them and tossed them in the back seat.

"Hey! Those are—"

"Shut up," barked Bush.

I said, "Great, I'm being kidnapped by Bush and Nixon."

"Close your eyes," said Bush. "And your trap."

I did and heard a ripping noise. Next, I felt tape applied to my face.

The tape held my eyes shut. Something cold and metallic clamped around my left wrist, then my right.

I started to scream, "No!" My words were muffled by another

piece of tape across my lips. I squirmed in my seat, panic flooding through me. "Mmm! Mmm!"

"Shut up."

It wasn't Bush. It wasn't Nixon. It was the man who haunted my dreams. I thought I could trust him. He looked like a businessman. But back at his car, he picked me up and threw me in his trunk before I could do anything. Now, it's dark. And hot. And smelly. The smell is awful. It's like a dead—no! No! I tell myself. Don't think about that. He's the one. The man that Mom and Dad have been talking about.

The car jerks forward, then bounces up and down. The floor is so hard. I feel my tree house key jam into my butt. The car stops. I'm going to die. Soon. My eyes begin to sting.

I shift position and feel the key jam into me again. My safety pin! It was huge. I reach behind me and fumble with the pin. I can hear footsteps.

The pin opens and I scratch myself as I pull it from my jeans. I hear a key in the trunk's lock. The trunk opens and I'm blinded. The man grabs me and pulls me from the trunk. He's got me halfway out of the trunk when I slash down with the safety pin.

I feel the pin rip through his skin.

"Son of a bitch!" His face screws up in pain. "What the—"

I slash again, this time catching his cheek. The pin pulls from my hand as he twists away, blood spurting from his face. He lands on the ground and hits his head. He lays there. Still. No movement. Blood pools from his face on the ground.

I turn and run, vowing never to trust anyone again.

CHAPTER TWENTY-FOUR

He said, "Where the hell did they go?"

Skip sat on the concrete wall watching Roxy wait on the bridge. It twisted his gut to see her having to handle this by herself, but they'd agreed that the kidnapper would bolt if she wasn't alone for the meeting. From his vantage point, which was about a quarter of a mile away, he had a clear view of Roxy. If she made a move, he'd know it the second it happened. If they told her to drive somewhere else, she'd have to go to the far side of the bridge, down the stairs, just to get to her car. It would take her five minutes. He'd need far less than that to get turned around and follow.

He'd been watching for about ten minutes when the expected happened. She pulled out her cell. He felt certain that the kidnapper was telling her to meet in a new location. He'd keep her moving around until he was sure she was alone. The trick was going to be for Skip to stay far enough away to make the other guy let down his guard.

They'd worked out a set of signals—rub her neck if the instructions were to go north, stamp her foot if she was going south. Either way, he'd be ready. In a way, it was a relief when the call came in. It meant the kidnapper was still willing to deal and felt comfortable enough that they could move the game forward to the next step. But Roxy gave no sign. No rubbing of her neck, no stamping of her foot. Instead, she glanced north, then hopped the concrete barrier and started across the road.

Skip swore as she checked traffic coming from the south. What was she doing? He waited and watched.

When she crossed the center divider, he felt an overwhelming urge to throw up. Not only could he not see her when she started trotting north, his car was pointed in the wrong direction. He had to move, and fast.

By the time Skip got in his car, traffic had come to a near standstill. He yelled out the window. "Goddammit! Move!" But nothing happened. Didn't anybody want a goddamn parking spot? He caught a break when the car in front of him inched forward and a guy in a beat-up Chevy let him out. Skip gunned the engine. He crossed over to the left lane just as he approached the turnaround. He glanced in his driver's mirror. No Roxy. He couldn't see a damn thing back there. He made his U-turn as the last car in a long line passed him. He hadn't seen her in over a minute.

He drove north on Carlsbad Blvd. and across the bridge, but there was no sign of Roxy. His stomach flip-flopped. Blood pounded in his ears. She was gone.

Now they had her, too. How could he have let this happen? His biggest concern was no longer whether they could free Richard Tanner, but how he could possibly tell Evelyn that her daughter had been taken also.

Would they let Roxy go or just take the money and kill her and her father? Could she lie and stall until he found her?

He pounded the steering wheel as he sat at the red light at Tamarack and Carlsbad Blvd. He stared, dejected, straight ahead and asked himself, "Where the hell did they go?"

And why in the hell had he let this happen?

CHAPTER TWENTY-FIVE

She said, "I'm here to save you."

"She okay?"

"Looks like she had a panic attack."

I realized that Bush and Nixon were talking about me. My breathing was returning to normal. My head ached in back and on the right side—it felt as though I'd been slammed into something.

"Glad that's over." It sounded like Bush.

"She's pretty screwed up."

Was that Nixon? I didn't know. I didn't care. The side of my head was killing me. I must have banged it on the passenger's window when the panic set in. I thought about Skip's soothing voice. Use what you learned, I told myself. Focus on what happened. I replayed Skip's induction with Mom. Yeah. Calm down. Concentrate.

I pictured how things had happened. These guys were smart. They'd left nothing to chance. I realized I'd heard them both speak, Nixon when she'd ordered me into the car and Bush after that. That's right, Nixon, was a woman.

How long had I been incapacitated by my fears? Probably not long, but—it felt like we'd just pulled into a driveway.

I heard Nixon shift in the seat next to me. "I'm going to remove the tape from your mouth. If you make a sound, your dad is dead. Got it?"

I nodded. She removed the tape slowly.

I muttered a hoarse, "Thank you." I heard my door open and felt cool air.

Bush commanded, "Out."

The voice wasn't muffled anymore—they'd ditched the masks.

I twisted sideways and put my right foot onto the pavement. A hand grabbed my right arm and guided me out of the car. I felt something get thrown over my shoulders. If there was anyone watching, they'd see a couple helping what appeared to be a blind woman—or a drunk—walk. But where?

In the background I heard traffic noises—cars accelerating, the hum of tires. We must be close to a major intersection. Maybe I-5? A hand seized my arm and pushed me forward. I stumbled on something hard and started to fall. Hands grabbed each of my arms and pulled me up before I could hit the ground.

"Be careful," Bush said.

Was he speaking to me or to Nixon? We'd only walked a short distance when we made a right turn. We walked a little more, then stopped and I heard a key in a lock. A door creaked and one of my captors pushed me forward. We were inside now and the air was heavy with the scent of anticipation and fear. I heard rustling noises of some sort. Someone pulled the coat from my shoulders and took the sunglasses off my face.

The last thing I expected was for them to pull the tape from my eyes. "Ow!" Having the tape removed hurt, but the brightness in the room was overwhelming. I closed my eyes and then opened them slowly. Still bleary-eyed and handcuffed, I took in the scene around me.

There were four other people in the room. Besides Bush and Nixon, who had donned their masks again, there was another captor wearing a Bill Clinton mask. Clinton was about five foot eight and stocky. He probably weighed around a 170 pounds. The three captors were dressed identically. All wore black turtleneck shirts and blue jeans. Clinton wore a pair of black tennis shoes I surmised to be brand new, whereas the other two wore old white ones. The other difference was that Clinton had a holster on his hip with a gun at the ready. The other two wore theirs in their waistbands.

The fourth person was tied to a dining-table chair. He was hooded, but I recognized one of Dad's shirts and trademark khakis. He, too, was handcuffed, his hands held behind the seat back.

I summoned my best confident tone. "Dad? Are you okay?"

A muffled, "Roxy? What are you doing here?"

Handcuffed and helpless, I smiled at the irony. "I'm here to save you."

Dad was silent for a moment, probably trying to process what was happening. "Let her go! I'll give you whatever you want. Just don't hurt her."

Clinton spoke for the first time. "You don't have anything we want. She does." He glanced at me. "Do you have it?"

I nodded. "Just like we discussed. I can do a transfer. But I have to be sure you'll let him go."

"You'll have to trust me on that."

The muscles around my mouth tightened in a grimace driven by the absolute preposterousness of the idea. I, a con artist, had to trust a kidnapper. "In a perverse way, that's almost funny. You really expect me to just turn over five million without a guarantee?"

From beneath Dad's hood, I was sure I heard a groan, then something that sounded like, "Oh, Roxy."

Clinton unhooked the safety strap on his holster. My gaze remained on the gun.

He crossed his arms. My heart pounded. My throat went dry.

"Good," he said. "You understand. Your only guarantee is that if you don't transfer the money, you and daddy die right here, right now."

The room started to spin. Everything I'd worked for was going to be gone and I couldn't even be sure my dad would be safe.

"Give Miss Tanner a chair. I think she needs to sit down," Clinton said.

Nixon crossed the room and dragged a chair to where I stood. "Here."

That voice. It was muffled, but familiar. I sat.

"You have two minutes to decide," Clinton said.

I didn't need two minutes, my answer was obvious. "I can't transfer the money if I'm handcuffed."

Clinton shook his head. "You think I'm that stupid?"

Did that mean he knew about my martial arts training? Did he expect me to take on three of them when they had guns? Either this guy wasn't that bright or he knew me better than I knew myself. "I don't have my computer," I whined.

He nodded in the general direction behind me.

I stood and crossed the room to the computer. "Internet and all, huh?"

"Get to it."

Though I couldn't see their faces, the other two kidnappers appeared nervous. Nixon fidgeted with her mask, then took up a position I recognized immediately. The voice. I realized who that voice belonged to. "Ste ..." I caught myself. If they realized I knew who one of them was, Dad and I were dead. I studied Bush.

He stammered, "What are you looking at?"

"Nothing," I spat. "I'm looking at nothing."

Bush charged in my direction, but my kick caught him squarely in the groin and sent him screaming to the floor. He curled up in the fetal position, but before I could even think about enjoying my small victory, a kick from behind took my legs out from under me. I landed with a thud that drove the air from my lungs.

"Roxy! Roxy! Are you okay?" Dad yelled from beneath the hood. He jerked in futility against his restraints.

Clinton stood over me, the barrel of his gun pointed at my head. "You shouldn't have left your back exposed."

He was right, I'd made a beginner's mistake. And he knew it.

"Roxy! If you've hurt her—"

Clinton said, "She's fine." The mask stared at me. "Pull another stunt like that and you'll be dead before you hit the floor. I'm not an amateur, Miss Tanner. I let you have that one to teach him a lesson. There'll be no next time. Understood?"

His voice was calm and devoid of emotion. My insides churned with a dangerous combination of rage and fear that pumped my system full of adrenaline and dulled my senses. I nodded, not sure if words would come out.

I glanced at where Bush lay on the floor and realized that Nixon, the person I thought was Stella, was tending to him. Did they know each other? How well?

Underneath his hood, I heard Dad sobbing. "This is my fault. Roxy, are you okay?"

Clinton shook his head. He pointed at Bush. "Get him down to the car. This is only going to take a couple of minutes."

Nixon helped Bush to stand and they hobbled toward the door. Meanwhile, Clinton backed away. "On your feet, Miss Tanner."

"Roxy?" Dad's sobs grew louder.

"I'm fine, Daddy. This will all be over soon enough." But would we be alive?

It was just Clinton and me—odds I might be willing to chance if he didn't have a gun, if my hands weren't locked in these damn cuffs, if he didn't have fifty pounds on me and if he didn't know how to fight at least as well as I did. Rationalizations—all of them.

Clinton pointed the gun at my dad's hood. "What's it going to be, Miss Tanner?"

Using both hands, I pushed myself up and stood. "I'm up. Now what?"

"You need to log into your bank account and transfer the money. After that, I'll leave you two alone—and alive. You'll be free to leave. I'll even give you this." He held up a small key, which he probably wanted me to believe was for the handcuffs.

"Right." I could feel the tears welling. I couldn't let this man see me cry.

"As I said, it's your only choice. Your money will do you no good in hell."

The brutal truth of his statement stunned me. The silence in the room was the sound of my world crashing down around me. Clinton was right. I had nothing to lose. My nest egg was lost either way. An uncontrollable trembling preceded the first tear. I loathed the idea of showing my captor that he'd broken me, but I couldn't stop it. I'd lost control over everything in my life. *Everything.* And this man had brought me down. I wanted to kill him.

Clinton motioned with the gun.

For the first time since I'd gotten out of diapers, I had to completely trust another human being. In one swift lesson, I'd learned to never trust a soul. And now, I had to trust this—this criminal—someone not that different from me. My alternative was to die with my father, his death on my conscience. Through bleary eyes, I realized the most basic fact of all. In the game of life, I'd failed.

I held up my manacled hands. "You win." Tears streamed down my cheeks. My voice caught. "Whatever you do to me, please, let him live?"

He motioned with the gun again. "My half of the transfer is already set up. Add your information and you two are free."

I closed my eyes and turned toward the computer. As I sat there, trying to bring the screen into focus between my tears, I kept hearing my mother's voice. "You keep that watch. It's a fake ..."

CHAPTER TWENTY-SIX

He said, "Blow this and you'll be dead."

The light at Tamarack turned green and Skip gunned the Porsche. He drove home as fast as he dared and made it in seven minutes. He rushed into his condo, woke up the computer and quickly typed in the address for the GPS locator service. Thirty seconds later, he knew where Roxy's phone was located. If she still had her phone, he knew where she was. What if she didn't?

He knew if he called the police now, he risked putting both Roxy and her dad into a hostage situation. It was also possible that the kidnappers had ditched her phone. No, he needed to be sure. He'd drive to the location. If he saw something suspicious, he'd call the cops. If he didn't, he'd poke around, pretend to be lost. Once he was sure of her location, he could move.

Less than ten minutes later, he pulled into the parking lot of a rundown apartment building. Five cars were scattered around the lot—a blue Buick that was missing a wheel, a beat-up red Mustang, two Honda Civics, both tan, and a white Ford Focus. All of the cars were empty as far as he could tell, but there was a woman walking away from the Focus. In her left hand, she held something that flopped around as she walked. Skip got out of the car and watched her closely, his stomach knotting as he realized that the object she carried was a Halloween mask and that she had a gun in the waistband of her jeans in the small of her back.

He could take her out, right now. That might give him leverage.

Skip walked quickly toward the woman and said, "Miss? Hey, can you help me? I'm kind of lost."

The woman faced him, irritation etched on her face. She had dark hair that stood up in back as though she'd been necking. Or taken off a mask, he thought. The sleeves of her black turtleneck had been pushed up and she had perspiration on her forehead. He pulled a business card from his wallet.

Skip did his best to sound sincere. "I'm looking for this apartment. My friend wrote down his number, but I can't read his writing and don't know this place. Maybe you could—"

He leaned into her as if to show her the card. She put her left hand behind her, in a weak attempt to hide the mask. She grimaced, obviously unhappy with the intrusion, but unwilling to make a scene by refusing him help.

She jerked her head. "The manager's place is over there. She can probably help you." She started to back away.

"I'm sorry. I didn't mean to intrude. If you could just read this." He leaned in again, now less than a foot away.

She made another face and shook her head. "Whatever."

Skip's blow struck with a force that sent the woman sprawling. The mask flew from her hand and landed in the bushes. She fell sideways, then hit the ground face down. I hope that hurt, Skip thought.

He landed on top of her and pulled the gun from her waistband. "Where's Roxy Tanner?"

He flipped her over. Her eyes were glazed and her vision obviously blurred. He'd hit her harder than he'd intended, but the blow had apparently taken away her will to resist.

She sputtered a mouthful of blood. "Four. She's in four."

"How many others?"

She held up one finger. "He's got a gun."

He flipped off the safety and checked the magazine. "You're going in first. Blow this and you'll be dead. Don't tip him off."

He hauled her up and shoved her toward Apartment 4, which had the drapes drawn. To his left, in a different apartment, he noticed the drapes slip closed, like a gentle wave—someone had been watching.

At the door to Apartment 4, he whispered, "Do you need to knock first?"

She shook her head. "I think I'm gonna puke."

"You'll have plenty of time for that. Just remember to be cool."

She turned the doorknob. Skip took a deep breath. This one's for all the marbles, he thought. Winner takes all.

CHAPTER TWENTY-SEVEN

She said, "You've got it all wrong."

No sooner had my finger pressed the send button than I heard the front door open. I shot a glance over my shoulder. Stella stood in the doorway. She had no mask on. Blood stained her chin. Behind her stood Skip, in his hand, a gun. From the corner of my eye, I saw Clinton reach for his holster.

In two seconds, Skip and Stella would be dead. Then, me. And Dad. I took an off-balance leap from the chair toward Clinton. He swatted me away like a fly, but this time, I was prepared for him. I landed on my side and rolled to my right. Too late, I realized that I'd rolled into the chair where my dad sat. His chair fell sideways and Dad went with it. Without thinking, I pushed myself up and jumped to my feet. Two gunshots echoed throughout the apartment. I gave Clinton a kick to his back and he spun toward me. My next kick caught him in the jaw. He stumbled backward. Then, instead of shooting me, he turned back to the front door, instinctively knowing the intruder was the greater danger.

I grabbed for the gun in his hands as he aimed at Skip, but his elbow caught me in the jaw. Clinton's gun went off and Skip went down. He rolled and started to bring his gun up, but Clinton kicked it away and then hit Skip with his pistol hard enough to slam Skip's head into the floor. I kneed Clinton in the side and jarred the gun from his grasp. He stumbled away. I readied myself for his attack.

Instead of attacking, Clinton scanned the room. He seemed to be assessing the situation. Gunshots fired, Stella dead, Skip down. If he dealt with me, the cops would be here before he could escape. He said, "Next time, kid." He turned and ran out the front door.

Behind me I heard my dad groan. To my left, Skip struggled to his feet. Before me, Stella lay bleeding. In the distance, I heard sirens. I stood in place, torn, not knowing what to do next. Those few seconds were the longest of my life. Clinton's words echoed in my mind. *Next time?* He intended to find me—at a time and place of his choice.

I rushed across the room, grabbed the key Clinton had set next to the computer, and tried it on the handcuffs. I unlocked both cuffs, then grabbed Skip's gun, determined that if Clinton and I were to meet again, it would be on my terms. I'd catch him now. Those were my terms.

I knelt next to her and put my cheek against Stella's mouth. I felt nothing. Blood splattered the walls, soaked her chest, and pooled on the floor. I'd never seen so much blood. As much as I wanted to chase down Clinton, my feet seemed cemented in place by the chaos surrounding me. Skip was still dazed, my dad moaned, and Stella—poor Stella.

My resolve rose. I couldn't do anything for Stella or the other two. Bile rose in my throat as I lunged out the door. To my right, I heard a car engine race. I ran toward the sound. Sirens in the distance grew louder. They could only be a couple of blocks away. I swallowed my fear and made it to the parking lot in time to see a motorcycle revving up to my left. On it was a man wearing a black turtleneck. Even without the mask, I recognized Clinton. The bike turned onto the street. I crouched and took aim. It was now or never. My hands shook. I fired. One. Two. Three shots.

Just as the third shot went off, two police cars screeched into the lot. The cops angled their cars into the lot, then took up positions behind the cars with their guns aimed at me.

"Put down your weapon!" The command came over the car's loudspeaker.

My heart seized as I realized what the cops thought was going on. Slowly, I set the gun on the asphalt and raised my hands.

"Walk toward us. Keep your hands where we can see them."

"You've got it all wrong. That man kidnapped me. He's the criminal, not me!"

One of the officers shifted his position. "We'll sort that out later. Right now, we need you to step over here."

Across the street, I saw small faces peering out of windows. An overwhelming urge to vomit washed over me as a mother appeared and pulled her children away. I whispered, "Oh my God." I could have killed a couple of kids.

My knees nearly buckled as I stepped toward the cops. Officer Stenheim was the first to approach. For the second time in less than an hour, I was in handcuffs.

I swallowed hard. "There's a dead woman in one of the apartments. And two men who are injured."

Little lines around the officer's eyes deepened. "Which apartment?"

"I don't know."

Behind me, I heard Skip's voice. "Apartment 4. Officer, she was going after the man who kidnapped her."

Another officer stepped between Stenheim, me, and Skip. A third took up a position to Skip's right. Skip's face had a nasty gash where he'd been pistol-whipped.

Stenheim began reading me my rights and moved me toward the car with firm, steady pressure.

I heard Skip explaining. "Skip Cosgrove. I'm a criminologist. I've done work for Carlsbad PD before."

One of the officers piped up. "I've heard the name. ID please."

Stenheim guided me into the car. I glanced up at him and pleaded. "My father's in that apartment. He may be hurt, please help him."

Stenheim's tone was stern. "Ma'am, you should have thought of that before you came out here and started shooting a gun."

I heard another siren. Across the street, I saw an officer knocking on the door of the house I'd shot up. Another police car and an EMT truck pulled into the lot. The place began to swarm with activity. They were like bees around a hive, checking my gun, patting down Skip, rushing to the apartment.

The car door closed and I watched as someone photographed, bagged and tagged my gun. The swarm continued to buzz. Two EMTs rushed a stretcher into the apartment complex, returning a few minutes later with a woman's body that they loaded into their truck. The sheet covering the body was already red. It was Stella. I must have been wrong and she was still alive. I said a silent prayer in hopes that Stella would pull through.

The truck pulled away, sirens blaring. Seconds later, another truck took its place. Two more EMTs rushed into the apartment complex. Another car pulled into the lot. The occupants got out, flashed badges to an officer who protected the perimeter, and went into the complex.

I still didn't know if my dad was okay. Stenheim and his partner approached the car. They got in and sat in grim silence.

As Stenheim started the car, I said, "How's my dad? He was the man who was tied in the chair."

Stenheim glanced at me in his rearview mirror. "He's fine. It looks like the woman you shot is still alive."

"Thank God."

"Don't get your hopes up. The EMTs don't think she'll make it to trauma."

CHAPTER TWENTY-EIGHT

He said, "I've only broken half the rules. So far."

It was nearly 4 p.m. when Skip got Roxy released from jail. He'd had to call in Wally and the only thing that pissed him off about that was now he owed Wally a favor. Who knew what he'd have to do or when he'd have to repay that one. They were halfway to the Tanner residence when the question that had been gnawing at him bubbled to the surface. He decided he couldn't ignore it any longer.

"Where'd you get the money?"

Out of the corner of his eye, Skip saw Roxy staring out the passenger's window. The memory of her face when she'd walked out of jail had been etched into his psyche. Lips drawn, complexion pale, eyes fearful, Roxy Tanner's world had been destroyed. In that moment, he resolved that he'd give anything—even five million dollars if he had it—to fix this.

He waited for an answer. When he got none, he asked the question again.

"What's it matter?" she said without looking at him.

Skip kept his eyes on the road. "I called a source this morning to check out your business. I was concerned about how you—"

"You *what*? You checked me out? Son of a bitch. You were hired to help, you—you—"

"Cool your jets, Hot Rox."

She glared at him. "Don't you call me that. Don't you *ever* call me that!"

"Sorry." He decided to gamble to get at the truth. "Alright, *Miss Tanner*, my source tells me your business is a scam. It looks like the money you've been collecting for this ocean-wave technology project of yours has been sitting in the bank waiting for you to use for some sort of disappearance. Are we close?"

She laughed and stared out the side window again. "Your source is so wrong."

"Why's that?"

"Because I don't have that five million anymore. It's gone. Vanished. It's off in some bank account halfway around the frigging world. No, your source has old intel. I'm broke."

Skip exited at Tamarack and pulled the car over. He twisted sideways so he could watch her face. "So you did use the money from the business to free your dad?"

She looked him in the eye, bit her lower lip and said, "Yes. But you know what? I'd do it again in a second." Her eyes and face grew red, her cheeks quivered, but she didn't break. God, she was tough.

Skip said, "I don't blame you. I'd probably have done exactly the same thing. If I had anyone left who mattered that much."

She swallowed hard. "What about Stella?"

"She never made it to the hospital."

"They—they think I killed her, don't they?"

He nodded. "That's the current line of thinking. Fortunately for you, they've only got enough for the weapons charge right now. The cops aren't buying the whole victim-turned-conqueror bit. A nosey neighbor saw you coming in with the kidnappers."

"That's great! Then she can testify. Prove that I was the victim."

"She says you were on drugs. That you were weaving all over. It took two people to help you into the apartment. There's no third man or the car you said was used to kidnap you. I never saw them grab you so I can't testify about that. The only kidnapper is Stella and the cops think you shot her."

"But you *saw* what happened."

He shook his head. "They're not sure about me either. I was behind Stella when she was hit. They think maybe we formed our own little vigilante party and went charging in there with guns to kill the bad guys. Which is kind of what happened. I should have called for backup. I know—knew—better."

"I'm screwed, aren't I?"

He reached across the car and wiped a tear from her cheek with his thumb. He grimaced. "You could be tried for fraud, embezzling money from your company, discharging a firearm in public, manslaughter, and, oh yeah, killing a fish tank."

She let out a nervous laugh. "What?"

"The cops say you put three tight ones into an eighty-gallon aquarium the neighbors had across the street. Shots went straight through the window and took out the tank. Thankfully, nobody was hurt—unless you count the fish. The kids were hysterical because someone murdered their fish. Of course, the parents want you put away since you could have easily gotten one of them or their kids."

Roxy groaned. She slumped back in her seat and laid her head against the headrest. "I've made such a mess of everything. You were right. We should have called the cops when the first ransom note came in. Now I've dragged you into this."

"Yeah, I am kind of in the middle."

"Will this hurt your business?"

He turned away.

She demanded, "Will it?"

"They consider me an accomplice. My mistake was not calling them as soon as I found out where you were. So, yeah, this will hurt me."

"Why didn't you?"

He didn't dare tell her the truth. If he did, he was sure she'd use that to manipulate him somehow. "I'm not sure."

She reached across the car and put her hand on his arm. "Thank you for trying to save me."

Her touch sent a hot charge through his system. Though he found the rush addictive, he willed himself to pull away. Seeing her in this much pain tormented him—she shouldn't have to go through this. That raised another question. What would he do to make that happen?

He forced a weak smile. "Let's go see your parents. They're worried about you."

She wiped at her cheek and turned away. "Okay."

Skip started to put the Porsche into gear, but stopped. He turned sideways to face Roxy again. "Look, there's one more thing."

She let out an exasperated sigh as she turned to face him. New tears tracked down her cheeks. "Now what?"

"I want to help you find the bastard who's behind this."

"I thought you'd want to wash your hands of me." She started counting on her fingers. "I'm a liar, a thief, a—"

"A fish killer."

She smiled. "That, too."

"I know you're going after him."

"You think so, huh?"

"You need that money back and there's a guy out there who probably wants to kill you. Your secretary was in on the deal, so you were betrayed by an insider. You've got big problems and might not be seeing the outside of a jail cell until you're somewhere in the neighborhood of, oh, say, sixty-five."

"Thanks a lot. What's it to you?"

"Do you want help or not?"

"I can't pay you."

"I told you, my business is on hold until the police are satisfied. I kind of need to clear my name with the cops—paying clients are going to have to wait a bit."

Her lower lip trembled as the words spilled out. "Fine! You want to help? Tell me who the blackmailers were. We have no clue. Hell, we have no *clues*."

Skip said, "Well, not exactly." He reached into his pocket and pulled out a green cell phone. "While you were busy chasing bad guys and shooting up aquariums, I had a couple of minutes to think about this. Roxy, meet Stella's cell phone."

Roxy stared, wide-eyed, at the phone, then Skip. "You *lifted her cell*?" Her jaw fell.

He chuckled, amused at how everyone thought he was so straight—even he had skeletons in his closet. "It was an impulse thing. I haven't had a chance to check it yet, but I'm sure her address book will help us out."

"What about the cops? You don't think they'll have a problem with you stealing evidence? And you don't think they might just notice a call on Stella's phone after she's *dead*?"

"We don't need the phone, just the information. We can download whatever we need and not leave a trail. You can just drop it in her desk drawer tomorrow morning. If they show up looking for it, it'll be right there."

Roxy watched him closely. He thought he saw a twinkle in her eye. Maybe it was hope. Maybe she was seeing him in a new light.

"Besides," he said, "I've only broken half the rules. So far."

CHAPTER TWENTY-NINE

She said, "What's one more lie?"

When Skip showed me Stella's phone, I recognized it immediately. Hers and mine were identical with the exception of color. The fact that he had taken evidence from a crime scene confused the hell out of me. This straight-laced guy, this guy who'd wanted to be a cop his entire life, this guy who barely knew me had broken the law to help me. That thought warmed my heart for about two minutes—then the anger came. It was a seismic wave directed at myself for what I'd done—and what I'd become.

Strangely enough, seeing my dad handcuffed in that chair and Skip coming through the door to fight off the guy in the Clinton mask seemed to have freed me from the old demons. That didn't mean I didn't still hate the man who'd ruined my life. But the fact was that as I sat in jail contemplating how I'd ended up there, my thoughts shifted away from the fear I'd felt for the past twenty years to something that scared me even more. I found myself wanting to track him down. To make him pay for what he'd done to me. And maybe even for all the other little girls who's lives he'd ruined.

I'd faced death a second time and fought it off. The hot streak running through me was there because I'd let other people control me. No more. No, from now on, Roxy Tanner would do what she wanted to do. And that, in some weird way, scared me to death because I might be turning into a female version of the man behind the Clinton mask.

The idea of going through Stella's cell phone to harvest her contacts, however, gave me some sort of perverse thrill, a sense of being empowered to legitimately snoop on another person. Now that we were actually getting to the task, trepidation filled my veins.

"How are we going to tell who's who? Stella had a lot of calls. It looks like she's got hundreds of names in her address book."

Skip sat next to me at Mom and Dad's kitchen table. "We're looking for patterns. You said it was like she knew the guy you decked in that apartment, right?"

I recalled that moment right after my kick to his groin, how it had sent him to the floor, how Stella had rushed to him, how she'd tended to him. "Could be. I mean, she was all over him when she thought I'd hurt him. It was like she was really concerned about a friend."

"Or a boyfriend." Skip pointed at a number. She called it three times the day before your dad was kidnapped. But there were no calls that evening."

Dad limped into the room. "That's about the time I met him. He was a nice enough guy. I was so drunk by then. I don't remember his name, though." Dad pulled out a chair and started to sit. He winced as he lowered himself to a seated position.

I hated seeing him in pain. "You should be resting. You've had a grueling couple of days."

"We need to talk." He watched my face. "I know, Roxy. I know what you did."

Skip came to my rescue. "Richard, I'm going to do my best to help Roxy make this right. If we don't find that money soon, nothing's going to matter. You can bet the calculators will be running full speed at Carlsbad PD tonight and by tomorrow morning somebody's going to be asking how your daughter came up with five million bucks. We have to get a jump on this, otherwise—we all know what otherwise might be."

Dad used the table for balance as he stood. "I'll leave you two to your work." He looked me in the eye. "When this is done, we're having a long talk."

Geez, how did he still make me feel like a little girl? I started to say, "I'm not a child," but gave up and went with, "I understand." With Dad out of the room, I turned to Skip and whispered, "I understand how he figured this out, but Stella? She wasn't that bright. She had, like, no business sense at all. I thought her biggest interest was in getting married—or laid."

"She was probably conning you."

I gritted my teeth. "That bitch. I can't believe she betrayed me."

Skip stared at me.

I gave it right back to him. "What?"

"Aren't you the one all filled with righteous indignation?"

I planted my elbows on the table and buried my face in my hands. I massaged my temples for a few seconds and sat up straight. "You're right. I did this. I have to fix it."

"Let's begin with that number she kept calling. It belongs to Jimmy Dane."

I checked back further in the call log. Sure enough, Stella called Jimmy Dane regularly. Very regularly. I checked the address book. "Holy shit!"

"What?"

"I think that's Stella's address. Might be a different apartment, but they both lived on Chinquapin."

"This one's down the street a block or so from where they held your dad. Where the hell did someone come up with that name, anyway?"

I rolled my eyes and watched the ceiling as I parroted 2007's Loser of the Year. "It's a shrub and a tree and a water plant—the American lotus, to be exact." I caught Skip staring at me, his mouth hanging open. "What? I dated a guy who tried to turn me into a freaking arborist. This guy thought plant sex was—"

Skip formed a T with his hands. "Time out! Too much information." He glanced at his watch. "It's too late to be skulking around. We'll have to wait until morning."

"He could be gone by then!"

"If he's leaving, he's already gone. Besides, we need to get the rest of the info off this thing so you can drop it on Stella's desk tomorrow morning."

I thought about it for a minute. Skip was right. If we went chasing around now, all we'd do is raise suspicion and alert the cops that he'd stolen Stella's phone. And that we were snooping. They'd probably charge me with obstruction or tampering with evidence. The bottom line was that *us* visiting Jimmy Dane tonight was a bad idea. Nothing in that thought meant that I couldn't do a little reconnaissance on my own. No one had to know. "Okay, let's export everything to my Dad's computer."

Skip shook his head. "A disk. It'll make the trail just a bit harder to follow—just in case."

I had to admit one thing, Skip was sharp. Too bad, with a business partner like him we might have spotted Stella's plan. But then, he would have known mine also.

It didn't take that long for us to get the information onto a disk.

We made two copies, one for me, one for Skip. By the time we were done, it was after nine. Skip left right after that and within about fifteen minutes, I snuck out of the house without saying good night to Mom and Dad, who had both fallen fast asleep in front of the TV. I left them a quick note, got into my car and, instead of heading home, went straight to Jimmy Dane's apartment. From my parent's place, it took just a few minutes to get there. Turn onto Tamarack head toward the beach. Left on Adams, do the street-parking search, and there I was, ready to roll.

The apartment building had minimal exterior lighting. The pathways to the apartments were dimly lit and only a couple of the units had porch lights. Most appeared to have had the bulbs removed by tenants who'd grown tired of living in artificial twilight after dark. With grocery and other necessity-type shopping just a block away and the beach less than a mile down Tamarack, I could see where this would be a popular location. On one of the upstairs apartments where the lights shone brightly, I saw a couple of surfboards propped against the wall along with the shadowy outlines of wet suits suspended in midair like dark knights watching over the street.

Dane lived in Apartment #14. I stood on a narrow walkway between #6 and #7. The night air felt silent. Serene. The marine layer blanketed the sky above, the reflection of city lights gave the sky a dull sheen reminiscent of dirty white linoleum in a half-lit room. The only sounds were those of TVs from inside the apartments and an occasional loud vehicle on I-5, which was just a couple of blocks away. But there was something else, too. A sense that I wasn't alone.

I spun on my heel and surveyed the complex. No people. No movement. My pulse quickened as I continued on. I glanced over my shoulder again, this time catching just a hint of movement behind me in the shadows. My body tensed involuntarily as I wondered if perhaps the kidnapper had come here also. My jaw felt like a steel trap clamped shut by the tension. I was unarmed. My usual confidence had been shattered by the man who had so easily escaped earlier today. Where was the manager's apartment? It was so late. And dark. Would people come if I screamed?

I pushed away my fears and continued my search for Dane's apartment. I stopped at Apartment 10, closed my eyes, and listened. Just the normal traffic and mindless entertainment sounds. I concentrated on relaxing my shoulders and on being ready if something should happen. As I moved deeper into the complex, my sense of confidence returned.

At Apartment #12, I heard a swish behind me. I spun around. A shadow disappeared between the buildings. I strode to the walkway where the shadow had been and checked for people. No movement. My breath felt ragged as I stared into the darkness at nothing. Someone was there. Stalking me. Maybe it was just a resident from one of these apartments—then why were they following me? Why disappear? "Get a grip," I muttered.

I retraced my steps and found Apartment #14 just one unit from the end of the row. There were no lights on in the apartment, no porch light outside, and dead silence everywhere. I jumped at the sound of a voice behind me.

"Adding breaking and entering to your list?"

"Jesus Christ!" It was Skip. "You scared the crap out of me!"

"I intended to. I knew you couldn't stay away."

I hissed, "And what about you? Why are you here?"

He smiled. His eyes moved constantly, scanning every direction in the half-light. "Someone has to protect you from yourself."

From one of the upstairs units, someone yelled, "Move it along! It's late."

I glanced at my watch, it was barely ten. I started to yell something back, but Skip clamped his hand over my mouth. I rolled my eyes and nodded. Only then did he remove his hand.

Even in the dimness I could make out the slight shaking of his head. I whispered, "Okay. I'll be nice."

Skip motioned with his head, I followed. We walked to the street, turned left, and ended up at my car. I realized that his was just a few spaces away. "Can't believe I didn't see the Porsche."

"I'll follow you home. Dane's not here, anyway."

"How do you know? We didn't even try."

"I knocked. He didn't answer."

"He might be asleep. He might be hiding out. He might—"

"I took a quick tour of the apartment."

"You got the manager to let you in?" I snickered. I could just see that one.

Skip reached into his jacket pocket and pulled out a small case. "Let's say I have a master key. A graduation present from a buddy in college. He thought it was funny, but I've always loved tools. Don't you love tools?"

A giddy wave washed over me. "You *picked* the freaking lock?" Mr. "By-the-Book" had surprised me again. I half-laughed. "You hypocrite." This guy was never going on my Loser list.

He slipped the case back into his pocket and gave me a self-satisfied smirk. "Call it resourceful. I'm a little out of practice. I used to be able to pop one of these old locks in thirty seconds—took me twice that to get this one."

"You frigging broke in. I can't believe it."

Headlights approached from a couple of blocks away on Chinquapin. Suddenly, Skip was all business again. "The creepy sensation you felt back there was your common sense kicking in. Let's get you back to your place. Tomorrow morning you can drop off Stella's phone at work and then we'll come over here. If Dane's not around, we'll get the manager to let us in. That one can be on you."

"You want me to lie?"

"Until this is over, we don't know who we can trust. Yeah, you've got a license to lie."

Skip followed me home, his headlights never far behind. As we drove, I considered what he'd said. He was right. We didn't know who we could trust. For all I knew, I couldn't trust him either. Sorry, Skip. I watched his headlights in my mirror. "What's one more lie?"

CHAPTER THIRTY

He said, "Greed. It just drives the whole system."

Skip arrived home at about 11:00 p.m. He'd spent time helping Roxy check her place for an intruder, then excused himself and drove home. Exhausted, he'd stripped and fallen into bed. At midnight, he still lay awake, bothered by what he hadn't told Roxy and by the steps he was taking on behalf of a woman he barely knew.

Jimmy Dane's apartment had been pitch dark. There had been no lights on and, with the blinds and windows shut, the place had a closed, hostile feeling. He eased the door shut behind him, subconsciously gave the latex gloves he wore a tug to check their fit, and drew his .357 Sig from the back of his waist band. He held a small flashlight in his other hand, but wouldn't turn it on until he was sure the place was empty.

From where he stood, he could see that the apartment had a living room and a small galley kitchen with an adjacent dining area. A single doorway to his right led to the bedroom. Before he went any further, he needed to know if someone was sleeping in that room. He crept across the carpet as though he were a cat stalking prey. His every sense became razor sharp as the adrenaline rushed through his veins. He listened for the slightest noise, knowing that not sensing a change—any change, even a breath or a heartbeat other than his own—could cost him his life. He reached the door and craned his neck to peer into the room. The bedroom, too, was dark and unoccupied. Next, he checked the bathroom. Clear, also.

Skip flipped on the flashlight and flicked it around the bedroom. Dane had little in the way of furniture. The bed had a comforter haphazardly thrown over the top and a few pieces of clothing strewn around. One side table had three items—a lamp, a clock, and a sci-fi paperback. Another lamp stood atop the dresser, where he also found a framed picture of a man and a woman, a business card, some jewelry, and two drawers left half open. Skip inspected the photo first. It was Stella, which meant that Roxy had been correct about the relationship. The jewelry was also probably hers since he doubted Dane wore earrings in the shape of hearts or a dainty gold chain necklace.

Skip picked up the business card and read it. It was for a local fertility clinic. The card doubled as an appointment card. The appointment was for next Tuesday. Were he and Stella trying to have kids? He placed the card back on the dresser. The drawers were empty.

Dane was gone, probably panicked after things went wrong this afternoon. Skip went to the kitchen to confirm his suspicion. The refrigerator contained milk, eggs, some leftovers, beer and wine. He found food in a small pantry. Yes, Dane had definitely fled in a panic.

Skip returned to the bedroom, where he'd seen a computer monitor, keyboard and mouse. He heard the whir of the computer below the desk. Skip jarred the mouse and the monitor lit up.

Line after line of gibberish filled the screen. Skip suspected that it was a programmer's or a hacker's code. He briefly considered having it checked out, but decided it would just be a waste of time. If Dane was truly gone, he wouldn't leave anything of any importance behind. Or would he? It depended on how big of a hurry he'd been in. Skip stared at the screen again. It had lots of weird characters. Forget it. He left through the front door and made sure to lock up on his way out.

Skip was about to cross the grassy strip to his car when he spotted Roxy. He slipped into the shadows and watched. She stood by her car door, glancing up and down the street, then quick-stepped to the front of the apartment complex. So he'd been right, he thought. She couldn't stay away. Time for a little cat and mouse. A way to teach her a lesson.

As he lay in bed, he realized that his biggest problem was that he'd enjoyed those moments. He'd enjoyed stalking Roxy, then meeting her on his terms. It was the worst case scenario—he enjoyed being with her.

He forced himself to think of other things—of how Dane, Stella, and a kidnapper had gotten together. Stella had obviously been the inside source, but how were they connected to the kidnapper? And now that his girlfriend was dead, what had happened to Dane? Was he on the run with his share of the money? Skip drifted off to sleep, annoyed with himself for not being able to solve the puzzle. Annoyed more that he couldn't even focus on it. And annoyed with Roxy that she kept intruding on his thoughts.

Skip's alarm jarred him from a deep sleep the next morning at 6:00. He felt groggy and tired, as though he were falling down a bottomless shaft in the earth's surface. Although a hot shower helped wake him, every time he thought about Roxy, that helpless feeling returned. He downed an extra cup of coffee and was getting ready to leave when his cell phone rang.

"Cosgrove."

"Herman Nordoff, Skip. Sorry I didn't get back to you yesterday, but this took longer than I expected. This is quite an operation you've uncovered. I haven't seen one this ingenious in a while."

"What do you mean?"

"I mean, it's a scam. She's collecting money for a project that's already funded. Maybe she just came to the party late and is going to return the money. I suppose that's a possibility."

Acid from his coffee churned in Skip's stomach. Shit. Now Herman Nordoff knew, too. What would he do with the information?

Everything made sense now. The pieces of the puzzle had fallen into place and he saw it all so clearly. Roxy *was* pulling a con. And Richard Tanner had figured it out. He'd gone drinking to forget what he knew. The kidnappers had used him just as Roxy had used the ocean wave technology project.

"Skip, you still there? You want the details?"

"Have you got a synopsis?" Skip sat at the dining-room table, just sure he wasn't going to like what he was about to hear.

"Fair enough. Ocean Technologies has filed for a patent on a system to turn ocean wave movement into electrical energy. Lots of people are working on this, so it's getting lots of attention. They wanted to put together a demonstration project where they could produce enough energy to power a hundred homes. They started searching for capital and found a block of investors. There is a Tanner Investments that's part of the team, but they're East Coast. I happen to know the principal. That's the only reason we realized this was a scam. This company you asked me about is playing in the shadow of a legitimate firm."

Skip stared off into space for a minute. Finally, he said, "Herman, I want to thank you for this."

"No problem. It was kind of interesting. If you need any help in nailing these bastards, you let me know. I could always call Tanner myself. He could get the feds in on this in no time."

"Hold off on that for now, Herman. We're working through this. I'm sure it'll all come out soon enough."

"I understand. You want the glory. No problem. You're the one who found this. I'll let you handle it your way for now."

Thank God for reprieves, thought Skip. How far into this was he? He'd probably already damaged his business beyond repair. He'd lose his consulting contracts. What police department would want to deal with a criminologist who was a criminal himself? He thought about possible charges. They'd go for obstructing justice, assault, and breaking and entering. As he disconnected, he thought that he should walk away while he could. Cut his losses. Go to the cops, explain what had happened—tell them how he'd been conned himself. And how would that look? It was easy to judge if you weren't the victim—and how the self-righteous would judge him. Two days ago, he'd probably have agreed with them.

Skip stepped out onto his back deck. It was tiny compared to Nordoff's and his view wasn't elevated like theirs. Still, it was his home. And if he started losing work, he'd lose this, too. Sooner or later the bills would catch up. "Damn you, Roxy Tanner!" He took the few steps down to the sand and walked to the shore. He stood, coffee in hand, watching the waves.

"Greed. It just drives the whole system," he said.

A wave lapped at his feet.

"I've never felt this way before. She's a complication I don't need."

Skip watched a large greenish-brown mass of seaweed drift in on the waves. It was like a spider's web, ready to catch the unsuspecting. Unlike a spider's web, this mass had no organization, no symmetry, and no real threat for its victims other than being an annoyance. Roxy's web had symmetry. It was organized. And it held danger. Roxy was a financial black widow and the consequences of being around her were far more than just a little clingy stuff around his ankles. So far, the consequences were bad, but were they critical? If there was anything that he knew from personal experience, it was that those consequences could turn seriously ugly almost overnight. He had one foot in the web and that put him close enough to be bitten. The solution was obvious. He should pull away. Get the hell out as fast as he possibly could.

The problem was that he couldn't do that. He couldn't walk away from Roxy. He had to help, had to find out who kidnapped Richard

Tanner and get the money back where it belonged. He'd force her to return it to its owners. He laughed. He'd already learned that forcing Roxy to do anything would be about as easy as getting out of quicksand alone. Despite that, he had to try to turn her around. Or go down with her.

He stared out over the water. "Cosgrove, you're a moron. She'll toss you away like yesterday's garbage. She doesn't even like me."

His face went hot when he realized a jogger had just passed him by. He glanced after the jogger. It was a young woman—long hair pulled back in a ponytail, a sweatshirt, shorts, and running shoes. Fortunately, she also had on headphones, so he doubted that she'd heard him.

"And I didn't even notice her." That in itself bothered him.

The ocean she-devil chuckled. She seemed to mock him. Did she find his predicament funny?

He turned his back on the waves. Within the next day or two, the cops would uncover Roxy's scam. She'd disappear forever or go to jail. His only solution was to find the money and undo what she'd done. It was the only way he could save her. Even if she didn't want to be saved.

CHAPTER THIRTY-ONE

She said, "She wasn't smart enough to be a crook."

The following day, Thursday, I got to the office just a few minutes after eight. It was another gray day on the California coast. The gray in the sky would burn off later—the gray in my heart, not likely. When I opened the door and saw Stella's blank desk, a sudden urge to turn and run overcame me. Without the money, though, how far would I get? Overnight, I'd developed a new goal. It wasn't elegant. It wasn't pretty. It wasn't even original. I wanted my money back. Yes, *my* money. And actually, it wasn't even a new goal. And no one was going to stop me.

Stella's cell phone hung like an anchor weight in my purse. Though the phone weighed just ounces, the mental drag was substantial and enough to make me anxious to rid myself of the weight. I locked the front door behind me, crossed the room to Stella's desk, and pulled the little anchor from my purse. I remembered Skip's caution—wipe it clean.

I set the phone on the desk and pulled a plastic baggy from my purse. The baggy contained a damp lintless towel, which I used to wipe off the phone's display, keypad, and back. I set the phone in the top drawer of Stella's desk and stared at it.

Head cocked to one side, arms across my chest, one leg slightly in front of the other, I began to wonder. Should it look more like it had been tossed in? Or placed on purpose? Would the cops think it had been planted if it rested neatly against a corner of the drawer? Would they wonder why she hadn't had it on her? I scooched it sideways. No better. Tried an angle. This wasn't working for me. I glanced around Stella's desk. I looked behind me at her credenza.

My eyes got wide as I spotted the solution. Stella had a charger stand for the phone. I pulled the phone from the drawer using the towel and dropped it into the stand. It lit up, happy to be home. I think my face lit up also, happy to have a solution to the problem. The towel went back into the baggy, the baggy into my purse. I'd find a trash bin somewhere later today and dump the evidence.

Next, I went to the file cabinet and pulled Stella's employment file. I took the file to my desk and sat, suddenly bummed that I'd forgotten to get myself a cup of coffee on the way in.

I muttered. "Focus, Roxy. Focus."

Stella Robbins' employment application listed two years at Texas A&M University. She'd told me she'd wanted to be a teacher but that she'd eventually had to leave school when both of her parents died and left her with more bills than money. Her application indicated a string of temp jobs that stretched back a couple of years starting six months after she left college.

Her address was on Chinquapin. It was a different street number, down two blocks from Jimmy's place. According to her application, she lived in Apartment 6. How had they met? Had they known each other before?

I'd chosen Stella for exactly the reason no one else would hire her. No solid work background. No skills. No potential for getting in the way. I rolled my eyes. So much for my employee-hiring skills.

Stella had told me she was new to the area and that's why all of her previous employment had been in Texas. Stella had been exactly what I'd been searching for, or so I'd thought. As a result, I'd never even considered calling to verify her previous employment. In fact, I hadn't even verified her address, not that it would do me much good now. On second thought, maybe it would. I glanced at my watch. It was nearly 8:30. Surely someone would be working by now. I dialed the number for Stella's landlord.

"Hello?"

Nice way to answer a business line, I thought. "Hi, my name is Roxanne Tanner. One of your tenants, Miss Stella Robbins, submitted an employment application. I'm way behind, but trying to confirm her address. Does she live in Apartment 6?"

"That one? She's a—hey, who'd you say you were?" The voice on the other end was gravelly, probably from a few too many packs of cigarettes. Whether it was a man or a woman, I couldn't tell.

"Roxanne Tanner. I'm the owner of Tanner Investments."

"Oh, you. She rented 6. That's all I can say on the phone, though."

A mental picture of the landlord formed in my head. She was a sixty-plus-year-old woman who had a smoke burning in one hand and a Bloody Mary in the other. Between sips and sucks, she'd hack her head off. She'd be dressed in a frumpy robe and fuzzy slippers. The way she phrased her response, though, made me curious. "What do you mean you don't want to do this over the phone? Is there something I should know?"

"Didn't you hire her already?"

I heard the phlegmy cough as she held the phone away. Ugh.

"I'm just trying to cover myself. You know, document everything. I'm way behind. C'mon, I'll just keep this between us."

"Sorry, honey, think I already said too much." She disconnected.

I didn't rule out another run at her, but the next attempt would be in person. She was dying to tell me something, I just needed to—I stopped, realizing what word I'd used—dying. "Sorry, Stella."

If the landlord wouldn't tell me anything, maybe the Internet would. I turned on my computer and did a search for "Stella Robbins." That returned somewhere in the neighborhood of 700,000 records. No help there. Women with that name were scattered around the country, probably the globe. I needed to narrow this down.

I was contemplating my next search when the door shook with a loud banging.

Was it the cops? I had nowhere to go.

"Roxy! Open up, it's Skip."

I snarled under my breath, "Asshole." Last night he'd pulled that stupid stalker routine on me and this morning he was practically beating my door down. I strode to the locked door and wrenched it open. "Who the hell do you think you are, banging on my door like that?"

"I tried quiet, but you didn't answer. I could see that the lights were on from under the door so I knew you were here. Sorry if I scared you."

"Whatever." I stomped away. I muttered, "Moron." Behind me, I swear I heard him chuckle. This guy *wanted* to piss me off?

"A bit touchy today?"

I whirled on him. "No, it's not that time of the month," I barked. "I'm trying to find information about Stella. What have you accomplished? Anything?"

He held out one of two cups he held in his hands.

I'd been so intent on chewing him out that I hadn't even noticed what he carried.

"I thought you could use one of these." His tone was smooth and consoling. "I accomplished not getting much sleep. Probably a lot like you. So, truce? And coffee?"

Ten minutes later, with a bit of caffeine kicking in, I was feeling less angry. "Sorry I yelled at you. I guess if I didn't answer, you didn't have much choice."

"Don't sweat it. It's understandable. You were busy looking for something on Stella." He pointed at the papers on my desk.

"This? It's useless. I called the landlord, she hinted that there's something about Stella she might like to say, but wouldn't tell me over the phone. She seemed to know who I was, but I don't think she knows that Stella's dead—yet."

"Did you search for her online?"

"I didn't have any luck. But I'm out of my element there. I mean, what am I looking for? I don't really know."

Skip leaned back in his chair. He sipped the coffee. "I've been thinking about yesterday—when I hit Stella. The funny thing is that when I hit her, she went down, but she didn't react. She's taken some hits before. And when I forced her into that apartment? She didn't cry or freak out. Instead, it was like she was thinking of how to turn that situation around. In fact, I almost think she wanted to help you. One thing's for sure, that girl wasn't a first-timer."

"Stella?" I laughed. "She wasn't smart enough to be a crook."

"Maybe that's what she wanted you to think." He tapped his chin and seemed lost in thought for a few seconds. "Where was she from?"

"Texas. She went to A&M."

"She finish?"

"She told me a family emergency forced her to leave. After that, she worked some temp jobs."

Skip set his coffee on my desk, then stared at the floor. "Try a search for 'Stella Robbins Texas news.'"

I typed in the search terms and pressed the enter key. A few seconds later, the screen filled with search results for people named Stella, but not Robbins, and Robbins, but not Stella. On page three, I stopped. "Here's something for a Stella Robbins on a web site called The Texas Blotter."

"Check it out."

I clicked the link and started to scan the article. "This is just some guy ranting about criminals."

"Keep going. The guy rants, but he does report the news."

"You know this guy?"

"Hello? Criminologist? Besides, we need everything we can get. Try to find her name on the page."

I did the PC search thing by holding down the Control key and the F key and then typing "Stella" in the little box that popped up. Halfway down the page, her highlighted name appeared. "Here it is. 'On Tuesday, Stella Robbins and Marty Horvath were arraigned on armed robbery charges. Horvath and Robbins allegedly held up a local convenience store at gunpoint. Horvath has also been arraigned on charges of assault and manslaughter for his role in beating one of the employees.'"

Skip nodded. "Bingo. That's our girl. I'll bet she made a deal with the DA to help nail this guy Horvath."

"Why would she do that?"

"That's the way the system works. It rewards those that rat out their friends. Stella wasn't stupid, she knew that."

His argument made sense. "Then she bails out of Texas and shows up on my doorstep. And I pay for her makeover."

Skip's chin puckered. "What makeover?"

"Stella was a new woman in all senses of the word. Lips, hips, boobs—"

"I thought she looked good. Damn good, in fact."

I glared at him. Was he deliberately trying to piss me off again? Raving about that bitch's looks?

He winced. "Sorry. Not real bright on my part—telling one woman how good another one looked. Besides, you're much more attractive."

I gave him the evil eye my mother always used on me. "You can't get off that easily."

"Maybe not, but it's true. You are. You're gorgeous."

I ignored the compliment. It was one of those weak too-little, too-late attempts by a man to appease a woman. What did I care how he thought I looked, anyway? A tinge of warmth radiated into my neck. Gorgeous? He thought I was—I muttered, "Whatever."

"You like that word, don't you?"

"*It fits.* Besides, we need to go see that landlord."

"You do realize where Stella lived, don't you?"

I gave him a blank stare. "What?"

"It's the same building."

"As what? Jimmy was two blocks away." I glanced at the application and read the address. My lips parted and I whispered, "Are you sure?"

Skip nodded. "The kidnapper had a unit in that complex."

My breath caught and I swallowed hard. "You're positive?"

"I know. You never saw the address. When the cops took you away, I doubted that you even noticed what street you were on. Believe me, it's the right complex. A different apartment maybe, but the same street address."

"Maybe that's why the landlord knew me."

"And why she was reluctant to talk on the phone. She might think you're a reporter snooping around."

"Why would she live there? I mean, why rent in the same building as the kidnapper?"

Skip shook his head. "Maybe it was the other way around. The kidnapper might have come later. The manager could tell us. We might even be able to get back in."

Shivers ran down my spine. "What the hell for? That's a crime scene. I'm not going in there." The last thing I needed was to add another felony count to my list of recent transgressions—or relive that experience.

"We don't have to go inside the apartment, I guess. I just wanted to see if there were any witnesses. Maybe someone can describe those kidnappers, sans the masks. I can talk to the neighbors."

Shit. My head pounded at the thought of getting anywhere near that apartment again.

CHAPTER THIRTY-TWO

He said, "Can I talk to you for a second? Without the gun."

Skip pulled the Porsche into the parking lot and took a spot two spaces down from where Roxy had parked. He tried to recall the details from yesterday—the vacant white car, Stella leaving it, the altercation. Had she been in that white car? Where had it gone? At the time, he hadn't thought about where she'd been coming from. But the car hadn't been in the lot when the police arrived. And it had been empty when he saw it. Hadn't it? Had the windows been up or down? He couldn't recall. He left the top down, but locked the Porsche out of habit. Why hadn't he told the cops about the white car? Had he forgotten about it? Or was it another bad decision? Roxy's arrest must have rattled him more than he cared to admit. It was the only rationale for the lapse that made sense.

He noted that Roxy picked a spot in the lot marked, "Tenants Only." A rental moving truck with a ramp extending down in the back took up five of the other tenant-only spaces. Maybe the truck had permission to be there, but Roxy must feel the rules didn't apply to her. As he approached her, he said, "That spot is for tenants."

She locked her car door. "We're not going to be here long. There are plenty of spaces."

Skip counted two tenant spaces left. He considered using Roxy's favorite word, but decided against it. Mentally, he countered. *Whatever.* "You find the manager. I want to see if I can locate anyone who might have seen something."

She laughed. "You just want to see if someone saw you smack Stella."

"Yesterday, I saw drapes move in one of these places. And that's when some busybody called the cops. Maybe I can get a description of the kidnappers."

"I'll see if I can get the manager to tell me who rented that apartment."

Roxy took one walkway, Skip the other. The kidnappers had been holed up in an apartment on the far end of the complex and this was the only parking lot. Skip surveyed the area from the spot where he'd met Stella. Only four units overlooked this spot, so he might as well try them all.

At the first apartment, he got no answer. At the second, the door was open. Stacks of boxes crowded the room. Pieces of furniture stood against one wall. He was about to knock on the doorjamb when he heard a high-pitched squeaking behind him and turned to face the noise. A dolly piled high with boxes inched in his direction. Behind the dolly, a man in jeans and a white T-shirt guided it along the narrow walkway.

"You're doing great, just keep coming straight on about three feet," Skip said.

"Thanks."

When the dolly reached the walkway in front of the apartment, the man eased the stack of boxes to a vertical position. Skip put a hand on the top box to steady it.

The gangly man, who was probably no more than twenty-five, stood to one side of the stack. "Thanks again." The guy's chin was covered in a thin mat of whiskers, about the only hair on his head other than his thin eyebrows.

Skip extended his hand. "Skip Cosgrove."

"Dave Brewster. Call me Davy. That load was a heavy one." He stretched his back for a second. "One too many boxes, I think."

"Just moving in?"

"Yeah, just drove in from Vegas. I'm glad to be back in San Diego, man. But traffic's a bitch. By the time I hit the 78 I thought that thing was gonna shake apart." He jerked his thumb over his shoulder in the direction of a rental moving truck.

Skip smiled. "Looks like that one's seen better days." He started to leave. "Well, good luck with the move in."

"Thanks. I'm almost done. Hey, you lookin' for somethin'?"

"My car got dinged, I just wondered if anyone saw it," Skip said.

"Can't help you, man. Try the old lady two doors down. I hear she sees everything."

"I'll do that." Skip nodded his thanks. As he passed the next apartment, he thought about how easily the lie had rolled off his tongue. What was happening to him? Well, it was probably better to tell the guy a lie than to tell him there'd been a kidnapping and shooting in the complex. On the other hand, the guy was bound to hear about it sooner or later. Skip snickered as he walked away from Davy. Let the poor guy get unpacked, then someone can tell him about the neighborhood.

When he knocked on the door Davy had told him about, the drapes to his right fluttered open and closed. Skip had a sudden realization that maybe Roxy should be doing this. If this was the woman who had reported him yesterday, she might already be on the phone with the cops. The door opened a crack, the deadbolt chain stretched tight.

"I've got a gun and a phone to call 9-1-1. What do you want?"

Skip swallowed hard. "My name is Skip Cosgrove."

"I know who you are. You're the one hit that girl yesterday."

He'd found his witness. "I'm a criminologist."

"That's why you decked a woman?"

"She committed a felony."

"Let me see some ID."

He reached into his back pocket.

"Slow there, mister. Real slow." The voice came from the door opening, through which the barrel of a Colt revolver pointed at him.

"I'm just getting my ID." He extracted his wallet and opened it, then showed her his driver's license and a business card.

"You said you was a cop, where's your badge?"

"No, no. I'm a criminologist. I contract with the Carlsbad PD and others, but I am not a sworn officer. Can you, um, put that gun down? I just have a question about yesterday."

The gun didn't waver. "Why the hell you think I got this pointed at you? I saw you clobber that poor girl yesterday."

"As I said, that poor girl was a kidnapper. If you saw the news last night, you probably heard about a man named Richard Tanner. He was kidnapped and held for five million dollars ransom. The kidnappers were using one of the apartments."

"Yeah, yeah. I seen that on the TV last night. Wait a minute. You're the guy who found that kid a coupl'a days ago. Right?"

"That's me." Local folk hero, thought Skip. How long would he be hearing about this one? "Can I talk to you for a second? Without the gun."

Skip stared through the opening between the door and the jamb. Her eyes darted down and to the left as the gun wavered. "I suppose." The chain went slack, he heard the chain clank, and the opening widened.

To his right, Skip caught the gangly guy hauling in another load of boxes. "That girl I hit was part of the kidnapping scheme. She would have been with two men. Did you ever see them?"

She stuck her head out the door and glanced around. She nodded and her chin puckered. "I seen 'em with that drunk." She scratched at her left cheek.

"What drunk?"

"Yesterday. A man and that woman from 6 was bringing in some blonde. She was wearing big sunglasses and stumbling all over the place. I couldn't believe it. It weren't much after noon. I figured they was gonna have some type of orgy or something."

She pronounced the word "orgy" with a hard "g," as in "go." Skip held back. He wanted to tell this woman that if she'd paid attention instead of prejudging, she might have noticed something was off kilter with the scene she'd witnessed. If she had called the police, she could have cut the whole scheme short.

He decided to press for more details. "Was this blonde woman wearing a white blouse and blue jeans?"

"Yeah, yeah, yeah. She was falling all over the guy. I thought she was gonna have him do both of them right there on the grass."

Skip took a deep breath. "She was the victim. Her eyes were covered with duct tape and if you'd looked closely, you might have noticed that she was handcuffed." He hadn't intended to do it, but he'd finished the sentence in a sarcastic tone.

The old woman's face paled. "Jesus. I missed all that?"

Skip nodded. "What did the man look like?"

She swallowed a lump in her throat. When she continued, her voice was less judgmental. "The guy was taller than her by a few inches. I guess he was kinda skinny, but not too much. He was definitely lighter than you."

Skip felt certain she was describing Jimmy Dane. "His partner shot at me yesterday."

"That's when I called the cops. I heard that gunshot and knew there was something wrong. I figured it was drugs. I thought maybe they was in that apartment—never mind, guess I was wrong. What else you wanna know?"

"This man, was he friendly with the woman from Apartment 6?"

"I couldn't say. Wait, yeah, later."

"Later?"

"Yeah, when she brung him out to their car . . ."

The scene flashed in Skip's mind. The woman prattled on in her recitation. He wanted to stop her because it reminded him of how *his* failure to observe had let one of the kidnappers get away.

"... and that was just before you showed up. That guy didn't look good at all when she put him in the back seat of the car. He was leaning all over her, kind of limping along like maybe he was hurting or something."

The memory came back. The windows had been rolled down, not up. He should have checked the car after getting Stella under control. He asked the question, but already knew the answer.

"Did this other guy drive the white car away?"

"Yeah, right after the gunshot. I seen him gettin' into the driver's seat while I was calling the cops. He pulled out of the parking lot just before they got here. Hey, mister, you don't look so good yourself. You feeling okay?"

He nodded. "I'll be fine." After he kicked himself, he thought.

CHAPTER THIRTY-THREE

She said, "You'll be the center of attention."

As I walked away from Skip, I smiled to myself. I hadn't intended to park in one of the tenant spots. The truth was that I didn't see the sign because I was gawking at one of the pieces of furniture in the back of the rental truck. The one that really caught my attention was an antique rocker with a red fabric back. It was made of dark wood and was small and squatty as though it had been designed for someone who might be considered tiny by today's standards. I know it was stupid, I could have hit something, but the chair in the back of the truck looked exactly like my mother's—and that was handed down to her from her mother, who stood a whopping five feet tall when she was young. Anyway, once I was in the spot and I saw that Skip was a bit tweaked by my parking faux pax, I decided to push his buttons a bit. He'd been hitting mine hard lately, so it was time to pay him back.

As I left him and headed off to find the manager's apartment, I swear he was watching me. He's cute, but his spring is wound way too tight. Guy needs to loosen up. If I wasn't going to be leaving as soon as I had my money—how's that for positive thinking?—I might be interested in taking the guy on as a project. You know, teach him to enjoy life a little. But right now, I had work to do.

The manager's apartment wasn't hard to find. Little "Office" signs all along the way guided me and there was even a little sign on the door. Talk about uptown. I heard music coming from inside. It sounded vaguely familiar. I knocked and waited.

A tall, heavyset woman opened the door. She had a full head of graying hair that she let hang loose around her shoulders. She should know it would look better up. That lioness hairdo might work on Lady Gaga, but on the sixty-year-old version? Not so much. Her makeup wasn't too terribly overdone—for a hooker. That went for her clothing, also. A cropped blouse tied at the waist and a pair of skin-tight capris completed the look. To top it all off, she was chewing gum. I wondered if this was the woman I'd spoken to earlier on the phone. She was certainly in the right age bracket.

"Hi, I'm Roxanne Tanner."

The woman's eyes twinkled. Beneath all that mascara and eye-liner, there was a spark of recognition. Then she coughed. That settled it, this was the voice. "I heard about that on the news just a few minutes ago. You're the one whose father was kidnapped and held in 4. I can't believe Stella's dead."

I nodded. Tears seemed to be pushing at my eyelids again. "I wondered if you might be able to tell me anything about the man who rented that apartment."

"They say you shot Stella."

"Actually, it was one of the kidnappers who shot her. I was trying to get the gun away from him when it went off."

The manager stared at the floor a few feet away for a moment. To my surprise, she started to blow a bubble with the gum she'd been chewing. She winked, "Got my 40th reunion in a couple of hours."

Oh gawd, I thought, a picture of a hundred seniors dressed like hookers and barflies rushed into my mind. "How nice," I said. "I won't take up much more of your time, but did Stella rent her own apartment?"

"She did, but she was hardly ever there after she met that ex-con boyfriend of hers."

"Jimmy Dane?"

"It was lust at first sight for those two. She'd been here a couple of months when they—what do you kids call it? Oh yeah, hooked up."

The thought of who the landlady might be hooking up with to-night was enough to make me swear off sex. I shoved that thought as far away as possible and it still wasn't far enough. "Did they know each other from before?"

She cocked her head slightly, then shook it side to side. "I doubt it. She rented the apartment after I evicted him. That was for nonpayment. It didn't have anything to do with his time in prison."

"Yeah, you said he was an ex-con."

"He'd been paroled after doing five years for attempted kidnapping."

"You knowingly rent to ex-cons?"

"Not usually, but in his case I did. He'd done his time. It wasn't like he was a sex-offender. He kidnapped his five-year-old son after his wife started doing drugs. Least ways, that's what he said. Course, then he didn't pay his rent, so I had to get rid of him. He was a nice enough kid, but he didn't have any money."

I thought about the news story Skip and I had read earlier. Had Stella and Dane gotten along because they were both criminals? I smiled. Here I was stereotyping people. And look at me. Would I get along with them, too?

"What's so funny?" she asked.

"Oh, sorry, I was just thinking how ironic life can be. Say, did you know that Stella might have had a criminal record also?"

"Not till after she was here. I met her one day in the laundry room. We started talking and next thing I know she's telling me how she got arrested for shoplifting, but she was innocent and it was someone else who looked like her that stole the stuff."

"It wasn't shoplifting, it was armed robbery. And it wasn't mistaken identity, she made a deal with the DA to testify against the guy she was with—Jimmy Dane."

Her jaw fell wide open. A few moments later, she recovered enough to speak again. "I can't believe how some people will lie to your face like that!"

I nodded. "I hear you. It's a bitch getting some people to tell the truth." Smooth, Roxy. So smooth. I was at the top of my game.

"Well, I'm damned glad they're both gone. What else do you know about them?"

"Not much, that's why I came here. I was hoping you might let me into Stella's apartment. I might be able to learn more about her."

She stroked her chin. "That's kind of irregular. Isn't that considered a crime scene?"

"Nothing happened in her place, just the other one. The crime took place in—" The words caught in my throat. I coughed. "In the other apartment."

"You're a tough one, coming back here like this."

I wasn't so sure about that, but put on a smile to reinforce the impression. "If I get something good, I can tell you and you'll have more to talk about at your reunion."

She stammered, "I—wouldn't."

I winked. "No problem. Just between us girls, this ought to be pretty spicy stuff. You'll be the center of attention."

She couldn't stop from grinning, much as she tried. Finally, she bit at her lower lip, but it didn't help. Her eyes widened. "You'll tell me what you find?"

I extended my hand, "Pinky swear."

Five minutes later, after having pinky-promised my new BFF Marjorie that I'd spill all the beans when I was done, I was standing alone in Stella's living room. A faded putrid-green couch with worn cushions took up most of one wall. Next to it was a rattan end table with a glass top, behind that, a torchiere lamp. On the wall next to the entry, a small entertainment center housed an old TV and a component stereo system, a couple of speakers sat on the floor on either side of that.

Stella also had a nifty collection of CDs in a wire tower. I'd had no idea that she was such a music buff. My opinion changed as I glanced through her collection. Her taste ran almost exclusively to country. I spotted a couple of the obligatory Kenny G and Michael Bolton cases, but other than that, this girl was country all the way, except for her surfboard and paddle.

Another thing I'd never realized about Stella was that she paddle surfed. And apparently, she was proud of it. I guessed her board to be about nine feet long, too tall to stand upright in one of these apartments. It rested horizontally on the wall on a couple of brackets. The paddle hung on a separate bracket just outside the bedroom door. The idea of using sports equipment as design elements had never occurred to me before, but why not?

The room was neat and tidy, nothing out of place. It was probably easy to keep the place this way because she spent a lot of time at Jimmy Dane's according to Marjorie. I went into the kitchen and checked the refrigerator, which smelled heavenly. The aroma of coffee flooded the room when I opened the door. I expected to find an open can in there, but it only contained a half quart of stale milk, two yogurts, and an orange. Closer inspection revealed a little sachet that hung on a lacy ribbon from the interior light. The little packet contained a few tablespoons of ground coffee. I took a last whiff before closing the door.

The freezer had the same heavenly scent, but the food supply wasn't any better. There was the can of coffee, another sachet, and a few frozen entrees. Stella obviously wasn't a gourmet cook. Of course, neither was I. We'd compared notes on that subject a couple of times while she'd worked for me. I chuckled at the memory of our last food conversation. We'd agreed that our best cooking skills were in picking good restaurants—and men who knew their way around a kitchen.

I checked a few of the cabinets, but found only a sparse sampling of cookware, dishes and glasses. With the kitchen a bust, I went into the bedroom. Stella's penchant for minimalism was apparent in this room also—a bed, a dresser, and a nightstand. She really had put all her money into cosmetic surgery and clothes. I checked the dresser drawers. Oh, Frederick's all the way. Everything from the latest in no lines to see-throughs. My eyes nearly bugged out when I found something Stella probably called a nightie. Sorry, but I just couldn't help myself. I pulled it out and held it up. Three pieces, sort of. A bra—if you could call it that, panties—which were almost nonexistent and I'm pretty damn sure had teeth marks, and a cover-up that left little to the imagination other than how long it would take to get it off. I felt my face going hot as I stuffed the set back into the dresser. I was about to close the drawer when I heard noises coming from the living room.

CHAPTER THIRTY-FOUR

He said, "Looks like we've got you boxed in."

Skip realized that his conversation with the old woman had given them both something to think about. Each seemed to be in some sort of contemplative state—she probably wondering how she could be so judgmental, he remorseful over letting two kidnappers escape—when Davy approached.

"Hey, Skip. Can you move your car?"

Skip started at the intrusion. He looked out at the parking lot and saw that another car had parked behind the moving van. "What happened?"

"I finished up. Everything else is going to storage."

"You can't get out?" The situation didn't look that bad to Skip, but he wasn't the one driving. His car was parked about ten feet in front of the truck, the new car about twenty feet behind, and Roxy's car—which was taking up one of those tenant spots—was almost directly opposite the new car. To get the truck out, Davy would have to move forward, jockey the truck to the middle of the lot, then back out through a space several feet wider than the truck itself. The last thing he needed was for Davy to hit the Porsche. If he needed to move the car, so be it.

Skip continued, "Looks like we've got you boxed in."

Davy's chest moved up and down rapidly. His breaths came fast and shallow. "So, can you?"

"Sure."

Relief seemed to wash over Davy. "Thank goodness." He crossed his arms over his chest and stared at the lot. He shook his head in a negative fashion as he turned back to Skip. "Man, I can barely drive

that thing forward. But backing it up between two cars? I need someone to guide me out."

The woman from the apartment stepped out to join them. "How
come you didn't tell that guy who parked behind you to move?"

"I tried, but he just ignored me. Acted like he was *deaf* or something. Asshole." Davy winced. "Sorry."

The other tenant said, "Don't worry, Davy, I even say 'shit' now
and again." She winked. "Barbara Allman. Welcome to the neighborhood."

Davy shook Barbara's hand enthusiastically. "At least I know
somebody now."

Barbara squinted at him. "Just no loud parties, understand?"

"Yes, ma'am."

"Don't ma'am me, either, I hate that. Along with loud parties."

"Yes, ma—sorry, Barbara." Davy glanced at his watch. "I hate to
rush, but I've still gotta get to the storage place and then return this
heap or they'll charge me for another day."

"No problem. I can guide you out. Let me move my car first," Skip
said.

As they walked to the lot, Davy pointed at the Porsche. "That's a
nice 911. I don't even want to take a remote chance of hitting it. Put it
on the other side of that guy's car, but park parallel. That way I'll
have an extra few feet."

"I don't know. What if another tenant comes in while I'm taking
up two spaces?"

Davy thumped himself on the chest. "Look, man, blame it on me.
Besides, I'll be backing up Big Bertha here. Who's gonna want to be
near that, huh?"

His laugh was nervous and he had beads of sweat on his forehead.

CHAPTER THIRTY-FIVE

She said, "You're not getting anything."

I stood stock-still in the bedroom of Stella's apartment. Maybe I was getting paranoid, but for some reason I didn't dare make a sound. The noises from the front room continued. I listened. Slip. Clunk. Slip. Clunk.

Whoever was out there was searching for something. My first reaction was to hide in the closet. While I'd lied to Marjorie about it, the truth was that the cops probably were interested in Stella's place. If the cops had sent someone up here, I'd have a lot of explaining to do. I could always lie to them and tell them I was thinking about renting the apartment, but they could expose that with one quick trip downstairs—a trip they would have already made. Marjorie knew I was here, why hadn't she warned me? Why hadn't the cop announced himself?

Maybe it was Marjorie and she'd decided to join in the hunt. But, again, why hadn't she called out when she'd entered the apartment? As the noises continued, I ruled out both Marjorie and the cops.

Either of them would have said something. That left Skip. I ruled him out, too. Skip would have wanted me to know he was here—unless he was playing another one of those stupid little mind games of his. That meant he wouldn't announce himself and would try to scare me. Well, as the saying goes, paybacks are hell. And that meant it was my turn. I considered my options, how I might return the favor for scaring me last night. But what if it wasn't him?

If it was someone other than Skip—oh, no. Clinton. I needed to be ready.

Slip. Clunk. Slip. Clunk.

I felt an adrenaline rush coming on as I crept to the open doorway and craned my neck to peek around the corner.

A man stood at the CD case, pulling and replacing CDs.

The man wore an unbuttoned aloha shirt over a navy T-shirt. He had on a pair of faded jeans. His height and weight matched Clinton's. His pristine black tennis shoes were identical to those I'd seen yesterday. I hadn't seen the face of the man behind the Clinton mask, but those shoes and build were unmistakable. It was my kidnapper.

I sucked in a breath.

He glanced in my direction as he pulled a CD from the rack.

Shit! I had less than two seconds to find a weapon. I scanned the room, frantically searching for something to use against him. Nothing, except for Stella's surfing paddle on the wall just outside the door. All I had to do was reach around and grab it.

The kidnapper said, "Well, goddamn. Hey, kid."

He started in my direction. I landed a kick to his solar plexus, which sent him staggering backward, stunned. He shook his head and fought for breath for a second, then came at me again. I grabbed the paddle and crouched, knees flexed, weight on the balls of my feet, ready to attack.

He chuckled.

The shiny tooth Mom had described gleamed, sending a chill down my back.

"Okay, Paddle Girl, I'm gonna tear you apart."

"Leave my family alone! You got your money."

He glanced at the CD in his hand. A half smile spread across his lips. "Now I do."

I caught a glimpse of the CD cover. It was black with some sort of flowing silver script.

He started to stuff the CD into the pocket of his jeans, but it wouldn't fit.

A key jiggled in the lock. We both heard it.

"Roxy? I'm going to have to leave soon."

It was Marjorie.

A flash of concern showed on his face. Now he had two witnesses to eliminate. He glanced at the door. I saw my opening.

I swung the paddle as hard as I could. It landed squarely on the side of his head with a loud crack and sent him tumbling into the CD rack. CDs spilled from the rack onto the floor.

The door opened and Marjorie shrieked. The kidnapper shook his head. Blood oozed from a cut under his right eye. I swung again. This time he instinctively blocked my blow, but the force of impact jarred the CD from his grasp. He staggered, then slipped on the pile of cases.

Marjorie stood aghast just inside the door. The kidnapper reached out and grabbed her arm. As he regained his footing, he shoved her in my direction.

I held onto the paddle with one hand and seized one of her flailing arms with the other just before she tumbled headfirst into the coffee table. The support was enough that she made a soft, but not very graceful, landing on the floor. I continued to grip my weapon, determined to take this guy down.

Clinton still seemed dazed. A trickle of blood from the cut under his right eye ran down the side of this face. Whatever he wanted was in that pile of CDs, but the case he wanted was now among fifty others. He shook his head as if trying to clear it.

Despite the adrenaline flooding my system as I inched closer, I made sure to keep my stance low, my knees flexed. My words didn't even sound like they came from me. They sounded more like those of a crazed fanatic. "You're not getting anything."

CHAPTER THIRTY-SIX

He said, "Who stole my car?"

It took Skip less than a minute to move the Porsche from in front of the van to one of the parking spaces on the opposite side of the car that was causing Davy's panic. He tucked the Porsche in nice and close to the driver's door of the other car and left the engine running. The guy had already been a jerk. He wasn't going anywhere as long as Davy was in this lot with that van. Once Davy got the truck out of the lot, the Porsche could be moved quickly back to its original spot.

Skip heard the moving van's engine cranking over as he trotted to the driver's door. The truck's engine rumbled to life and Davy stared down at Skip from the driver's window. Skip hoped that Davy's chin quivered from the truck's vibration, not fear.

"That's a mighty small space," said Davy.

Skip stepped back and checked the distance between the cars. "It's not that bad. I thought you drove this from Vegas?"

Davy's head bobbed up and down. "*Forward,* man. I never had to, like, *back up* or anything."

"Davy, you need to do this. You'll feel better once you've threaded that needle."

"It's that small?" Fear permeated Davy's voice.

Skip laughed. "Just a figure of speech, man. Relax. This van isn't that big and the space between the cars isn't that small. No problem. Pull forward to the end of the lot."

Davy followed Skip's instructions and positioned the truck.

Skip stood beside the driver's door. "Okay, you're going to crank the wheel to the left while you back up. It'll be like doing a seven-point turn on a narrow street. You've done those before, right?"

"Not in anything this big."

"Forget what you're driving. Just imagine this is a small truck and you've got complete control."

Davy bit at his lower lip. "That's kinda hard from up here."

"*Davy,*" Skip scolded. "I'll be at the back of the truck. I'll motion like this," he put both hands up with his fingers spread wide, "when it's time to stop. You can't crank the wheel too hard on this first turn because of the curb. Okay, let's go."

Skip stood by the vehicle that had caused the problem and motioned for Davy to back up. The truck inched toward him and gradually turned until it was at about a fifteen degree angle. He motioned to stop and the truck jerked as Davy jammed on the brakes.

Skip smiled as he approached the driver's door. "Good job. Now you're going to crank the wheel hard to the right and go forward."

It took a couple of more turns and some additional coaxing, but Davy finally got the truck positioned to where he'd be able to back out without trouble. Meanwhile, Skip kept an eye on the parking lot. He was thankful that no one showed up to park while he was playing driving instructor. He was also thankful that the driver of the other car hadn't shown up either. In retrospect, he wished that he'd just put the Porsche on the street.

He walked up to the driver's door and said, "Okay, you're ready to back out. Just keep the wheel straight and you should be fine. Ready?"

Davy shook his head. "That space is so small, man. I don't have any room over there on the right."

Skip stood on the running board of the truck and checked the right side mirror. He guessed that Davy had at least three feet of room on the other side, but in the mirror it looked nothing like that. "You've got plenty of room."

"It looks like six inches, if that."

"All right, I'll go over there. If you get close to Roxy's car, I'll signal you to stop. Will that work?"

Davy nodded. He took a deep breath. "Okay."

Skip went and stood next to Roxy's car and motioned for Davy to put the truck into reverse. The truck inched backward, generally in a straight line. Davy veered a little and with his view of his own car blocked, Skip's anxiety grew. He realized how Davy felt, this thing seemed bigger now. It would do a lot of damage if it hit something. He'd rather be on the other side of the truck so he could keep an eye on the Porsche. But the laws of physics were immutable. There were several feet between Roxy's car and the moving van, which meant, logically, there had to be at least two feet on the other side. No, his baby was fine.

Suddenly, the truck jerked to a stop and Davy began yelling. Skip couldn't make out the words over the truck's engine noise, but Davy was flipping out. Skip ran to the passenger door and jumped up onto the running board. Davy was hanging out the driver's window, desperately pulling on the door release. "I'm locked in. Goddammit! I'm locked in! Your car!" Skip jumped from the running board and ran to the driver's side of the truck, where Davy hung half-in, half-out of the window screaming. "Stop! No! Get away from there!"

Skip stood, his mouth agape, staring at where the Porsche had been. His heart did flip flops in his chest. "Who? Who stole my car?"

"That guy, the one with the car we had blocked in. He just ran out of the apartment and took it."

CHAPTER THIRTY-SEVEN

She said, "We've found something important. But, what is it?"

I stood just outside the apartment, searching in all directions. Clinton had already disappeared. I hurried back into the room and locked the door behind me. Two steps away I turned around and checked the lock, then stood and stared at the mess. CD cases littered the floor, one of the legs on the coffee table tilted oddly to one side, and Marjorie didn't look much better as she sat, eyes glazed, next to it.

Marjorie's phlegmy cough echoed in the silence of the apartment. When she'd finished coughing, she said, "Who the hell was that?"

"That was the man who kidnapped me and my dad. He was the leader. Jimmy and Stella were his helpers." I reached out and helped Marjorie to her feet.

She wobbled a bit and winced. "My leg. Oh, that hurts." She took a couple of tentative steps. "I think I'll be okay." She hobbled in a circle around the pile of CD cases.

"Careful," I said.

Marjorie looked down at the paddle in my hands. "I don't think you need that anymore."

I hadn't even realized that I still clutched my weapon. She was right, the guy was gone, but I felt a weird reluctance to relinquish it. "Sorry." A question formed in my mind as I hung the paddle in its spot on the wall. I glanced at the door. "Marjorie, that was the leader—or whatever he's called. He isn't the one who rented the other apartment?"

She shook her head. "I've never seen him before."

"If it wasn't him, who was it?"

"Martin Sylvester. Nice guy, tall. Good looking."

I glanced around. "I'm sorry about this."

"No need to be sorry, you were defending yourself. Hey, you were defending me, too. Where'd you learn that anyway?"

"My mother started me on martial arts training when I was six. She said it would help my confidence and maybe keep me alive if I ever got into real trouble."

Marjorie eased herself into a kitchen table chair. "My granddaughter's ten. I'm going to talk to my daughter about that. I've never seen a woman be able to—you know."

I stared down at the pile of cases littering the floor as she sat in the chair and coughed. Somewhere in here was the one the kidnapper had wanted. Despite her obnoxious hacking, I was starting to like Marjorie. I squatted next to the largest pile of CDs and glanced up at her. "The training's not cheap, but it can—but it can make the difference." And how it had.

She nodded. "I'll help her out with the cost if she needs it. What are you looking for?"

"He was after a CD. Black. Silver writing. Want to help me look?"

She hoisted herself up. "Sure." The pain on her face told me she wouldn't be doing any crawling around on the floor—or dancing at her party.

"I'm sorry I dragged you into this. This is going to ruin your reunion."

"Oh, crap. That's right. I forgot all about it. I came up to tell you I had to leave. Let's call the cops. I'll feel better once they're around."

"No cops!"

Her brow furrowed and her shoulders heaved as her breathing grew heavier. "Oh, man, do I hurt." She sat back down. "Why don't you want the police involved?"

"What are they going to do? The kidnapping is over. This is just some guy breaking and entering. You think they're going to care about some guy who wants a CD?"

Marjorie surveyed the floor. "What if he comes back?"

"The cops won't care. Besides, imagine all the paperwork."

"But you could give them a description of the guy."

"What about the publicity? That won't be good for you. You'll have everyone moving out because the building isn't safe."

Marjorie winced as she rubbed her leg. "Were you the debate captain, too? All right. After your run-in with them yesterday I guess I can't blame you. You stopped the guy—nothing was taken. Okay, no cops."

The adrenaline was washing out of my system as fast as water flowing out of an overfilled pond. I wanted to find that CD before my energy level died and my emotions kicked in. "Thanks." I knelt and began sorting through cases. "Look, if you want to go to your reunion, I can close up here after I'm done."

She stared at the mess, the glazed-over look still in her eyes. "I don't know. I was so looking forward to that, but now—after this."

I stood and went to her, rested my hand on her shoulder. "You don't get a 40th reunion every day. You should go." Besides, I wanted more time to snoop.

She motioned around her. "You don't get *one of these* every day either."

I pulled a chair next to hers. "Look, I feel responsible for this. If I hadn't been here, he would have found what he wanted and would've been gone just like that." I snapped my fingers for effect. "Nobody would have been the wiser." As much as I hated to say it, I followed that up with, "I'll take care of this mess and lock the place up. Don't you worry about it."

Worry, followed by another shot of pain, returned to her face. "I can't do much here."

It took a bit more coaxing and I thought I had her primed to leave when she made up her mind. She was going to supervise. Unfortunately, I was the one who gave in. Maybe I just didn't want to be alone. Besides, Marjorie wanted to help and it seemed like there was nothing I could do to talk her out of it. We put a chair next to where the CD tower belonged. Next, we had to decide on a methodology for sorting the CDs. Mine would have been to go with the tried-and-true efficiency method of first in the hand, first on the rack. But Marjorie would have nothing to do with that. She maintained that Stella had been an organized person. From what I'd seen at work, this was a stretch, but I went along. We ended up agreeing—actually, Marjorie decided, I acquiesced—to put the collection in alphabetic order by artist, then by year of production.

I righted the CD tower and put it in its proper place, then plunked down cross-legged on the floor and began sorting through the cases. Stella wasn't going to care what order these were in now that she was gone, but obviously it meant a lot to Marjorie. I began sorting by artist. Talk about tedious. All I really wanted to do was find the one the kidnapper had been after. Instead, I'd become Stella's CD librarian.

I examined each case before I handed it to Marjorie, who put it into a slot in the tower. It took about twenty minutes to get the mess cleaned up, but when we were done, we had five cases that resembled the one I'd seen the kidnapper holding.

I said, "Damn. Which one was it? I couldn't read the title."

Marjorie shook her head. "I was too busy being frightened out of my wits and trying to avoid killing myself on that damn coffee table."

"How did he know which case he needed?" The five cases all had a black background and silver lettering. "I wonder if someone told him to look for a specific CD."

"Probably. I wonder ..." Marjorie's voice trailed off.

"You think it could be Jimmy?"

Marjorie worked her jaw from side to side. "That's what I was thinking."

"That means he hooked up with the kidnapper." I shivered at the thought of the two of them coming after me again. I went to the door and checked the lock.

"What are you doing?"

The rationale seemed silly since we'd already been sitting here for twenty minutes sorting through CDs. "I just wanted to check it."

"I check mine about every half hour. I know the damned things are locked, but it just makes me feel better to be positive."

"I've never been paranoid before." The words sounded hollow to me because they were. I'd spent twenty years being haunted by a memory. No more.

"So you're not as tough as you let on."

"I feel better now that I've checked it." My phone rang. I glanced at the display. "Hey."

His voice sounded shaky. "Are you okay?"

"I'm in Stella's with the landlord."

There was a pause, then he said, "I'll call you back."

She winced at the abrupt cutoff.

Marjorie asked, "Who was that?"

"Um—a guy I'm working with on this case."

Marjorie's eyes twinkled. "A *special* guy?"

I felt my eyes roll nearly to the back of my head. Why did everyone assume there was something between us. I summoned my best business tone, but it sounded fake, even to me. "He's supposed to be interviewing tenants. But, it's been, like, half an hour. That's a long time. It shouldn't have taken him anywhere near that long. Maybe I should go down and see what's up?"

Marjorie nodded and gave me a little smile.

"*What?*"

"Don't lie to yourself, Roxy. You're too young."

I set my jaw and pushed the hair away from my face. "I'm sure he's okay. Let's check those CDs."

Marjorie and I sat at the kitchen table. Each of us took a case and opened it. Marjorie screwed up her face and said, "Wish I knew what I was looking for."

"Ditto." That wasn't going to stop me. I examined each cover, front and back. Nothing unusual. Country. I opened each case. Again, there was nothing unusual until I got to the fourth CD. A note fell out and drifted to the floor as I opened it. I leaned forward to pick up the note and realized that I, too, hurt from my encounter with the kidnapper. "You're right. I'm not as tough as I used to be."

"You're too young to have aches and pains."

"I need to get back in training."

I picked up the note and read. "S. Meet me at the designated place. J."

I handed the note to Marjorie. She read it and handed it back. "Beats me."

"Same here." For the first time, I looked at the disk itself. "Oh crap."

Marjorie leaned toward me.

I turned the case so she could see also.

"This is a computer disk, not music." My heart raced. "We've found something important. But what is it?"

CHAPTER THIRTY-EIGHT

He said, "This is getting dangerous."

Skip leaned against the car the auto thief had abandoned. The heat in his face and neck came from pure embarrassment. *What an idiot I was.*

His lower lip quivered as he thought about how he'd lost the one thing his uncle had left him. "Until one of us dies," he'd told Wally. "Until one of us dies."

A patrol car rolled into the lot. He cursed himself again. Stupid, stupid, stupid. More heat rushed into his face as he watched two uniformed officers exit their vehicle. Were they eyeing him? Wondering how he could have done something so—so—stupid? He knew better than to leave his keys in the car. Worse, he'd left the car running. An open invitation for a thief.

"Mr. Cosgrove?" said the first officer. His name tag said he was Eagan. He had short-cropped hair, stern eyes, and flared nostrils that reminded Skip of his junior-high gym teacher.

Skip gaped at the man who had spoken. "Sorry, guess I'm still in shock." Skip gestured with his head at Davy, who gave the two officers a meek smile. He continued, "I was helping Davy when it happened. He was backing this truck out—next thing I know, my car's gone."

Eagan said, "You left the keys in it?"

"Worse. I left it running. But I was *right here.* I can't believe someone would steal a car like that."

Eagan said, "Maybe he was in a hurry."

Skip forced himself not to snarl. "Is that supposed to be funny?"

Eagan shook his head. "No sir. Car thieves aren't usually so brazen. The fact that he stole your car while you were in the immediate vicinity suggests your thief was either acting on a dare, has sociopathic tendencies—"

Skip finished what he knew was coming next. "Or was running away from something. Crap." He'd been so focused on his car that he'd forgotten about Roxy. What if something had happened to her? "One second." He pulled out his cell and dialed Roxy's number.

He waited four long rings before she picked up.

"Hey."

He felt relief at the sound of her voice. She must be fine. "Are you okay?"

"I'm in Stella's with the landlord."

Eagan shifted from one foot to the other, his impatience obvious. Skip decided he'd have to wait for the story. "I'll call you back." He said to Eagan, "Sorry about that. She's in one of these apartments. I wanted to make sure my, um, friend was okay."

Eagan nodded knowingly. "No problem. Right now, we're looking for a car based on the description you phoned in. It hasn't been found yet, but as long as it's still on the streets, the guy won't get far. Let's go through the report."

Seconds felt like minutes, minutes like hours, as the police completed their paperwork. When they'd finished, they went on their way and Davy finished backing the truck out onto the street. As the truck rumbled away, Skip ran back into the complex. He found Apartment 6 and knocked on the door.

Behind the door, a hacking cough preceded a gravelly, "Who is it?"

"Skip Cosgrove. Is Roxy there?"

"Just a sec."

The dead bolt clicked and the door opened. An elderly woman with long, flowing gray hair opened the door. Her eyebrows arched as she gave Skip the once-over and smiled. She nodded as she turned toward Roxy, who sat at the kitchen table.

He breathed another sigh of relief, but then realized she winced as she stood. "I was worried about you," he said.

The woman nodded. "You should have been worried about her. She had to fight off a criminal."

Roxy's face flushed mildly as she glanced away. The woman hacked a few more times while Skip searched Roxy's face for an explanation.

"The kidnapper showed up. He was after this." Roxy held up a CD case.

So he had been here. Now he knew why the man had been in a hurry. "He wanted *music*?"

She shook her head. "It's not music. It's a music case, but it's a computer disk."

"What's on it?"

"We don't know—yet. Marjorie was going to let me use her computer to check it out."

He licked his lips. "You're not the only one who ran into this guy."

Skip saw her cheek twitch as she took in what he'd said. "You, too? You saw him?"

"More like he drove away—in my car."

Roxy's jaw dropped and Marjorie began to hack again. She chirped, "This just gets better and better."

Roxy said, "Your Porsche? He stole your Porsche?"

It was the first time he'd seen anything resembling concern on her face for someone other than her immediate family. The fact that she cared, even if it was only about the car, gave him some consolation. "He grabbed it while I was helping some guy back a moving truck out of the lot."

Marjorie chuckled. "Davy. He's new. He's a dork. Kid'll be lucky to land a job. That's why he left Vegas, no work for him. Poor kid's got a black cloud over his head. It's a little late, but stay away from him if you don't want to get rained on."

Skip ignored the comment. "He's not real good at driving a truck." Skip paused. "I can't believe the guy stole my car!"

"You called the cops?" Marjorie said.

"They just left."

"Too bad, could'a gotten a twofer. You want to see what's on that CD? We can go down to my place."

"How do you know that's what the guy was after?" asked Skip.

Roxy held out a piece of paper. "Here's the note that was in the case. The CD is marked MH with a marking pen. And he was holding a black CD case with silver lettering in his hand when I interrupted him."

Skip held Marjorie's gaze. "Are you sure you want to be involved in this? Maybe we should leave. This is getting dangerous."

"Not at all," she hacked. A small cough followed.

"You need to see a doctor," Roxy said.

"Forty years of two packs a day, honey. Doc says I won't live to see my fiftieth, but I'll have a helluva time till then."

"I'm sorry to hear that." Roxy looked at Skip. "Marjorie had her fortieth reunion today. She missed it because of me."

"Don't worry about me. I haven't had so much fun in ages."

Fun? Skip wondered how anyone could call this fun. It took only a few more minutes to finish straightening up Stella's apartment and then they followed Marjorie to hers. Inside, Marjorie sat Roxy in front of the computer and excused herself.

"I gotta check messages." She limped across the room and pushed a button on her answering machine.

Roxy glanced up at Skip. "She's been really sweet." She lowered her voice to a whisper and Skip leaned closer to hear her. "That guy could have killed her, but she's a trouper."

Skip gawked in disbelief at Roxy.

"What?"

He couldn't believe what he was thinking. When had she morphed from a self-centered, uncaring—he tried to wet his lips, but his throat felt waterless. Nor could he explain how he'd felt in that moment when he'd thought she was in danger. He nodded in agreement. "She's tough." He looked her in the eye and realized how exposed he felt. "So are you."

Roxy snorted and turned away. She put the CD into the drive.

In the background, Skip heard a voice blaring. "Margie? Where the hell are you? You're gonna miss the reunion. Call me. If you don't, I may just have to call 9-1-1 and have 'em send some big hunky firemen over to save you. On second thought, I'm hanging up and calling 'em right now to have one sent over here. I think I got a case of the vapors coming on." The woman leaving the message cackled. "Anyway, call me."

Roxy tapped on the keyboard, seeming to ignore him while she stared at the computer screen. She giggled. "Too much."

Skip watched the contour of her face and felt loneliness encroaching on the perimeter of his confidence. She'd gotten to him. He had to distance himself. Starting now. He took a deep breath and watched the screen. "So, what've you got there?"

"Still waiting. This thing's so *slow*."

"So why do you think this guy came back for the disk?"

Roxy shook her head. "Dunno. It's got to be something important. He must have picked the lock, just like you did at Dane's apartment."

"Maybe he had a key. He knew Stella. They were in on the kidnapping together."

"I hadn't thought of that." Roxy's face fell. "Damn. I can't believe the luck I'm having."

Skip turned his attention to the computer screen.

Roxy buried her face in her hands. "It's password protected."

CHAPTER THIRTY-NINE

She said, "Why would he leave her a CD, but no password?"

My afternoon had gone to hell. I'd met my dad's kidnapper again and failed to take him down. I'd gotten the disk the kidnapper wanted, but couldn't read it. I'd nearly gotten an old woman I liked killed. I'd had to spend time reading back issues of *Popular Mechanics* in Skip's insurance agent's office while he reported his car stolen because he just *couldn't do that* over the phone. And the final blow was that now we were having dinner together at Keller's.

Don't get me wrong, I like Skip. Actually, I like him a lot. It's just that, well, I'm probably leaving town soon and the last thing I need is a complication. Besides, he thinks I'm just another SSB—a spoiled, snotty bitch. Maybe he's right. Whatever.

During dinner we hadn't said much, which suited me because I was famished and not feeling particularly sociable. Skip had a burger. I went with the turkey sandwich. Both of us opted for the Crispy Fries, which I reasoned I was allowed to have because I'd gotten the sandwich without mayo. I'd just finished the last of my fries when Skip's phone broke the silence.

I could either go to the restroom or eavesdrop on one side of the conversation. What the hell? Last time—when Skip was having that conversation with Tommy—I went to the ladies room and got left out when I returned. I hate making the same mistake twice, so eavesdropping won out.

"Cosgrove. What?"

Skip's voice had gone up a few notes. His face turned blotchy.

"It's totaled?"

Ouch, I thought, not the car.

"When? Where?"

His eyes were turning red. This hadn't been good news at all.

"Thanks."

I decided to pry. "What's up?"

"They found my car."

He sounded morose and his eyes glistened. OMG, he wasn't going to cry on me, was he? I considered heading for the restroom after all, but decided to press on rather than bail on him. "Was that the cops? They found your car and it was totaled?"

He nodded. His jaw was getting tight and his neck was kind of bulgy.

"I'd kill the son of a bitch, but he died in the crash," he said.

I nearly choked on my Chardonnay. "He's dead? That should be some consolation." Even to myself, I sounded like a snotty bitch. "Sorry, that wasn't what I meant to say."

"CHP spotted the car on I-5 right near the 78. When the cop turned on his lights, the driver took off. He changed lanes in front of a semi and clipped the front end. The cop thinks he was doing about 100 and trying to hit the off-ramp."

"Jesus. A hundred? At the 78? That's, like, suicide."

"I-5 is a mess. You know what pisses me off the most?"

My attitude? SSBs in general? I wasn't sure I wanted to hear this.

"This guy kidnapped your dad, beat you up, stole my car. And we don't even know who he is. Or who he was working for."

Not that I was keeping score, but on that list, I had two of the things that pissed him off. And mine came first. Wow. Another wow—something I hadn't thought of. "You think he was working for someone?"

"I think he was a hired gun. You saw him. You didn't know him, right?"

I shook my head. "Never seen the guy before—except in a Bill Clinton mask."

"Think about it. One of the kidnappers meets your dad in a bar, gets him drunk, and then ransoms him off for five million dollars."

"But that was Stella's doing."

"This guy killed his boss? The one who set it all up? I don't think so."

"Maybe it was Dane?"

166 ~ Terry Ambrose

Skip took a long swig of his beer. "Who's he? Where is he? How did he suddenly hook up with Stella for this? Last time I checked, the phone book didn't have a category for kidnappers."

The waitress showed up to clear our plates. "Everything okay here?"

Skip gave her a thumbs-up signal. I smiled. "As usual, the best."

With the waitress gone, I sat back in my seat, stunned. There it was. The answer had been right in front of me since I'd first seen the CD. Skip was right. Stella had known the kidnappers before. "MH— Martin Horvath."

Skip stuck one of his fries in his mouth. "Stella's old boyfriend."

"Shit. So what do you think is on that CD?"

Skip held up another fry and pursed his lips. "My guess? Five million dollars."

"Excuse me?"

"I think it's the bank transfer information."

I wasn't sure whether I should laugh or cry. If my bank account was on that disk, I could get the money back. In order to do that, though, I'd need the password. Without it, the disk was useless. And my five million was history.

"Why would he leave her a CD, but no password?"

"Insurance? That's a lot of money. Maybe he was worried about a double-cross."

"But he knew Stella. He was her boyfriend."

Skip leaned forward and put both elbows on the table. "You're assuming he's Horvath."

I remembered Marjorie's description of Jimmy Dane. "That guy today wasn't Dane. He doesn't fit the description. He has to be Horvath."

"Dane's probably the third kidnapper."

I nodded. "He kind of fits Marjorie's description."

"What if there's a fourth guy? What if the guy you ran into was getting the disk back because Horvath told him to?"

I didn't want to think about that possibility. "You think he was there under orders?"

"Maybe."

"That would mean the disk was there for safekeeping. Who put it there? The guy in Stella's apartment? I saw him leave, remember? I shot at him."

"Maybe it wasn't him. Maybe it was Dane or the fourth guy."

I felt like I was on a merry-go-round and unable to get off. "This is ridiculous. We're going in frigging circles. We have nothing."

Skip rubbed the back of his neck. "I'm pissed. I want these guys. I want your money back. And I want to bring whoever started this to justice."

His voice held a sinister tone, a menacing and ominous current that made me glad I wasn't the one he was after. "What are you going to do?"

"I'm going back into Dane's apartment."

"For what? So you can get busted for burglary?"

"If Dane's behind this, I need to access his computer. I saw one the other night. It looked like it had a lot of programming code or something on the screen. I didn't think it was important at the time, so I ignored it. I have a friend who can help me, though."

I half laughed. "Of course, you know a hacker, too." I lowered my voice. "You're a criminologist, you can pick a lock, you steal cell phones from crime scenes and you know a hacker. Why not?" So he wasn't Mister Straight. Skip had a bad boy side and I liked that. He'd also given me an idea. Maybe that password was right in front of me? I thought about Stella's phone, her e-mail. Would he have sent it to his girlfriend?

Skip said, "Look, Tanner, I don't know about you, but I've got work to do."

And so did I, but not in the same place as Skip.

CHAPTER FORTY

He said, "Can you crack a password?"

Skip stood in the shadows watching Jimmy Dane's apartment and the surrounding area for activity. The apartment itself was dark. Most of the others had lights on, but drapes closed. The one exception was a second-floor unit where two couples sat on the deck playing cards. Their raucous laughter filled the night air. It was the type of private party that caused neighbors to count the minutes until the noise let up. It was that attention that worried Skip. He didn't need someone peering out to check on the card players and spot him breaking into Dane's, so he'd resolved to wait for the party to end. Given that it was nearly 10 p.m., he guessed that it wouldn't be long before that happened, one way or another.

Sure enough, five minutes later, the group finished their card game and began sliding their chairs back. Apparently, the game had been men against women and the men won. The women promised payback next week. As they went into the apartment through the sliding door, Skip checked the area again. It would take them a few minutes to say their good-byes. He had a brief window of opportunity or he'd have to wait for the visitors to leave. He donned a pair of latex gloves and made his move.

It took him less than thirty seconds to pick the lock to Dane's apartment this time. He still wouldn't use lights, but had his flashlight ready. He'd become familiar with the apartment layout on his previous visit and quickly walked toward the bedroom. About halfway there, the refrigerator kicked on. In the dark room, it sounded like a freight train.

At the bedroom door, Skip paused. Footsteps thumped overhead. He took a breath and crossed the room to Dane's computer, which whirred in the dark. He moved the mouse and light from the screen filled the room. Skip stared at the gibberish he'd seen the other day for a couple of minutes. He wished he'd paid more attention the last time he'd seen this, but as near as he could tell, there was no change.

The longer he stared at the screen, though, the more patterns he began to recognize. He could make out words that were separated by some sort of code. Outside the apartment, he heard a man and a woman talking. Their voices grew louder. Skip went to the living room. The voices were right outside the front door. He waited and listened.

If they came into this apartment, his only option would be to go out one of the windows, probably the slider to the patio. Skip positioned himself by the door and eased the latch open. His pulse shot up at the clacking of metal meeting metal. He watched the front door and waited for it to open. When he heard a door close, he realized that the couple had gone into the apartment next door and let out the breath he'd been holding.

Skip locked the latch and returned to the computer. So what was he looking at? He was almost afraid to touch the keyboard for fear of disrupting something important. On the other hand, he had the sense that whatever he was looking at was important to finding the ransom. Skip pulled out his cell phone and dialed.

On the second ring, a man answered. "Dude, speak to me."

"Hey, Baldorf, howzit dude'?"

"Sweet, man. I'm into final testing on Baldorf's Revenge."

While he didn't understand even the basic details of the programming behind a virtual reality program such as Baldorf's Revenge, Skip did know one thing. Baldorf was a computer genius. If anyone could become one with the machine, it would be Baldorf. He was a twenty-two-year-old geek who immersed himself in the computer world for eighteen hours a day, six days a week. On his off day, he meditated. All day—or so he said. Skip was willing to bet money that some of that meditation time was spent on a computer.

"I have a technical problem," Skip said.

"You've come to the mountain, my friend. Speak and I shall cure your ills."

Skip chuckled. "You're a maniac, you know that?"

"Oh, I am so offended. And here I thought you sought knowledge."

"What I seek is someone to tell me what the hell I'm looking at."

"I have great powers, true, but I am unable to see through your eyes."

Skip gave himself a light tap on the forehead. "You are a genius man. Let me send you a photograph from my cell, maybe you can tell me if this is important or not."

"Beam it up, dude, I'm ready."

Skip laughed as he disconnected. Baldorf's real name was Barry Finkledorf. He'd constructed the name Baldorf as a way to market his product while maintaining his identity. Skip had tried an early proto-type of the game and gotten blown out on Level 2. Baldorf had prom-ised Skip that, with practice, he could easily make it to Level 3 or 4. The game had ten levels. Skip figured it wasn't for him.

He snapped a picture of the screen and sent Baldorf a text mes-sage with the image attached. Two minutes later, his phone rang. "Cosgrove."

"Dude, it's a base 64 encoded key logger output stream delivered via FTP."

Skip stammered, "A—a what?"

"That computer you're looking at is monitoring someone else's computer. It's logging key strokes."

"How do you know that?"

"You want me to *explain* it?"

Skip listened to his pulse echoing in his ear. He wet his lips and said, "Uh, not really."

"Didn't think so. But you do want me to decode it for you."

"You can do that?"

"Child's play. It could be a cool diversion for a few minutes."

Skip shook his head. Only Baldorf would consider something of this nature and complexity child's play. Or a cool diversion. "Sure. Decode it."

"Well, I can't, like, just look at it and decode it. I'll need your help."

"I don't even know what you're talking about, Baldorf. And you want me to help?"

"Think of it as a little male bonding and a bit of computer training. Use the mouse to scroll up on the screen."

Skip did as Baldorf instructed. He was stunned to realize that he was looking at pages of data. "How much of this stuff is there?"

"Looks like someone was playing spy games. Very cool. Dude, there are two ways we can handle this. You can bring the computer to me, which could be problematic if you have to shut it down. If that thing has any security at all, it might take a little time to hack in."

"Can you crack a password?"

"Dude, this is me. Of course I can. It just might take awhile."

"I don't have lots of time. What's the other option?"

"We set up a remote monitoring session. Once I'm connected, I'll have complete control over that machine."

"I think I like that option better."

"Awesome. I can expand my network."

"Huh? What's *that* mean?"

"I'm just going to tap into the brainpower of that machine for a little while. I'll use the resource whenever the machine is in an idle state."

Skip's mind raced with questions as he considered his predicament. Baldorf had also tried to explain the concept of virtual networking to Skip and he'd zoned out. How one computer could use another computer's resources might as well be some galactic mystery. "Is this, um, legal?"

"You're giving me access to the machine, right?"

"It's, um, not really mine."

"Very cool, my friend. I take it you did not have the consent of the owner to access this machine."

"Not exactly."

"Awesome. I'm proud of you. Welcome to the dark side."

CHAPTER FORTY-ONE

She said, "Who needs a hacker, anyway?"

Skip's insurance company, of course, had a loophole that they interpreted to mean they didn't have to provide Skip with a rental car. That meant getting rid of him wasn't going to be nearly as easy as I'd hoped. For starters, I'd driven us to dinner. I couldn't leave him at Keller's without transportation and he didn't have a second vehicle. It had already dawned on me that if I didn't help him find something to drive, I'd be playing taxi for days—maybe weeks. Thank goodness he remembered that his hot-shot lawyer friend had a motorcycle he could borrow before I got to months or years.

I got stuck driving him down to Del Mar to the lawyer's house, but that was better than having to drive him all over for eternity while he sorted things out with his insurance company. Traffic wasn't too bad, but the drive down Pacific Coast Highway, while pretty, was a pain in the ass. Basically, we had what seemed like half of Southern California on the road. There were all the surfers who had run out of daylight. And don't forget the sunset seekers. Or the commuters who'd rather go slow on PCH than fight the weirdos on the 5. And then there was everyone else, those like me, who were just plain in the wrong place at the wrong time.

Once we got the drive out of the way, the next obstacle became the lawyer. Wally has the gift of gab and could talk chicken off the bone if he set his mind to it. He's also hugely impressed with the money he's made. If it wasn't for the fact that he was Skip's friend and a big-shot attorney who loved high-profile cases, I might have even considered him as a potential client. He had the bucks and the attitude I was looking for, but if I conned him, he'd probably set Skip on my trail.

And if there was anything I'd learned in the last couple of days it was that Skip had a bad case of Mountie syndrome—he always got his man. Better for me to pass on Wally and go after someone who had less-persistent friends.

I'd also learned another of Skip's problems—he took things personally. That was good for his clients—my present role, but bad for his quarry—my role if I went after his friend's money. No. It would be better to keep him on my side rather than on my trail.

It was almost eight when I finally got away from Skip and Wally. I was relieved when Skip said he needed to compare notes with Wally about the Nordoff case. That meant he wouldn't be following me and I'd get to my office to check out my hunch.

My guess was that Skip might be having Wally do some checking on my business. But unless Wally enlisted the help of some high-powered financial investigator, it was unlikely he'd turn up anything negative since I'd done everything in the shadows of legitimate companies. Even so, if Skip was checking my operations out, that meant there was another reason to get my money back quickly—the less people poking around my affairs, the better. I got to the office in the minimum standard San Diego commute time, thirty minutes. I was relieved when I slipped the door closed behind me and saw Stella's phone sitting on the credenza charging. Good, right where I'd left it. And that meant no cops yet.

My guess was that if Jimmy Dane was Stella's boyfriend, he'd have sent her an e-mail with the password for the disk. He'd left the CD in her apartment, so why not send the password under separate cover?

I started reviewing e-mails on her phone. The most recent were spam. At least, that's what they looked like to me. She had emails for cosmetic surgery and beauty products along with the standard bedroom promotions of "make your man pant like a dog in heat." With all the work Stella had done and the lingerie I'd found in her dresser drawer, I'd be surprised if a couple of quick poses in a candlelit room didn't do the trick.

The first e-mail that wasn't spam was from Jimmy Dane, himself. "Where are you? Been calling for hours. Call me."

There was another from someone named Caroline. Her e-mail address was caroline@liketosurf.com. It turned out to be an invitation to meet this Saturday morning for a few hours. Sorry, Caroline, Stella won't make it.

Other not-so-innocent offers invited Stella to "hook up," "catch up," and "party around." If they only knew what I knew about Stella.

Further down the list, I saw Jimmy Dane's next e-mail. It had no subject and had been sent yesterday afternoon within an hour of the time I'd been taken in by the cops. I opened the message.

"P2xek3o!$FQ."

That looked like a password to me. My fingers began to shake so much I think I nearly dropped Stella's phone. I reached into my bag and pulled out the CD. In an effort to bolster my confidence, I said, "Who needs a hacker, anyway?"

Finding out if this gibberish was really the password I needed would only take a few minutes. If I was correct, I could put this all behind me. That was a big if. I sat staring at the e-mail, unable to bring myself to actually try the password. The last thing I wanted was to be wrong and in this short moment, as far as I knew, I was right. I was rich again. I wanted to savor this moment and couldn't bear the thought of being wrong.

Finally, I gathered up my nerve and took Stella's phone and the CD into my office. I booted up my machine and got the disk into the CD drive. A dark-blue screen with a password field filled my monitor's display. Slowly, I tapped out the characters in the e-mail. I clicked the submit button. A little disc rotated on the screen, the CD in my drive clickety clacked. The machine went into thinking mode.

I held my breath. The screen went dark and then filled with the contents of the disk. I'd expected to see some elaborate conglomeration of data. Instead, it had four little lines. The first line was a web site address. The second was labeled "Account" and was a twelve digit number. The third was labeled "User" and it was a series of characters. The fourth was labeled "Pass" and contained another series of characters.

By now, my heart pounded in my chest so hard I thought it might explode. I was one step closer and almost free. I started up Internet Explorer and waited ... and waited ... and waited. Finally, when it was ready, I typed in the web site address from the disk.

The address came up as "Amalgamated Worldwide Bank."

I whispered to myself. "Oh my God, Roxy, you're there."

I searched the page for some sort of login form. Nothing on the Home page for that, but I did find a page called "Client Accounts." I clicked the menu item and landed on a page that had a field marked Account Number on the right side.

I typed, "198724887743" and clicked the button labeled "Submit."

The box I'd typed the account number into slid down to reveal two new fields. One was labeled User Name, the other, Password. My palms felt sweaty as I rubbed my face with my hands. Tears welled in my eyes.

I typed in the user name and password and clicked the "Login" button. The screen blurred.

I clasped my hands together and mumbled, "Please make this right."

On my screen, the image of rotating gears superimposed itself over the page content. Below the gears was a two-word message. "Please wait ..."

CHAPTER FORTY-TWO

He said, "Somebody's changed the password."

The butterflies in Skip's stomach danced in circles as he watched the blue lights to his right. The modem blinked some sort of coded message, one that he had no desire to understand. The first light was solid, the second blinked once every second. Another alternated between flashing and solid patterns. First it flashed rapidly, then glowed, then flashed again. On the nightstand, the red numbers of a digital clock cast the bed in an eerie glow. Green dots from a printer and a shredder added to the dimness. But the biggest single source was the computer screen in front of him.

The half-light from the screen hurt Skip's eyes when he looked directly at it and left glowing imprints that slowly dissolved when he glanced away into the dark shadows. He'd never learned to type accurately by touch, so he kept his little flashlight in his mouth and watched the keyboard as he followed Baldorf's instructions.

He had just clicked the mouse to make the connection with Baldorf's computer when he heard a thud. He realized that he'd been so focused on getting the computer connection made that he'd lost track of what was going on anywhere other than on the computer before him. There it was again.

Was someone in the apartment?

Another thud. Skip turned off the flashlight and whispered into the cell phone, "Baldorf, hang on."

He slipped the phone into his jacket pocket and stood. His back felt stiff from having been hunched over for too long. Thud. Thud.

Skip glanced into the living room. Dark.

He stood stock still in the shadows of the darkest part of the room.

If someone else was here, would he have time to get to the slider and escape?

Thud, thud, thud.

Skip's heart pounded as he forced himself to breathe. He willed his body's mechanism to calm itself, to be more quiet. His efforts were to no avail. He closed his eyes and strained to listen for the slightest movement. Was there a rustling? A footstep?

He now heard the ticking of a wall clock coming from the kitchen. A motorcycle in the distance. Now the room was silent except for the occasional banging noise. Another noise. There it was again. A moan. Voices. A man's.

He thought he could make out the muffled words. "Oh, baby."

A woman's voice, "Yes. Yes!"

Skip leaned against the wall. He breathed in slowly, then let the air out just as slowly. He focused on the noise. It was upstairs. It was a headboard banging against the wall.

The voices grew louder.

He pulled out his phone. "How's it going, Baldorf?"

"Fine on this end, dude. You sound tense."

"There was a noise. I thought I wasn't alone, turns out I am, but someone else isn't."

The thuds grew more insistent. The murmurs, emphatic.

Skip rubbed the back of his neck. Here he was, forced to listen to this couple get it on while he tried to concentrate. It didn't help that he was between girlfriends or that he couldn't get Roxy out of his mind. He shook his head. Roxy was bad news and had no interest. He began to pace. He snapped, "Can I get out of here, now? Are you done?"

Baldorf chuckled. "Dude, sounds like you need to relax. Yeah, I have what I need, come on over."

Skip double checked the apartment to make sure he'd left nothing behind. He realized that the banging had stopped. "Glad I don't live here," he muttered.

He went to the front door and peered out the peephole. The space was empty. He slipped out the door and pocketed his gloves while the damp coolness of night air welcomed him. With each step he took away from Dane's apartment, he felt more relaxed. By the time he got to Wally's motorcycle, he'd put the closeness, and the tension, of the apartment behind him. He donned his helmet and started up the bike, then took off for Baldorf's condo in Oceanside.

Baldorf rented a studio apartment just a few blocks from the beach, a place that, to Skip's knowledge, he never visited. He could walk to the Oceanside pier easily, but preferred to spend his time staring at a monitor. Skip kept hoping that Baldorf would meet the right girl and develop other interests, but the kid seemed to get his enjoyment from tackling computer challenges.

It took about fifteen minutes to reach Baldorf's place. Traffic was light at this time of night, but not nonexistent. In Southern California, someone was always going somewhere. He found a spot between two cars that hadn't wedged themselves into the street's parallel-parking spaces and backed the bike in. This time, he took the helmet with him. He'd wanted nothing to carry when entering Dane's place, but here, he could always go back to Baldorf's should he leave something behind.

Baldorf had rented the studio apartment for about three years. The unit was actually an illegal addition that had been built by an owner back in the '80s. The owner had never admitted that the unit didn't meet building codes, but Baldorf had gotten suspicious when his equipment kept blowing fuses. Finally, out of frustration, he'd checked with the City. With that bit of leverage, he'd persuaded the owner to do some wiring upgrades that resulted in the power supply becoming reliable and Baldorf becoming a very satisfied tenant.

At the door, Skip was about to knock when he heard Baldorf's voice. "Come in, Skip. It's open."

He opened the door and stepped inside. Baldorf sat at a bank of monitors. One of the monitors was split into four quadrants. He instantly recognized Baldorf's new addition. "You've added security cameras."

Baldorf smiled and leaned back in his chair. "I did some work for a local outfit that installs them. We did a trade. I feel way more secure now."

"Turning into a recluse?"

"Like a Howard Hughes? No, man, I haven't got that dude's money—yet. Wait till Baldorf's Revenge hits the stores, though."

"I know, you're gonna be rich."

"And famous."

Skip snickered. Like Baldorf would care about either of those, he thought. He noticed that the monitor in front of Baldorf displayed more of the gibberish he'd seen on Dane's computer. "What'd you find?"

"This guy is way into spyware. The funny thing is he's only been monitoring one computer."

"Is that unusual? Stupid question. Of course it is. People who do that go after as many machines as possible, right?"

Baldorf nodded. "That's the norm. It's unusual to put in this type of effort on one machine unless you're carrying out some sort of industrial or commercial espionage."

Skip wondered who Dane could be monitoring. "Can you tell what computer?"

"One geographically close to where you were. Maybe two blocks away."

"*Two blocks?*" Skip felt like a giant hand had just slapped him on the side of the head. He practically fell into the chair next to Baldorf. "The guy was planning to double cross his boss. It was a kidnapping and he was going to steal the ransom."

Baldorf winced. "Who got snatched?"

"My client's dad. They held him for five million ransom."

"Electronic transfers?"

"Yeah, how'd you know?"

Little lines around Baldorf's eyes crinkled in a self-satisfied smile. "It's all here. This guy was tracking keystrokes so he could intercept the banking transaction and reroute it. Very cool. Once you know what the login information is, it'd be simple, quick, and best of all, couldn't be reversed."

"So he moves the money to another account and it just disappears?"

"You'd know the number for the other account, that could be traced, but you'd never discover who had the account. Or the money. Sweet."

Skip wet his lips. Could it be that he'd found Roxy's money? "So can you decode this stuff?"

Baldorf let out a puff of air between his lips. "Dude. That was done before you were out the door. I got intrigued by this." He clicked one of the buttons at the bottom of his screen.

What was on the screen reminded Skip of an e-mail in some ways, but there were no little fields to put an address into. Skip said, "It looks like an e-mail printout."

"It is. It's going to a Gmail account, sp5445. Like I said, it was generated from a place just a couple of blocks from this computer." He pointed at the screen. "Here's the message. It says, 'Target en route. Money transfer should be complete within the hour. Will expect payment tomorrow noon at designated location.'" Baldorf continued. "I figured you were involved in some sort of kidnapping when

I read that and a couple of the other messages."

"What can we do about it? The guy who owns this computer is gone. Disappeared. The kidnapper stole my car and totaled it. The other kidnapper is dead."

Baldorf smiled. "You're gonna love this. The answer to all your problems." He clicked another button at the bottom of his screen. "Your bank transfer, voila."

"You have it? I have to call Roxy."

"Is that the target?"

Skip nodded. "Yeah. No, wait. Let's see if we can get into the account."

Baldorf winked. "Awesome. I thought you'd never ask."

He turned and opened an Internet browser. He typed in an address and a screen for Amalgamated Worldwide Bank came up.

Skip said, "You're amazing, Baldorf."

Baldorf nodded. "Yeah, I know. Wait until I'm amazing, rich, *and* famous."

Skip searched the page frantically, but was nowhere near as fast as Baldorf. He'd already selected one of the menu items. A new page, this one labeled Client Accounts came up and Baldorf quickly scanned the page. His head and eyes moved like a metal ball in a pinball machine. His eyebrows went up as he clicked in a field and began to type.

"This is the account number," he said. "Once I click this button, we should get ... aha."

Skip glanced at the screen. He watched as Baldorf clicked in the user name field.

He typed again. "There's the user name."

He tabbed down and typed again. "And the password. Ready?"

Skip glanced at Baldorf. "Go for it."

Baldorf clicked the login button.

The image of gears turning appeared on the screen. He raised his eyebrows. "Sweet graphic."

A moment later, a message appeared. "The user name and password you entered do not match our records. Please try again. Your account will be locked after three unsuccessful login attempts."

Baldorf got an irritated look on his face and swore. "Shit. Maybe I had a typo." He retyped the information. The result didn't change. "Well, damn."

Skip glared at the screen. "Somebody's changed the password."

CHAPTER FORTY-THREE

She said, "Time for Roxy Tanner to disappear."

The balance in the account at Amalgamated Worldwide Bank was $4,877,946.32. In the short time that my money had been there, I'd made a bit of interest. My one consolation was that we'd never completed my mother's transfer so she still had her $50,000. Actually, there was another bit of good news—I was getting $10,000 of the kidnapper's money that had already been in the account.

A little surge of self-satisfaction made me smile. "Serves you right, asshole."

For the first time since my dad had disappeared, I felt good. I found myself humming a Jimmy Buffet song while I performed my first official duty as the new custodian of the money—changing the password on the account.

Tomorrow, I'd move the money to the account I'd set up when I was planning this operation. Amalgamated and my bank offered similar services—online banking, anonymity, and security—unless, of course, someone got hold of your login credentials. The credentials for my account were in my head, not written in a stupid email. What a bunch of amateurs.

I wasn't going to need Stella's phone for anything else, so I put it back in its charging stand. My next step was to implement my long-planned exit strategy. I was supposed to have a bit more money, but under the circumstances, it was time to pull the plug. In fact, I was surprised that the cops hadn't already started investigating my business. Once that started, leaving would be nearly impossible. No, when they showed up on my door, I wanted my door to be unanswered. I'd be in the Caribbean, somewhere where these local guys had no jurisdiction. A strange longing weighed on my heart, but I'd do what had to be done.

My business records all resided on my laptop, which I unplugged and set in its carrying case. Usually, I just left the machine here, but I'd take it along to avoid having records of my dealings accessed easily. No sense in giving the cops their case. I also went to Stella's desk and started up her computer. As long as she hadn't changed the password, which I'd told her not to do, I could check to see what she had there and clean up any incriminating evidence.

As it turned out, Stella didn't have much on her computer, just a record of my calendar and an address book. It still amazed me that she'd gotten involved in this kidnapping scheme. She'd just seemed so—could she have really conned me that well?—no, Stella was dense. Or was she?

I'd learned enough about computer records to know that the only safe hard drive is a missing hard drive. Without that, the forensic guys would have a helluva time reconstructing anything. Just to be sure, I cleared off the calendar entries and the address book. There were some documents I'd had her work on to help drum up business. Those marketing materials wound up getting trashed also. Finally, satisfied that it would take a forensic review of the disk to find anything of value, I shut it down and pulled out my trusty screwdriver set. I'd pull the hard drive and take it with me. I could drop it in the ocean somewhere and the evidence would be harder to find than the Titanic.

A few years ago, I learned the ins and outs of computer forensics by visiting a computer store and sweet-talking the tech into showing me how to remove a hard drive. Removing the drive on Stella's machine took me just over ten minutes. I glanced over at her cell phone. Just to be safe, I'd toss that, too. I placed her phone and the hard drive into a cloth shopping bag that I kept in my desk drawer. It took twenty minutes to shred the signed documents for my clients. Everything else was in electronic format and those documents were on my laptop.

I checked my exit strategy list and congratulated myself. Forty-eight minutes. I gazed around the room. Forty-eight minutes. I'd destroyed my entire business in less than an hour. It was as though all the sins of my life suddenly came crashing down on me. The need to let it out grew until I plopped down into my chair and cried. And cried.

The last time I cried like that was when my dog Brandy died. My parents bought a Golden Retriever shortly after I was born. I'd never known a day without Brandy, had never walked in the house without her greeting me at the door, licking my face and my fingers and giving me her unconditional love. She died when I was fourteen, two days before I graduated from 8th grade.

I cried for Brandy, for the mistakes I'd made, and for the ones I would make in the future. The tears rolled down my cheeks in a river that couldn't be stopped. My head began to pound and that made me cry more.

I wailed, "Stop it! Dammit, stop it." But the tears wouldn't stop. My body and emotions had taken their own path. I'd turned into a perpetual crying machine and felt like I was producing tears that could be packaged and sold. And that made me cry more, because, for the first time, the realization that I'd sold my soul hit me.

With my head pounding, my eyes wet and hurting, and my little bag full of the soon-to-be discards, I headed for the door. There was little time left. My stupid crying-jag had cost me more valuable time. If I didn't move now, if I didn't get out of town before morning, my instincts told me I'd be discovered, arrested, jailed, and would lose everything. I was not about to let that happen. If nothing else, I'd have the money.

By the time I made it to the car, which was one of several parked on the street, the tears let up enough that I was able to get my key into the door, unlock it and toss the shopping bag onto the back seat. I needed to get home to pack a few clothes into an overnight bag. I stuck the key in the ignition, but my vision blurred again as the tears returned. My head was killing me. I tried breathing deeply and soon I was able to see clearly enough to drive.

A car and a motorcycle approached in the opposite direction. The car continued on, but the motorcycle did a U-turn and parked in a spot in front of the car ahead of me. The street was dotted with parked cars. Several of the buildings here had been turned into work-live lofts. But there was something familiar about this guy. I bit at my lower lip. Who would be out at this hour? I waited.

At this point, my Toyota was hidden from his view by the car between us, but I could just make him out through the front and rear windows of that car. I slipped down in my seat as he walked away from the bike. He strode toward the door of the building, but stopped about halfway there. He glanced up at the window of my office. I followed his gaze. I'd forgotten to turn off the lights on my way out. The guy glanced at my car, apparently noticing it for the first time. My heart pounded again. He took another look at the window above. He started in my direction, and my breath caught. Then, he turned and ran through the building's front entrance.

I gave him another few seconds, then started the Toyota and pulled out of my parking space. The guy on the motorcycle had been Skip. He'd figured everything out, I was sure of it. The fact that he'd come here made me believe he'd either been to my condo already or would be going there soon. Should I trust that he'd already been there? No. I'd use the back entrance.

Fortunately, my condo building isn't gated. That lack of security had concerned me on several occasions, but tonight I praised my decision to not move to a more secure location. There were a couple of ways into and out of my building and, once in, I could exit out the patio slider and Skip would never be the wiser—if he turned up there.

It only took a few minutes to drive to my place. I parked my car a block away on a side street in the middle of a row of cars relegated to the street each night.

A few of the apartments around here, mine included, had their own parking lots, but many didn't. Consequently, this hodgepodge neighborhood had a few little "secret" pathways that were known only to exploring tenants or those who were clued in by a neighbor. In my case, I'd met my neighbor, a little old man of about eighty who walked to the nearest market each day and carried his groceries home. He'd told me about the back way in and out of the building. I'd used it a couple of times for that same run, so I knew the route. I went in the front entrance and grabbed my mail, sure that I had a few minutes lead on Skip. When a business card fluttered to the floor as I pushed the door open, I knew that Skip had already been here. How long before he came back?

"Pull yourself together, Roxy," I muttered. I hadn't even noticed the card wedged between the door and the weatherstripping. I stuck the key between my teeth, kept a firm hold on my laptop with my left hand and grabbed the business card off the ground with my right.

On the back of the card, he'd scrawled, "Call me."

I got inside, locked the door, and turned on the lights. Diversion. If he showed up, I'd need a diversion. If he saw lights on, he'd try and get in. Who knows how long he might bang on the front door while I slipped out the back.

I went to the closet and grabbed my overnight bag, which was a combination notebook case, briefcase, and suitcase. I put the laptop into its compartment and sealed that up. Next, I needed some underwear, two changes of clothes, my toothbrush, razor, and makeup. No gels. No liquids. No hassles with TSA at the airport.

With clothing packed, it was time for my exit cash, passports, and credit cards. I had three fake credit cards in different names that I'd never used, but kept for a time when I'd need the convenience of credit without being discovered—at least for a while. I'd charge airline tickets on one, hotel on another, and keep the third for another escape should it be necessary.

I put $250 of the exit cash in my wallet. The remaining $750 went back into its envelope, which I secured in my carry-on bag. The burbling of the phone nearly sent me through the roof. I muted the phone and checked caller ID. It was Mom. Shit. Had he gone to my parents' house, too?

"Roxy, honey. It's Mom. Skip was just here and he's worried about you. If you're around, call me. Your dad and I are worried sick about you, too. Please, call."

I waited, listening to a silence that spanned my lifetime. She sniffled, then finally disconnected. It was 11:37 p.m. Mom and Dad were usually in bed by ten. I felt the tears coming again, but found the will to hold off. I had to move and had no time for emotions. Once I got to the Caribbean, I could cry for days. Until then, I had no time.

I jumped again at the knock on the door. No! It was too soon.

Skip's voice came through. "Open up, Roxy."

I took a last look around my apartment. I loved this place. I liked my neighbors.

Another knock.

Damn you, Skip Cosgrove! I glanced at my image in the mirror. I looked like hell. My face was blotchy, my mascara had run, and I was sweating and breathing like a marathon runner at the end of a race.

The image was enough to make me hate myself and everything I'd become. I took a last look at myself. "Time for Roxy Tanner to disappear."

CHAPTER FORTY-FOUR

He said, "I'm done chasing you."

The butterflies that Skip had felt in his stomach were gone, replaced now by a rancid mix of fear and anxiety. Emotions were truth. Skip believed that. "Trust your gut," didn't become a cliché because it was wrong.

Skip sat in the chair adjacent to Baldorf and leaned back. Try as he might to act calm, he knew what this meant. With the password to the killer's bank account changed, one thing was certain. The game was over. Someone had the money and the likelihood of getting it back was somewhere near zero. Who was he kidding, he knew who the someone was.

Baldorf watched Skip with an expression that said, "I'm sorry."

Skip shook his head. "It's not your fault. I know who did this."

Baldorf seemed to perk up. "Let's check his browser history. We'll know if he visited that site."

Less than a minute later, the browser history showed that Dane hadn't accessed the AWB web site.

Baldorf said, "Dude, he couldn't have changed the password."

"I know. Two people might know how to access this account—the kidnapper and Roxy. The kidnapper is dead. He died before he got hold of the CD. That leaves Roxy. Somehow, she hacked that disk. I have to find her, Baldorf."

He sat for a few seconds until Baldorf said, "What are you waiting for, dude? Go! Find her. You're, like, a major downer on my space." He winked, then made a shooing motion with his hands.

After leaving Baldorf's, Skip had gone directly to Roxy's apartment. When she didn't answer the door, he stuffed his card into the doorframe and went home to use the GPS locator on her phone. He quickly discovered that she was at her office. He could think of only one reason she'd be there at this time of night, she was after the money and getting ready to run. He got on Wally's motorcycle and drove there. When he arrived, he spotted her car, but it looked empty. The office light was on so he charged up the stairs to her office and realized—once he'd picked the lock on her door—that she was long gone. The inside of the office had a normal appearance, except for the lights blazing away in the middle of the night.

When he came back to the street, her car was gone. It was the second time this week he'd made that mistake. At first, he'd assumed she'd go to her parents. He drove there and learned that they'd been asleep when Richard answered the door. He'd asked Evelyn and Richard not to call Roxy, but knew what would happen next. Evelyn had probably been on the phone to her daughter before he'd mounted the bike.

He drove to Roxy's apartment again. This time, he scoured the lot for her Toyota. When he didn't find it, he assumed she was gone, but decided to be sure. At her door, he found the lights on and his card gone. He wondered if she was pulling another trick or if she was still here.

Skip knocked—lightly, at first, then louder. "Open up, Roxy."

He considered banging even harder, maybe yelling, but that would only make the neighbors angry and bring the cops. For all he knew, Roxy also had a snoopy neighbor who had a revolver and 9-1-1 on speed dial. He paced back and forth on the walkway in front of her door. He didn't know what to do. He could go home and check the locator service, but if she was inside, she could leave the moment he walked away. What he needed was someone to check the locator for him. Baldorf.

He dialed the number.

"Dude, speak to me."

"I need another favor."

Baldorf chuckled. "You're going to owe me. Big."

"Whatever you want. Can you check a GPS locator service for me?"

"Do I have to hack in or are you giving me access codes?"

Skip smiled. "I suspect it doesn't matter much to you."

"Only in the amount of time it takes to get in. Some systems are more secure than others."

Skip gave Baldorf his user name and password and the URL to

access his account. About a minute later, Baldorf said, "I'm still waiting for the results. You still trying to find that woman?"

"Roxy Tanner."

"Right. The one who's been making you crazy."

"You're a pain in the ass, you know that?"

"Dude, I've, like, never seen you in love before. It's kind of cool."

Skip rubbed the back of his neck, which felt suddenly hot. Was he that obvious?

"Hey, here it is. She's on the corner of Washington and Juniper. Where are you?"

"At her apartment on Acacia. This thing can't be off by that much."

"Hey, man, I take that back. She's on Juniper. She's moving, man. Looks like maybe she's in a car."

"Son of a bitch! There must be a back entrance to this place. I'm gonna try to catch her."

"Car chases are a bad scene, man. Wouldn't you rather, like, use the technology? Let her run. You show up once she stops. How cool would that be?"

Where would she be going? To see her parents? She hadn't been there yet. "Baldorf, you really are brilliant. Is she headed toward Tamarack?" He was already at the bike and had the key in the ignition.

"Yup. Dude. I know this isn't very cloak-and-dagger like, but, um, I gotta tinkle."

Skip revved the engine on the bike. "You what?"

"I gotta go, man. Be right back!"

Skip found himself listening to dead air as he guided the bike down to Garfield, then left. She was probably headed to her parents' house. He'd hold back and show up just after she got out of the car. No more running then.

He was about ready to turn onto Tamarack from Garfield when his phone beeped. He glanced at the display.

Low battery.

Baldorf still hadn't returned, so he disconnected. He stuck the phone in his jacket pocket and made his left. Traffic on Tamarack was light at this hour and he wanted to make sure he didn't land on Roxy's tail at one of the stoplights, so he drove slowly. As he crossed the overpass for I-5 he noted the traffic, which, even at this hour, resembled a steady stream of ants invading a picnic.

He passed Rite Aid and Vons and had just crossed Adams when

his phone rang. He pulled it and checked the display. Baldorf. He snickered as he chided his friend. "Tinkle time over?"

"Yeah, man, oh that's so much better. Too much coffee."

No wonder he was always wired.

Baldorf asked, "So, did you follow her onto the 5?"

"What?"

"She turned north on the 5, man. She's halfway to Oceanside right now."

Skip pulled the bike to the side of the road. "What the hell's she doing there?"

"I dunno, man, looks like she's hauling ass wherever she's going."

Skip sat back on the bike. He cursed his luck. She wasn't heading for her parents, she was going—where?

His phone bleeped. "I'm about out of juice." And he was. The way he felt, if Roxy didn't want his help, forget her. The phone bleeped three times and shut itself down. Skip glared at it.

A car cruised by, windows down, radio blaring, sparkly lights in the back window lighting up the rear like a Christmas tree. Shit! He couldn't track her. He could take the 5 north to the Canadian border and never see her. He put the bike back into gear and pulled forward and drove to the Tanner residence.

He passed their home, did a U-turn and stopped on the opposite side of the street from the house. Dark. He wasn't about to wake Richard and Evelyn again. His throat felt tight as he noted the street-light glinting off one of the front bedrooms. Had that been hers as a girl? How had she turned into a criminal? He sat until the fog began to drift in, wondering when he'd become just another dumb guy who'd fallen for Roxy Tanner. How many others had there been?

The streetlight glowed with a cold halo in the heavy blanket of fog. He could sit here until the night chilled him to the bone, or he could go. He didn't know that it mattered. He felt numb inside as it was.

Skip put the bike in gear. "To hell with you, Roxy Tanner. I'm done chasing you."

CHAPTER FORTY-FIVE

She said, "Are there any seats left on the New York flight?"

Some things in life just seem to be patently unfair. I had nearly five million in the bank, a grand in cash, and fake credit cards to muddy my trail. I had a head start on anyone trying to follow me and the dead-on cunning to work out contingency plans on the fly. What I didn't have, however, was gas.

There was no way I'd make it to LAX without filling up. Not safely, anyway. I started watching for gas stations and found one in Aliso Viejo. Stopping for gas pissed me off because it made my car more visible. Stay low, under the radar. That meant minimize human interactions whenever possible.

I paid cash for the gas and used the restroom—which reminded me of a cross between an outhouse and a garbage dump. It was the kind of place my mother would say, "The five-second rule doesn't apply, honey. If it gets within a foot of anything, it's contaminated." Restrooms like this make women envy the male plumbing system.

Given that I was already here and visible, I grabbed a cup of coffee before getting back on the road. With caffeine in hand, it was back to the late-night driving routine of watching taillights come and go while keeping an eye out for those pesky Highway Patrol cars. The cities came and went also—Cypress, Lakewood, Compton, and Lynnwood. With my coffee drained and the turnoff for LAX in view, I should have been feeling as though I had mastered the world, but didn't. I found a spot in long-term parking, grabbed my overnight case from the trunk, and headed for Terminal 7. With any luck, I'd be able to catch a flight destined for a warm climate.

Inside the terminal I found a bank of monitors and checked for departures. My choices were slim. Take Cathay Pacific to Vancouver—not happening, Asiana to Seoul—wrong direction, Aerounion to Guadalajara—too many people, or Sky West to San Diego—like I wanted to *fly* back to where I'd just *driven* from. Definitely not happening.

Way down the list, I found what I was looking for, a United flight to New York. I made my way to the ticket counter, which was staffed by a sleepy-eyed employee. His face brightened when he saw me—this guy was so bored he actually wanted to see a customer. Now that's desperate.

"Morning," I said.

"Indeed, it is. Can I help you?" His name tag said he was James.

"Are there any seats left on the New York flight?"

James got a bewildered look on his face. I doubted that he had many customers walk in at 2:00 a.m. wanting to buy a ticket, so my first order of business was to give this sleepyhead something to focus on before he spent the rest of his night wondering if he should call the cops about a blonde terrorist.

I set my bag down and let the pain from my fight with the kidnapper show through. "My boyfriend beat the crap out of me. The cops came and took him away, but I want to be gone by the time his asshole attorney posts bail in the morning."

James seemed at a loss. Maybe I'd come on too strong. He hesitated, then said, "I'm sorry to hear that. Pretty bad?"

"Not as bad as the last time. I told the SOB that if he did it again, I was gone."

"Good for you. Does he drink? I had an uncle that got real nasty when he drank."

I rubbed my shoulder and put on a pained expression. "No, we went to a restaurant. The waiter was talking to me just like you are right now. When we got home, he went ballistic."

James shook his head. "That's terrible. Let's get you out of here. You're in luck. I have some seats left to New York. Do you have a credit card?"

I pulled out my credit card for Lucy Kravatz and handed it over. The fake credit cards and passports had set me back a considerable amount, but it was a far cry from what it would cost me to hang around here.

"Ms. Kravatz? Hang on. Oh, I'll need some ID also."

"It's Miss. I just got a domestic-violence divorce—dial 9-1-1 and run like hell."

He smiled. "No problem." As he ran the card, he said, "You know,

192 ~ Terry Ambrose

it's going to be several hours before your flight. Maybe you'd like to rest up a bit in our International Lounge?"

"Could I—do that?" I was stunned. I hadn't expected him to care much about my personal tale of woe, so this guy's willingness to help shocked me. All because I'd told him I'd been beaten up? His kindness touched me. "How can I get in?"

He winked. "It'll be our secret. It doesn't open until five, but I can sneak you in now. That way you'll have some peace and quiet until it's time to check in."

I smiled, in fact, I think I even blushed. "Thank you, James."

He winked. "My pleasure."

We finished the financial transaction and James met me on the other side of security, where he guided me to the lounge up on the mezzanine level. The doors to the elevator closed and James broke the silence. "My wife has a friend who just had to separate from her husband for the same exact thing. There's just so much violence in the world today."

I agreed. The elevator reached the mezzanine and we walked to the door of the lounge.

James opened the door wide and flipped on the lights. "Here you go. It's all yours, for a while."

"Thanks." I kissed him on the cheek.

It was his turn to blush. "I—I need to get back to my station. Bye-bye."

He closed the door and left me alone. The lounge wasn't stocked with anything like coffee or tea or other stuff yet, but it was quiet and the seating was far superior to the standard airport-issue backbreakers out in the terminal area. It was also away from public view and that fit my plan precisely. I pulled off my jacket and settled down into one of the chairs, covering myself with my jacket to ward off the cool air coming through the vent above. If this was home-sweet-home, I might as well get comfy.

I must have fallen asleep in the chair because I don't remember anything until around four. That's when someone turned the doorknob, which sounded like a gunshot in the otherwise silent room. I practically jumped out of my chair. Being basically paranoid, I immediately assumed that James hadn't fallen for my act and had reported me to the cops. To my surprise, it was James again.

"Thought you might like a newspaper. Sorry if I woke you."

"It's okay." I rubbed my face and neck. "Guess I fell asleep."

"Well, you'll be able to board in about three hours. I'd better warn you, the flight might get delayed a bit. Restrooms are over there and they'll be bringing in the coffee and snacks soon."

"Will you get in trouble if I'm here?"

He shook his head. "If anyone questions you, which I seriously doubt, send them to me." He tapped himself on the chest and winked.

Wow, I thought, look what one kiss on the cheek had done for him. "Okay. Thanks again."

James left and rather than settling down for some more sleep, I started flipping through the pages of the Times. It wasn't often that I saw the *LA Times* and I'd probably see it even less once I had relocated to the Caribbean.

Most of the stories were insanely boring. The typical BS. Political posturing, international squabbles, and more. All of which were driven by people who would rather fight than work out their differences. When had compromise become a dirty word? Whatever. Not my problem.

I was bored as hell by the time I got to the back of the A section and spotted a headline that struck close to home. "Oceanside Man Found Dead at Beach."

Oceanside is an old military town that's trying desperately to find their way in an environment that's not so heavily dependent upon the military. The shift from bars and brothels to malls and tourists wasn't coming easy, but it was happening. I read the story, wondering in that morbid way people do when someone from near their hometown dies—did I know him?

> On Thursday afternoon at about 5:00 p.m., LAPD received a call that the body of James Dane of Oceanside had been found on the beach in Newport. According to LAPD, Dane had been shot once in the back of the head, execution style.
>
> LAPD sources indicated that they have no witnesses and said that the motive did not appear to be robbery because Dane still had his wallet in his back pocket. They also noted that the body did not appear to have been dragged to the scene.
>
> Witnesses are encouraged to contact LAPD Detective Wallace.

The reporter had apparently gotten to the scene quickly because there was a picture of Dane's body in which he lay arrow-straight in the sand, face down. The photographer had also gotten a mini-forest of bare legs that surrounded the body in the picture. My hand trembled as I set the paper in the chair next to me.

Someone was cleaning up. First Stella, now her boyfriend. It couldn't be the kidnapper because he'd died in Skip's car. Or was it him? Maybe I had the sequence wrong. Had the kidnapper followed Dane? Found him and learned about the CD? Was that why he'd been at Stella's?

Who else knew about this? Was there a fourth man, a boss, as Skip had thought? Stella's phone might have the answer, but I'd dumped it—no, I hadn't. It was sitting in the back of my car. I slumped down into my seat. Shit. I'd forgotten to dump the bag with the phone and my hard drive. Now what? It was 4:34. This room would open shortly anyway. I put on my jacket, grabbed my bag and left my little hideaway. I'd handle the rest of my wait in the public arena.

As I made my way back past security, I noticed that the TSA line was already growing. It had been easy earlier—returning through security would take much longer. Instead of going straight to the car, I decided to see if James was still on duty. My breath caught when I got near the ticket area and spotted Skip wandering around. Son of a bitch—how had he found me? I searched frantically for a courtesy phone and spotted one about twenty feet away. I waited until Skip was pacing the opposite direction, then dashed over to the phone and picked it up.

An operator answered, "LAX operator."

"I need to speak to James at the ticket counter in Terminal 7 for United."

"One moment."

The phone rang twice and James picked up.

"Oh, thank God. James, this is—" I almost said Roxy, but caught myself. "This is Lucy Kravatz. That guy who's wandering around the terminal wearing a blue jacket, that's my boyfriend. He must have gotten out of jail somehow. Maybe they didn't hold him."

"He said he was looking for a Roxy Tanner." His voice was tinged with suspicion.

"This is LA, James. I'm trying to become an actress and that's my stage name, the only one he knows me by. My real name is Lucille Jennifer Kravatz and I was born in Ithaca, New York. Now, who's going to hire an actress with that name? Everything's got to be sexy these days. That's why I've been using Roxy Tanner since I got here."

"Okay, well, I told him I couldn't give out any information about customers. I think he's about to leave anyway. What are you doing on this side of security?"

"I realized I left something in my car that I need."

James interrupted my tale, "He's leaving."

"Thank goodness. Thank you again. I won't bother you anymore."

I watched Skip exit the terminal and noticed that he was headed for short-term parking. Since I was in long-term, I felt relatively safe and made my way back to the car. I'd opened the back door and had pulled out the bag containing Stella's phone when I realized how Skip found me. He'd been using that GPS locator service. He'd know every move I made until I got rid of my phone. I'd intended to get a replacement within the next day or so, but not while waiting for the plane at LAX. Then it hit me. Maybe I already had a replacement, thanks to Stella.

What would happen if I put the little do-hickey they called a SIM card from her phone into mine? Wouldn't that make mine a different phone? It was worth a try, but first I needed to go through her address book one more time.

I powered down my phone and pulled the SIM card, then went back to the terminal. I figured the safest place for me was on the other side of security. Skip could always buy a ticket, but I doubted he'd go that far. Besides, the line was growing longer with each passing minute. Inside Terminal 7, I found a quiet spot and began looking through Stella's address book.

If I'd known that my flight was going to be delayed when I bought the ticket, I might have done something different. As it was, I'd already waited for hours and had two more before my flight. I was checked in and ready to go, so I might as well tough it out. They wouldn't start boarding for at least an hour. I had plenty of time. I went through the entries one by one. It looked to me like she had in the neighborhood of 200 contacts, so I didn't have a lot of time to spend on each. I found the entry for Jimmy Dane and further down the list, I found an entry for her old boyfriend, Marty Horvath. That seemed odd. Was it just an old entry or was she still in touch? It was an area code I didn't recognize. I checked the time. I was down to an hour and a half. Curious, I dialed the number.

CHAPTER FORTY-SIX

"It doesn't matter, just looks like I was wrong again."

On the drive home from LAX, Skip realized that he knew exactly how Richard Tanner had felt when he'd started drinking a couple of months ago. Just like Richard, Roxy had disappointed him beyond his wildest expectations.

He'd driven to LAX in hopes of finding her and talking some sense into her. He'd checked every ticket agent in Terminal 7, where the GPS signal was coming from, and had come up with nothing. He'd walked the terminal several times. If she had been there, she'd either caught an earlier flight or had used a fake ID and had already slipped through security.

The southbound Friday morning traffic was light, allowing Skip to make it home in less than two hours. On the drive he questioned his sanity yet again. Why had he spent five hours chasing after a woman he barely knew? Or three days letting her ruin his life? By the time he arrived home his mood was as glum as the skies were cloudy.

Today was definitely different than most days. Seldom did he notice the grayness. Today, it depressed him. The damp air depressed him. And the time that dragged. Yes, that did, too.

He skipped his beach walk and sat at the kitchen table drinking coffee. The phone rang and he considered letting it go to his answering machine, then made a quick decision to pick up when he saw that it was the Carlsbad Police.

"Cosgrove."

"Mr. Cosgrove, this is Sergeant Grimes from Carlsbad PD. I thought you'd like to know that we just got a match on the guy who stole your car."

There, thought Skip, another reason to be depressed—the Porsche was gone. "Who was he?"

"Lawrence Eugene Sproutman, aka the Wizard. He'd done some minor time in Arizona, and Texas, but was on his third strike here."

"Too bad he didn't get that third strike before he stole my car."

"Apparently, he's well known for masterminding scams. He got his start boosting cars. Eventually, he graduated to banks and a little extortion. Looks like this was supposed to be his ticket to the big time."

"It's comforting to know he was getting better at his trade." Skip tried to retract his sarcasm, "Sorry."

"I just thought you'd like to know."

"It doesn't matter, it's over," said Skip. And it was. The car was gone. Roxy, too. Knowing that the guy who'd stolen his car was a career criminal didn't help his crappy mood. At least the bad guy got what he deserved, permanent deletion from Skip's life.

"One more thing," said Grimes. "We're going to keep this quiet for a few days as part of the Tanner investigation—just as a precaution."

"Fine." Skip hung up and decided to take a shower. After that, maybe he'd visit the Tanners. No, he thought, stay away from them. It would just remind all of them that Roxy had run. Instead, he'd call Wally to see if there was any work to do.

He logged into the GPS locator service web site and searched for Roxy's phone. It was gone. She must have caught a flight already. He cursed himself for ever letting himself care about her. What the hell was he thinking? That he could change her? Make her go straight?

He closed the drapes to the bedroom windows and stripped, then stepped into the shower. He let hot water pummel his face until the physical numbness seemed to match his mental state. He took his time shaving and getting dressed. He checked the time, hoping that he'd been in the bathroom for an hour, but was disappointed. The whole cleanup process had taken just 38 minutes. More depressing news. Today was going to be a long day—the kind of day Richard Tanner hadn't been able to face. Skip wasn't sure he could face it either.

He opened the bedroom window a crack to let in the ocean air and returned to the kitchen. He poured the last of the coffee into his cup. He stared at the pot for a few minutes as he sipped, then decided it was time to call Wally.

But it wasn't Wally he called. It was Roxy. The phone immediately went to voicemail.

"Hi, you've reached Roxy. Leave a message."

Skip hung up. There was no point in leaving a message, he knew she wouldn't return his call. She must have forwarded her phone to avoid calls or she was, as he suspected, already in the air and somewhere over the Midwest. He lifted the receiver again and dialed. He waited until Sergeant Grimes answered, then said, "Sergeant, this is Skip Cosgrove. I wondered if you might tell me a bit more about this Lawrence Eugene Sproutman."

"I may be able to help, what would you like to know?"

"You said he did time in Texas, right?"

"Two years back in 2003."

Right about the time that Stella had been arrested. "Can you tell me which prison he was in?"

"I could find out, but why do you need that?"

"I think he might have met another criminal named Stella Robbins while he was in jail."

"That's unlikely. Most of their facilities for men and women are separate. Hang on." A few minutes later, he returned. "Just as I thought, he was in a different facility than Robbins. Same time frame, but different locations altogether. Looks like Robbins only got six months. She also got released early, probably as part of a plea agreement."

"Crap."

"Not what you expected?"

"It doesn't matter, just looks like I was wrong again."

CHAPTER FORTY-SEVEN

She said, "Amen to that."

I waited while the number for Marty Horvath rang. It was at least thirty seconds before an older-sounding woman with a strong southern drawl answered the phone. "Hello?"

"Hi. Could I speak with Marty please?"

"Why, he's not here."

"When will he be back?"

The woman laughed. "Honey, I don't think Marty's ever coming back. After what they done to him here, he hates Texas."

"Are you his mother?"

"Yes, I am. And who are you?"

"My name is Lucy, Lucy Kravatz. I'm from the Department of Corrections. We met while I was doing some rehabilitation work with the prisoners. He promised me he was going straight when he got out. I just wanted to check on him."

"Well, that's sweet. I didn't know the state had a program like that."

"It's still a bit experimental. Say, he didn't by any chance hook up with Stella again, did he?"

"Lord knows, I hope not. That girl is nothin' but trouble."

That might be the truth, but I had a hunch trouble had come back around. "At one point, he was talking about moving to California to get a fresh start. Did he do that?"

"Sure thing. He said he was going to someplace called Carlsbad. He was gonna live real close to the ocean and learn how to surf. I told him he'd best get a job first."

"Amen to that."

And what kind of job had Marty Horvath gotten? Kidnapper apprentice? I'd never asked Marjorie, but I'd bet money that Stella had taken Jimmy Dane's apartment almost immediately after he'd been evicted. I still wasn't sure what had happened to her son, but felt sorry for Mrs. Horvath. I didn't have the heart to tell her I feared her son might be dead.

"Do you have a forwarding number for him? I'd like to catch up. You know, see how he's doing."

"Golly, I just can't believe how nice you are. You just hang on."

Papers rustled in the background as I waited, but soon she returned and gave me Marty's new number—a 760 area code with a prefix sounding like ours in Carlsbad. I didn't know what I'd do with it, but suspected my call to Texas hadn't been wasted.

I went to the monitors to check my flight status. As James had predicted, the New York departure was delayed. A line extended back from the gate. In the midst of the line stood a woman who conveniently ignored her three screaming brats while they circled in attack formation and terrorized the rest of us. As someone who wasn't a parent, it was easy for me to judge her as an insensitive, half-deaf bitch who made a practice of letting her offspring run wild. That assumption was probably highly inaccurate, but my nerves were on edge and I didn't care who I insulted at this point.

I got in line behind a young couple. The man held a small girl in his arms. When he tweaked her nose, she giggled. I had flashes of days when my dad had done that same thing to me. The woman gazed at the two of them with adoring eyes. My throat went tight and dry. The woman with the screaming brats finished her business at the counter and took her brood off to the windows, where they continued to run in circles and scream like tortured cats.

The couple ahead of me finished up and left. As I approached, the United representative nodded in their direction. "What a cutie, huh?"

I smiled and nodded. The words barely came out of my mouth, "I'm supposed to be on the flight to New York, how long is the delay?"

"There's a mechanical problem on the plane. We're bringing in another one, but it could be a couple of hours."

I rolled my eyes. Just my luck. Here I was trying to make a quick exit and I'd picked the flight with a broken plane. Lack of sleep was making me grumpy, but I dared not take a nap for fear that I would sleep through the boarding call. In that case, it was time for coffee. Lots of it.

As I sat at one of the tables, I thought about Marty Horvath. Was he really Jimmy Dane? Curiosity was eating me up, almost as much as the airport acid mix in my cup. I hated the thought of diluting this stuff with creamer and sugar, but the concoction in my cup was better suited to testing lab rats than drinking.

I dumped a mound of creamer and a packet of sugar into the cup and stirred the brew. It still stunk. I must have gotten the last of yesterday's leftovers. A girl dressed in a brown uniform began wiping off the table next to mine. "You don't look like you're enjoying that very much," she said.

"This is awful."

She glanced over her shoulder. "I'll bet they gave you the old batch. I'll get you a fresh cup, okay?" She returned a minute later and gave me a cup that still had steam coming off the top.

I took a sip. "Much better. Thanks."

She smiled and moved on to the next table.

I pulled my note with Marty Horvath's number from my purse. The number looked familiar, but I was too tired to remember where I might have seen it before. What did I have to lose? I dialed and on the third ring, the answering machine picked up.

"You've reached the home of Marty and Jimmy. We're not available right now, but you all can leave a message right after the beep."

I recognized the voice, even though the last time I'd heard it the voice had come from behind a Halloween mask—it was Bush. I hung up and smiled. It was one of the oldest tricks around—create a fake voicemail message and tell the mark to leave a number. Jimmy Dane wouldn't be getting back to anyone right away. Neither would Marty Horvath. They were one and the same and they were both dead. Did that mean all the kidnappers were gone?

I spotted the couple that had been in line ahead of me. Seeing that little, happy family again reminded me of my mom and dad. I'd been in such a hurry to get away that I hadn't thought about what my leaving would do to them. They'd miss me. And I missed them already. They'd survive. Or would they?

The kidnappers had all died or been killed. A chill ran the length of my spine. If Skip was right, these guys were dying for a reason. We didn't know who'd masterminded the kidnapping plot. And that was the only person left. What if he wanted revenge because I had the money?

CHAPTER FORTY-EIGHT

He said, "It might be the only way to prevent her from making the biggest mistake of her life."

Skip stared out the slider window at the ocean while he contemplated his options. The heaviness that had plagued him on the drive home from LAX seemed to be lifting. Clinically speaking, he knew action would help. He could walk the beach or take a ride on the bike. If he simply sat here to sort out his life, the heaviness would probably return. Outside, patches of blue were already starting to show in the sky. Skip hoped that as the fog headed back out to sea, it would bring him a better mood. He needed sunshine, not a gray day. Walk the beach, he told himself. Meet the day.

The phone rang. He answered without checking Caller ID. It was Evelyn Tanner. "Skip? Is Roxy there?"

"No. I haven't seen her since yesterday."

"Then, can you come see Richard and me? Roxy's disappeared."

Should he tell her that her daughter was on the run? "Evelyn, I don't know, I'm kind of busy this morning."

"The way you feel about her? You should make time for this or you'll regret it forever."

How did she know—how did everyone know—how he felt about Roxy? He started to make an excuse, but decided it was futile. "I'll be there in twenty minutes."

He took his time getting ready, not sure he could face the Tanners with the truth. He closed up the condo and donned his jacket and helmet, then rode the bike to the Tanner residence.

Both Richard and Evelyn greeted him at the door. He shook hands with Richard, but Evelyn gave him a tight hug. He found himself holding her also, wishing it were Roxy. When they pushed away, Evelyn said, "Where is she? You know, don't you?"

Richard added, "I've explained everything to Evelyn. Why I've been so depressed. Why I went on that binge. Roxy's been embezzling from her company. We want to help her."

"It's not that simple," Skip said.

Skip watched Richard's shoulders move ever so slightly. He was tense, but maintaining his calm. "We know—at least, we're fairly sure, that she used the money from her business for the ransom. I've suspected what she was up to for a couple of months now. She was building a nest egg with other people's money and planned to run. The kidnapping forced her hand."

"She couldn't let you be killed." Skip remembered the fear in Roxy's eyes when they'd first met.

Richard continued, "Now she thinks she's got to run because the money's gone."

"It doesn't matter, Richard, I can't reach her. She's forwarded her phone and she's probably ignoring e-mail. She's isolated herself from everything."

Richard said, "What kind of life is that? If she runs, it will look like she killed that girl."

"Stella. Stella Robbins was her name. She worked for Roxy. We think she's the one who passed along information about how much money Roxy had. Roxy didn't think Stella was very smart, so she may have gotten sloppy around her—oh, crap." Skip began rambling. "Stella—Roxy has Stella's phone. Maybe she figured out the GPS. She didn't want me finding her so she disabled it by destroying her phone. Or swapping SIMs."

Both the Tanners gave him a blank stare.

He let a smile creep across his lips. That was another reason he found her so attractive. The blonde hair and great body helped, but she was damned *smart*. She'd figured out the GPS locator and swapped SIMs with Stella's phone. Her phone thought it was Stella's.

"Maybe I do know how to reach her." Skip pulled out his cell. He checked the call history and the address book. His shoulders slumped as the realization hit him, "I don't have the number for Stella."

Evelyn's confusion was obvious. "But she's dead. Why would you call her?"

"Roxy might be using what's called the SIM card from Stella's phone. A SIM card is like a portable memory chip. Or a miniature hard disk. It's where your personal identity information and phone number are stored."

"So if you change that then the phone number changes?" Richard said.

"Exactly," Skip said. "Right now, I'll bet Roxy's phone will ring if I call Stella's number. The problem is I don't have her number."

Evelyn turned and rushed away. She called over her shoulder, "Well I do!"

Richard stared at Skip. "How the hell did she get that?"

Skip shook his head.

From the hallway, Skip heard Evelyn's voice. "I went to lunch with Stella a couple of times. We always talked on the phone and she thought it would be fun if we could get together. She was always so sweet. It's hard to believe she was involved in something like this."

"Did you know she did time for armed robbery?" Skip said.

Evelyn paused and glanced down to the right. "Um, no."

Richard smirked. "So what did you talk about at your lunch?"

"Roxy," she said. "The business. You—she had lots of questions about you. Her father died when she was young. She said she'd never gotten past his death."

Skip wondered what else Evelyn knew. "Sounds like you got to know her a bit."

"Now that I think about it, she asked more questions than she answered. She did like to talk about Texas though. I guess she liked it there."

"That's where she spent time in prison."

"She told me she lived with relatives. I think they were distant relatives, but she stayed with them when she went to college. She was pumping me for information, wasn't she?"

Skip nodded. "I think so. Did she ever mention their names?"

Evelyn shook her head. "Not that I recall. She did mention her old boyfriend. Michael? Manny? No, Marty."

Marty again. Again? Of course, Marty Horvath. "I need the number for the Carlsbad police."

Evelyn's face drained of color, her jaw dropped. "You can't do that!"

Skip shook his head. "Not about Roxy. Marty Horvath was Stella's old boyfriend. I'll bet he was in jail with the guy who masterminded the kidnapping."

"The guy who met me in the bar never said her name," said Richard. "But he kept talking about his girlfriend. I barely remember it, but he kept talking about how his girlfriend was coming into some money. They were talking about having kids. But he figured it would be a big test for his girlfriend—would she choose him or the money? That's why we got to talking. I knew what Roxy was up to. It resonated with me."

Skip watched Richard's face as he spoke, caught the pained expression as he recalled the mistake that had nearly cost him and his daughter their lives. "If he hadn't suckered you in that way, they would have done something else."

Skip noticed the color rise in Evelyn's face. She stormed away.

Richard said, "Yeah, but I went along willingly. It was just two guys commiserating over women."

Evelyn returned, carrying the phone book. She glared at him. "You could have told me, Richard."

He nodded. "I should have."

Skip interrupted. "It's too late for that. Besides, this was a well-planned operation. They were performing reconnaissance on every level. Even Roxy was taken in. But, I think we're a step closer to knowing who set this plan in motion." Skip dialed the number for the police. He prayed that he was right.

Evelyn asked, "Do you have to call the police?"

"It might be the only way to prevent her from making the biggest mistake of her life."

CHAPTER FORTY-NINE

She said, "That son of a bitch. He ruined everything."

I wasn't so bored that I was counting, but I was starting to wonder how many people Terminal 7 could hold. The domino effect was in play. The mechanical problem with my plane impacted the flight behind us. They moved that flight, but the move delayed two others. Now, there were five flights on the board that had a delayed arrival or departure. Unless this got straightened out, by my math, the entire airport would be shut down by late afternoon. My eighth-grade math teacher always said my math stunk, but I had five million in the bank and he was stuck with a lousy pension.

The longer I sat, the more irritated I became. It wasn't so much that my flight was delayed. The thing that irritated me most was that I was here at all. If I hadn't been forced to leave in the middle of the frigging night, I would have slipped down to San Diego and used the smaller airport. I could have hopped a cheap Southwest flight to anywhere in the country and quietly escaped to the Caribbean at my leisure.

The wait, in addition to giving me seething time, also gave me time to analyze what I knew. And what I knew gave me time to worry. It was a hopeless, endless cycle that might haunt me like the one from my childhood. That's when I realized that my childhood kidnapping no longer ruled my thoughts. Since the moment I'd thrown myself at Clinton to keep him from shooting Skip, that memory seemed to hold no more power. How long would I be free from that terror?

I considered calling Mom and Dad to warn them. But what would I say? That I'd gotten away with the money? That someone might want to kill Dad for revenge? What good would that do? As much as it hurt me to say it, if someone wanted to kill my dad, being careful would only delay the inevitable. The fact that I'd sunk so low that I couldn't, worse yet, wouldn't, save him had me wondering if I was still part of the human race.

My mind was in rerun state as it played back the episodes of the past few days. It was the episode from Stella's apartment that triggered one of those fabulous "aha" moments—the kind that seems so simple when it hits and makes you wonder why the hell it took so long to surface. The secret to who was behind the kidnapping lay somewhere in Stella's past. And there was a source of information about Stella's past that I hadn't even considered before, her rental application.

I remembered seeing Marjorie's number in Stella's address book. It only took a moment to find the entry and dial.

"Hello?"

"Hi Marjorie, it's Roxy Tanner."

I heard a rumble and knew what was coming next. I held the phone away from my ear and waited. A loud cough erupted from the speaker. "Sorry about that. How are you, honey? I was stiff for a day, but I'm good as new today."

"I'm glad to hear that. Hey, I have a favor to ask."

"Anything. You name it."

"Can you pull Stella's rental application? Then maybe read it to me?"

"Let me guess. You didn't sleep last night and need something really boring to put you out?"

"No, no. I think there's something in her background that will help this all make sense."

A few minutes later, Marjorie had read me about half of Stella's application. Marjorie had been correct, this was boring. Much of the information sounded almost identical to her resume, which I now realized was bogus. For references, she'd listed Jimmy Dane in Carlsbad and Marty Horvath in Texas. If I'd have called, I could have gotten two references and never realized that I'd gotten them from one guy.

Marjorie said, "There's another reference. A Sonny, uh, Panaman."

"What!" My voice was so loud that it caused a pall of silence to fall over everyone around me. "Sonny Panaman? Are you sure?"

"It's clear as day. His address is local, here in Carlsbad."

"That son of a bitch. He ruined everything."

"You know this guy?"

"He's a client—no, he was *almost* a client. That no good, lying, piece of—" I stopped cold when I realized that the little girl next to me was gawking like I was a freak in a circus. Her mother gave me a glare that made me cringe. "I'm—sorry about that. I just got really bad news."

The woman's stare darkened. Obviously, she was completely unimpressed by my apology.

I heard Marjorie in my ear. "Where are you anyway? Sounds like a train station."

"What was the date of that application?"

"Back in July. Hey, you know what? Stella took that apartment two days after I evicted Jimmy. You think there's a connection?"

"Oh, there's a connection alright. That was two months before she started working for me." Three months before she ever supposedly met Sonny Panaman. "What else is on that application?"

"Investments, right? That's what you do?"

Did. Whatever. "Correct."

"Looking at this reminds me. She was unemployed when she got the apartment. But she said she was going to be getting a job with an investment firm. Does that help any?"

"Yeah, it does. Thanks, Marjorie, I'll see you soon."

"Let's have lunch. That is, if you don't mind being seen in public with an old woman."

I smiled. "It would be my pleasure."

As I disconnected the call, I heard an announcement in the background. Boarding would begin in thirty minutes. The plane had arrived. Inside, I was madder than ever. I'd been played not only by Stella, but also by goddamn Sonny Panaman. I wondered if Bruno knew what his son was up to. Right now, I was mad enough to kill Sonny. The only downside I could see to that was that I'd miss my flight and have to drive back to Carlsbad.

CHAPTER FIFTY

He said, "We've got to stop her from doing something stupid."

Skip waited while the operator connected him to Sergeant Grimes. A few seconds later, he heard, "Investigations. Grimes."

"Sergeant, this is Skip Cosgrove. I have one more name I wondered if you could check for me."

"What, exactly, are you trying to find out, Mr. Cosgrove?"

"I believe I've found the connection between all of the kidnappers. We might be able to provide a lead to the person behind the Tanner kidnapping."

"This will have to be the last one. What's the name?"

Skip closed his eyes. "Marty or Martin Horvath."

Grimes put Skip on hold, then returned a minute later. "You're right. He and Sproutman were incarcerated together. What's the connection?"

"Horvath was using the name James Dane. He was Stella Robbins boyfriend. Their connection goes back to when Horvath and Sproutman did time in Texas."

"So you think someone hired them to kidnap Richard Tanner? Why wouldn't they just cook up this scheme all on their own?"

Skip grimaced. "At this point, I guess it's just a hunch."

"Who would have hired them? I'll pass this along to the detectives. Given that all three kidnappers are dead, I think they're closing the case. I'll let them know your concerns, though."

When they were done, Skip said to Richard, "It sounds as if they might close the investigation. If anyone's going to find the person responsible for this, it's going to have to be me. I've got a friend—

guy's a computer genius—who might be able to help. I'm going to visit him. I want you two to sit tight in case Roxy calls. If she does, get her to come home. We've got to stop her from doing something stupid."

"What about the money?" Richard said.

"I'll help her find a way to get the money back to her clients."

Evelyn wrapped her arms around Skip's neck. "Thank you. I have a good feeling about this."

As Skip pulled away, he wished he had that kind of feeling. He left the Tanner residence and called Baldorf. When Baldorf gave him the usual "speak to me" introduction, Skip did. "I need you to check that key log thing again to see if there were any e-mails sent from that computer."

"You coming over?"

"I'm on my way now."

"On it, dude."

Skip gunned the engine on the bike and headed for Baldorf's. Traffic was light on the way and he made the trip to Oceanside in fifteen minutes. As he approached the door, a mechanical voice said, "Enter."

Baldorf was dressed in a black T-shirt with "162" in bold, white lettering. He wore raggedy jeans and flip flops and his hair stuck out in every direction possible.

"You look like you didn't sleep," Skip said.

Baldorf shook his head. "Dude. I got a good four hours last night. I'm ready for the day. How'd you like my door sentry?"

"I thought maybe you used a synthesizer on your voice or something."

"Nothing so mundane. I'm tinkering with some facial recognition and text-to-speech software for Baldorf's Revenge. The security involved just a little recoding. I got your photo last night. My system does a comparison against the database and if it finds a match, it lets you in. Otherwise, it challenges you. For now I'm still monitoring the results, but it's got 100% reliability so far."

"Wow. No errors?"

Baldorf's shoulders shook as he laughed. "The system's only checked one so far, man. You. Hey, I found a couple of e-mail messages."

"And?"

Baldorf smiled like an overexcited child. His skin had a healthy glow—to describe him as pleased with himself would have been an understatement. "And I got two messages that were captured after the remote monitoring logs were initialized at 0617 on Wednesday and before session termination this afternoon."

"English, please."

"The key logger was added just a couple of days ago. I picked up two messages before I lost the connection. Somebody pulled the plug on the machine, dude."

"Today? Someone pulled the plug today?"

Baldorf nodded. "Looked like a maintenance guy to me."

"You *saw him*?"

"Dude, don't get excited. The guy's setup included a webcam." Baldorf flushed.

Skip started to ask why that embarrassed Baldorf when the monitor behind him went to a screensaver. The image on the screen was definitely Stella. He felt his own color rising. The negligee Stella wore left nothing to the imagination. Without realizing it, he muttered, "Holy shit."

Baldorf seemed to sense what had happened behind his back. He winced and said, "Went to screensaver, huh?"

Skip nodded. "Goddamn, she's hot."

"You have no idea." Baldorf turned around and jiggled the mouse. The Stella screensaver disappeared and was replaced by the image of a man in overalls followed by a woman who might be his supervisor. She pointed around the room, then directly at the computer.

Baldorf cleared his throat. "This looks a lot like the manager telling the maintenance guy to clear everything out. I captured the e-mails before he took the machine down, though. Look." He brought up details of an e-mail message on his screen. "I'm not sure what this means, but I have the address it went to."

Skip had questions about the video that must have been on Dane's computer, but he forgot them the moment he read the screen.

"Package picked up. Will have payment shortly."

Skip said, "That means they grabbed Roxy. You said you have an address?"

"Yeah, this one was sent to a Gmail account. The user is sp5445."

"So who's this sp5445?"

"That's the thing. I could try to hack Google's servers, but for what? If your guy was using this account to insulate himself, he'd give them fake information."

So far, it didn't sound like Baldorf had much to offer. "What was the other message?"

"It was a reply. It just said to confirm when the transaction was complete."

Skip began to pace. Baldorf had so much computer gear scattered about that there was little room to work off his excess anxiety. He needed to clear his head. "I'd like to send this guy a message, but it's not going to look like it came from that same computer, is it?"

Baldorf said, "Oh, dude, I'm disappointed in you. You underestimate me."

Skip stared at Baldorf, not knowing what to say.

Baldorf's smile grew. "So?"

Skip hadn't planned that far ahead. What should he say? "I—I don't know. Wait! I want to tell him the money is safe and I'll turn over a disk with the access information today at 3:00 p.m. He's to meet me in front of Starbucks at the Carlsbad Outlet Mall."

Baldorf positioned his hands over the keyboard, looked toward the ceiling and let out a cry, "Wahoooo! Field trip!" He began to type furiously.

"It's me. Alone."

Baldorf shook his head. "You owe me, man! This is my payback. Besides, don't you want this transaction on video?"

The mention of video reminded Skip about the webcam photos. "So did Dane's computer have, um, videos?"

When Baldorf ignored the question, Skip had his answer. He chuckled. "Call it a bonus. You deserve it."

In between keystrokes, Baldorf said, "Focus, man, focus."

"If things go bad, you stay out of it."

"Hey, man, I'm half programmer, half chicken. And this chicken don't want nothing to do with getting fried. You're on your own out there. But I'm very inquisitive—from a distance."

"Before we take down the bad guy, there's someone I have to call." Skip pulled out his cell and prayed that the call went the way he wanted it to.

CHAPTER FIFTY-ONE

She said, "That's the most idiotic plan I've ever heard!"

Sonny Panaman's name alone was enough to enrage me. And now, scare me to death.

I thought of our conversations about our parents. About what Stella might have overheard or learned from me in casual conversations. Christ, he probably knew everything about me. Killing him might not be the best option—then I'd have two reasons to run from the law. And the way my luck had been going, I'd probably get caught in the act before I finished the job. Still, it might be the only solution.

Boarding was scheduled to start in fifteen minutes and I still couldn't make up my mind—get on the plane, or not? People milled everywhere in this madhouse terminal. My anger burned. I couldn't stand the thought of sitting still on an airplane for a few hours while Sonny planned his next move.

The phone rang. I stared stupidly at the display. How did Skip get this number? My blood had nearly reached the boiling point when I considered an even stranger option. Had Skip been involved in this too? Had he played me just like the others? That thought sent a pang into my gut. No way. No.

I felt tears welling in my eyes. I didn't want to know the answer to that question. Didn't want to, but couldn't help myself. I punched the answer button and said, "Hello?"

"Thank God I caught you. Where are you?"

"Same place I was last night."

"You *were* there. You have to come back." Skip's voice sounded desperate.

He knew I couldn't do that. It would cost me everything.

"I've got an email address for the guy behind the kidnapping. A friend of mine is going to help me catch him. But if you leave—you'll look guilty."

I bit at my lower lip. "I have to go. I can't stay here."

Determination built in his voice as he spoke. "I know about the money. It can all be reversed. We'll get it back to the people it belongs to. I'll help you fight this."

I dodged a kid running through the terminal. Two seconds later, his father nearly knocked me over. "Sorry!" he called out as he ran after his son.

"Sonny Panaman," I said. "He's the one behind this whole thing."

"Who's he?"

"Someone who said he wanted to be a client, but never came through with the cash. He got Stella to take a job with me so she could be his spy." I stopped and laughed. It was a laugh filled with embarrassment brought on by another of those "aha" moments, but this one was sickening in its perversity.

"What's wrong?"

"I financed Sonny's operation. I paid Stella to spy on me. That sick bastard, I'd love to get him."

"We can. If you leave, you'll lose. If you help me out, we can beat this."

In the background I heard the announcement, boarding had started. "What's your plan? Make it quick, my flight's leaving soon." I walked slowly toward the gate.

"My friend faked an e-mail back to this Sonny Panaman. We're telling him to meet me this afternoon. I'll get the evidence to prove he arranged the kidnapping."

Overhead, I heard, "Now boarding rows 40 and above."

I snorted. "That's the most idiotic plan I've ever heard!"

"We'll work on that. We'll find a way. There is one thing. You'll have to give the money back."

Skip's idea wasn't a plan—it was a capitulation. From my perspective, it was also a time bomb waiting to go off. No, I was in this alone and had no one to trust.

I hoisted my bag on my shoulder and pulled out my ticket. I stood in line with the others. "Good luck. I hope you get him." I hit the disconnect button and shoved the phone back into my purse.

CHAPTER FIFTY-TWO

He said, "He'll suspect something's wrong as soon as he sees you."

When Roxy hung up the phone, Skip's last hopes for saving her disintegrated. He'd been sure he could convince her to return. He slid down into Baldorf's spare chair as he stared, his jaw slack, at his cell phone. "She's going to run. The temptation has gotten to her."

"You look awful, man. You okay?"

Skip shook his head. "She's leaving. Getting on a plane for—hell, I don't know where."

"We could see what planes are going out of LAX this morning."

"No. She doesn't want to be found." He straightened his back and took a deep breath. He felt a building pressure behind his eyes. "I said earlier that I was done chasing her. I am. But I'm going to nail this Sonny Panaman's hide to the wall for causing all this. The way I feel right now, he'll be lucky if I don't kill him on sight."

"You've got it bad, man. This is, like, epic."

"Are you going to video this guy or not?"

"You bet. I'll cut the feed if you do decide to commit a felony, though." Baldorf smiled.

Skip grimaced. "Good, you may need to. How do you want to handle this? Do you have the equipment you need?"

"Leave that to me. I got it covered. Wow, I haven't seen anyone this bad off in, like, forever."

"Pick you up at two." Skip cut off Baldorf and left.

Back at his condo, Skip turned on the TV, but stared past it. He didn't care what he watched, he didn't even see it. After about an hour, he decided to walk the beach. He had two hours before he had to pick up Baldorf and he needed clarity. He left his shoes at the edge of the sand and began to walk along the edge of the shore just out of reach of the waves. He made it to the jetty, turned around and headed home.

He stopped in front of Tower 37 to watch surfers test their skill against the waves, but the bodies bobbing on boards as they waited for waves held no interest for him. Further down, in an area reserved for swimmers, body boarders, and kids, he dodged them as they splashed along the shore. He took his time, hoping that the walk would clear his head, but darkness clung to his thoughts. He wanted revenge on Sonny Panaman for kidnapping Richard Tanner. He wanted revenge for bringing him in contact with Roxy Tanner. Yes, he wanted revenge for ruining his life. He'd been content. He'd had a solid business going. And now? What did he have now?

He turned away from the sea and began the trek across the sand to his condo. He sidestepped a girl learning to catch a Frisbee with another girl that looked like her older sister. Their throws went wide of the mark, their catches fared not much better. Still, they seemed to enjoy their play. He glanced up at his condo and froze.

Someone was on his patio sitting in one of the chairs. It was a woman bundled up under a coat, her face hidden by a floppy hat that she'd pulled down. At her side was a roller bag, its handle still standing upright like a soldier at attention. Skip approached cautiously, not daring to let himself speculate who she might be for fear he'd be disappointed.

As he closed the distance, he noticed strands of hair that reminded him of Roxy. He called out, "Can I help you?"

The woman started as though she'd been asleep. She lifted the hat from her head and blonde hair fell to her shoulders.

Skip thought his heart had stopped. He whispered, "I can't believe you came back."

"I thought I'd help you catch this guy."

What was she really here for? Did she want revenge also? "Sonny Panaman's a son of a bitch."

Roxy snickered. "Your plan stinks."

Skip watched her closely, trying to read her emotions, even her intent. "Unless you've got something better, at 3:00 p.m., I'm meeting Panaman to turn over a CD. I have a friend who's going to video the whole thing. I'll prove that he was behind this and get him arrested."

Roxy's cheeks colored, there was the faintest hint of a smile, and her head tilted to one side. She nodded. "I'd like to be there."

"He knows you. He'll suspect something's wrong as soon as he sees you."

"I can stay out of sight."

"It's too dangerous. Besides, how would you accomplish that?"

She stood and waved her hands in the air in a wide gesture. "Let's see. Maybe I could wear a disguise, hide behind a newspaper with a hole in it. I don't know. Tell me what a spy would do."

"What's this guy look like?"

"Five-ten, one-sixty, dark hair, pockmark left cheek. I could wear a wig. Or a hat." She glanced at the one she held in her hand.

"Even if I said no, you'd show up anyway, wouldn't you?"

She glanced at the condo deck. Her eyes glistened as she took in his gaze. She whispered, "You know me better than I do."

Skip swallowed hard. "I guess you could stay with Baldorf."

"Who's Baldorf? Oh, is that the guy who's got the camera?"

"You hate this Panaman, don't you?"

She shifted her weight from one foot to the other and watched the ocean for a few seconds. "I wouldn't exactly call it hate—that's a bit weak."

"Because he played you?"

"Because he kidnapped my dad. Because he got Stella killed."

"Because he lied to you and stole the money you stole from other people."

She recoiled and closed her eyes. "Am I in or did you just want to condemn me? There's proof of everything in my bag. Stella's hard drive is in there also. So if you want to send me to prison, take it." She shoved the bag in his direction with her foot.

It was all Skip could do to ignore the question.

"You have to do what I say."

"Of course."

Skip knew that agreement was going to last about ten minutes. He'd have to let Baldorf know about the change. All he needed was Roxy barging in during the middle of his meeting with Panaman.

"You're the boss. I'm too tired to plan, but I can follow directions."

"You look it—tired."

Her eyes were puffy and red, her expression dull. "Thanks. Just what a girl likes to hear. 'You look like hell.' I'm working on about three hours of catnaps since yesterday morning."

"You could stay here and rest." Skip regretted saying that the moment the words were out of his mouth. He needed to keep an eye on her now that she was back. She was just one step away from being a fugitive for life.

"No, I want to be there. I want to see him confess."

"Okay, you're in. But I have a couple of phone calls to make to get ready. Why don't you go crash on the couch and I'll call from out here?"

"I couldn't rest."

"You were asleep when I showed up."

"For a few minutes, maybe."

Skip let Roxy into the condo and got her settled on the couch. He went back out to the patio. He sat for a while and watched the ocean. Roxy's return didn't change anything. He was going to follow through on the plan. That meant he had calls to make. He called Baldorf first. "Hey, buddy, are you ready?"

"Almost, I've still got time, right?"

"We'll pick you up in about an hour."

"We?"

"Roxy's back."

"Dude, awesome, thought you sounded better."

"Not so much. Not after everything she's done. I have to turn her in."

Baldorf's tone turned suspicious. "Sounds like the vengeful lover talking. Don't do anything stupid."

"I've been doing stupid things all week. See you in an hour."

He disconnected from Baldorf and dialed the number for Sergeant Grimes. Yes, he might regret this next call for the rest of his life, but it was the only way.

CHAPTER FIFTY-THREE

She said, "You've thought of everything, haven't you?"

Apparently, I fell asleep on Skip's couch almost as soon as my head hit the pillow. I only know this because one minute, he was throwing a blanket over me, the next he was telling me that it was time to get up. My head felt as though someone had taken fluffy cotton and stuffed it into every available crevice in my brain. I'm sure a doctor would tell me all the space up there was filled with stuff that belonged there, but at this particular moment, all that "stuff" felt like it had been replaced by soft balls of white that went squish when I tried to think.

Skip showed me to the bathroom and brought in my bag while I began to freshen up. Twenty minutes later, I'd scrubbed my face, reapplied my makeup, put up my hair, and was ready to go. It wasn't the most meticulous job I'd ever done, but then I wasn't supposed to be recognized either. I found Skip staring out the slider window. He had a faraway look, the kind that people get when they're contemplating some life-changing decision. Did that decision involve me spending time behind bars?

"Hey," I said.

"Hey, yourself."

"You look deep in thought."

He spoke without looking at me. "I dumped the GPS locator service that I added to your phone."

The hairs at the back of my neck stood. Wow, was he crossing the ethics line again? Now that I could put my phone back together, my exit plan had gotten easier, if I even wanted to use it. I cleared my throat. "Thanks, guess that means I can put the SIMs back."

"I already did that, too."

And what else, I thought. I could always ditch the phone. I smiled. "You've thought of everything, haven't you?"

He got a pained look on his face and stared at me. "You ready to go?"

My cheeks felt tight, but I forced a smile. "As ready as I'll ever be. Should we take separate cars?"

"I don't have a car, remember?"

He wasn't going to let me out of his sight. Why hadn't I just gotten on the damned plane?

"I'll drive," he said.

I closed my eyes and bit my upper lip. "Sure. Go ahead."

"We'll pick up Baldorf first. He's in Oceanside, but then we can jump on the 5 from right near his place."

The last thing I wanted to do was talk, but I said, "From where the 76 and the 5 cross?"

"That's the one."

"There's not much traffic getting on there. Not this time of day, anyway."

Our meaningless small talk went on like that for the rest of the trip. When we ran out of directions and traffic to discuss, we hit on the weather. By the time we got to Baldorf's, my insides were shaking. I'd lost it all. For what? Because I'd been stupid enough to believe in Skip for a fleeting moment?

Skip led me to Baldorf's apartment. It was a separate bungalow in the back of the main house. The yard was neatly trimmed, the grass green, and there was a mechanical voice that greeted us at the door.

"Enter."

I shuddered, "Creepy."

Skip opened the door. "Baldorf? You ready?"

A tall, nerdy looking guy with dark hair hoisted a small knapsack onto his back. He wore a black T-shirt, black jeans, black tennis shoes, and a black baseball cap. The tee was emblazoned with yellow script that read, "Baldorf's Revenge."

"You changed shirts," said Skip.

He winked, "Dress up." He must have noticed me eyeing the shirt. "It's my masterpiece." He approached, his hand extended. "You must be Roxy."

"Nice to meet you. The T-shirt is your masterpiece?"

"Nah, the shirt is just for marketing. Baldorf's Revenge is a virtual reality video game. It's virtually ready, too." He smiled at his pun.

I gave him a weak smile back, not much in the mood for jokes. "What's in the pack?"

"You'll have to wait and see." His eyes twinkled, his pride about whatever gadget he had stashed in his bag spilling over.

It was 2:15 p.m. We returned to the car and drove to our destination, Starbucks, at the outlet mall. Skip had told me about the location during our directions conversation earlier. How or where we nailed Sonny Panaman didn't matter to me, I just wanted to see him go down. After that ... whatever.

Baldorf rode in the back seat, Skip drove, and I was a passenger in my own car. Baldorf prattled on about his video invention thing while I pretended to listen. He was your typical boy-genius, able to spend time talking on a level that only other geniuses understood.

At one point, Skip finally took part in the conversation. He glanced at me, "He must like you. He didn't explain any of this to me."

I wondered how well Baldorf could multitask and if he'd be willing to help me since I was making zero headway on an escape plan. Then again, he was a friend of Skip's. Scratch that idea.

Skip said, "Baldorf, should I be wearing a microphone so we get voice also? Or did you have something else in mind?"

Over my shoulder, I could see Baldorf straining against his seat belt. The guy was like a little kid on an outing to the zoo. "We'll do both. I have a wireless microphone that will handle the job, but we'll also have a directional mike going. The wireless will fit under a collar or you can drop it into a shirt pocket."

"And you have the CD?" Skip said.

"Oh, this is so cool. When he opens the CD on anything other than my laptop, if it ever gets to that point, he'll interface with a web site that mimics the bank's site. He could bring a laptop along, plug the CD in and even log in. Of course, once he does that, his laptop will be hosed. The next time he tries to log into the laptop, the machine will log into my server and give me his location by the IP address. Staunchly sneaky, man."

I blurted out, "Staunchly?"

Baldorf nodded. "Staunchly. As in firm, substantial."

I twisted sideways in my seat so I could see his face and countered, "You are totally into this, aren't you?"

Baldorf cocked his head from side to side and rolled his eyes. "Totally."

"Our exit, coming up," Skip said.

For a moment, I'd forgotten what was about to happen. For a moment, I'd gotten caught up in the thrill of catching Sonny Panaman. For a moment, I'd forgotten that I needed my own plan. And I still didn't have it.

CHAPTER FIFTY-FOUR

He said, "I got five million reasons to terminate this deal."

The Cannon Rd. exit took Skip by surprise. He started to give himself a mental admonishment for inattentive driving, but instead, muttered, "Screw it."

At least he'd stayed to the right and hadn't had to cut someone off to make the exit. He let up on the gas and at the top of the ramp, turned left and crossed back over I-5. Roxy and Baldorf said nothing as they neared the outlet mall. By the time he pulled into the parking lot, they were all as quiet as pallbearers. He parked well away from Starbucks just in case Sonny Panaman went trolling for familiar cars.

As they got out, Roxy said, "Can I have my keys back now?"

Skip shook his head. "I'll hang onto them."

He'd expected her to show anger, to threaten him, instead, the color drained from her face and tears welled in her eyes. "At least give me a fighting chance."

Skip stuffed the keys in his pocket. "Baldorf, you ready to go?"

Baldorf glanced at Roxy, then at Skip. His brow furrowed. "You two sure you don't want to talk about something before we do this?"

"No time. Let's get set up," Skip said.

Roxy gestured toward the trunk. "I need a couple of things. That is, if you don't want Sonny to recognize me."

Skip opened the trunk. Silent, Roxy pulled out the floppy hat, a scarf, and a light jacket.

The three began the walk to Starbucks. Outside the store, Skip said, "You two will need to be inside."

Baldorf beamed. "Perfect."

Roxy echoed him, but her voice sounded like that of a prisoner condemned to death. "Perfect."

Baldorf handed Skip a little metal disk about the size of a button. "Toss it in your shirt pocket, this side out."

Skip put the disk in his pocket.

"I'll give you a signal if there's a problem," said Baldorf. "There shouldn't be. I've got that laptop rigged up to act like the bank's system. There's also a CD in case he brings his own computer. I'll give everything to you inside."

Skip watched as Roxy and Baldorf entered the store. He spotted an outdoor table in the shade and leaned the chairs forward so the backs rested against the table. They were twenty minutes early, but he wanted to make sure he had an outside spot. He might as well get a coffee and get Baldorf's laptop and the disk. He also wanted to see how Baldorf was going to video everything.

Inside the store, he spotted Roxy standing at the counter and Baldorf unpacking at a table off to one side near the back of the store. At Baldorf's feet stood a two-foot high robot, which reminded Skip of a suited-up astronaut in miniature. He stared at it for a moment, then walked over to Baldorf. "You brought a toy?"

Baldorf tapped a button on a remote control. The robot craned its stubby neck to look up at Skip.

"Hel-lo, Skip."

"It's a souped-up QRIO," Baldorf said.

"A what?"

"It was an acronym Sony used after they renamed their dream robot. They stopped development, but I picked one up after RoboCup 2004. I've been toying with the little guy, get it? Toying with it?"

Skip glared at Baldorf. He needed surveillance equipment, not a toy—or jokes.

Baldorf ignored Skip as he continued, "He already had visual circuitry. Sony had designed these little guys to be able to walk and talk, they can even dance. I just needed to tap into their code so I could record everything and give him some limited intelligence." Baldorf pointed at a laptop screen before him. "See?"

On the screen, Skip saw his image, which appeared to have been shot from the ground. Again, he heard, "Hel-lo, Skip." That was followed by the conversation he'd had with Baldorf.

Skip took a deep breath. "You're sure this will work?"

Baldorf pressed another key. "Check it out."

The screen image changed to one of the front door, which became larger. Skip whirled and watched the robot walk to the front door and do an about-face. He turned back to the screen and saw himself standing over Baldorf. Skip turned back and saw the robot facing him from just inside the door.

"You've got to be—" Skip stopped midway through his sentence, realizing he was hearing his voice from the speaker of Baldorf's computer.

Baldorf winked and pressed another button. From across the room and from Baldorf's laptop, Skip heard, "Fol-low me, Skip."

"Are we good?" asked Baldorf.

Skip shrugged. "We're good." On the screen, the view shifted and he saw Roxy standing, holding two cups of coffee. He turned to her and said, "What are you laughing at?"

She approached the table, then sat with her back to the window. "I'm just wondering why I had to get the coffee."

Baldorf said, "Here's the extra laptop. Just start it up and use the desktop icon for AWB."

"But you're not really connecting to their bank's web site, right?" Roxy said.

"The machine will look like it's connecting to the bank's server, but it will be connecting to itself. You'll log in using the user name and password on the disk. The balance in the dummy account is approximate. I calculated based on the original amount of the transfer and adjusted for accrued interest using rates I got from the bank's web site. If their posted rates are accurate, this should be good to within a few cents."

Skip snorted. "You—you did all this between last night and now?"

Baldorf nodded. "Most of it was quite simple. And it was a nice little diversion from coding."

Roxy laughed. "What do you have, like a 250 IQ?"

"Oh, no. The highest practical limit is about 201 on the Stanford-Binet scale. I'm only 162, so I plug along."

"I hate to interrupt," said Skip, "but there's a chance he'll come inside. If he does, you need to disappear." He pointed at Roxy.

She jerked her head to one side. "Restroom is right there. I doubt he'll be checking that out." She flashed a smile, "I guarantee he can't outlast me."

Skip realized that he no longer had time to make his purchase, so he headed outside. In the front of the store, he sat at the table he'd staked out. To one side, he saw the robot take up a position next to a planter. The robot waved, then hopped from one foot to the other.

Skip turned away, but couldn't suppress a smile. That Baldorf, he thought, he's just a big kid. The rumble of exhaust caught his attention and Skip's gaze automatically went in the direction of the noise. A fire-engine red sports car with a Maserati emblem on the hood crept through the parking lot. Skip saw the pockmark on the man's left cheek and said, "I think he's here."

The robot raised its right hand and saluted.

The car turned in to the next parking lane and disappeared. A man to Skip's right shifted position. The man wore a leather jacket, a tan sports shirt, and khaki pants. Skip thought he detected the bulge of a gun on his right side. That would be one of the undercover cops, he thought. Where were the others? Was Grimes here also? Had Roxy spotted them? Probably. And she hadn't run. What had he done?

Skip leaned back in his chair and watched the lane where the Maserati had disappeared. Soon, the man who had driven the Maserati appeared. Skip recognized Sonny Panaman from Roxy's description and said, "He's coming. Walking this way." His pulse raced as he watched his mark stroll toward him, briefcase dangling from his right hand. As Sonny crossed the traffic lane, he glanced in both directions, but he also seemed to scan the area, as if looking for a trap.

Sonny stopped about twenty feet away and surveyed the scene. Creases lined the other man's forehead as he nodded to himself. He moved forward.

Skip motioned for Sonny to sit. "I'm doing the exchange." He pointed at the chair opposite his.

"Who are you?"

"The Wizard's delegate."

Sonny seemed to relax a degree at the mention of Sproutman's nickname. "Why'd he send you?"

Skip licked his lips. He checked both directions and motioned with his index finger for Sonny to come closer. "Trust is a funny thing, you have to earn it. And quite frankly, he trusts me more than he trusts you."

"So why should I trust you? I've never seen you before."

Skip stood. "Fine. You don't want the money, no problem. I'm here to fulfill an obligation to a friend. I got five million reasons to terminate this deal. Understand? You want me to go?"

Sonny grabbed Skip by the arm. "Wait!"

Skip glared at Sonny. "Maybe you want me to break your arm?"

Beads of sweat formed on Sonny's forehead. "Sorry. Sorry. It's just—you're not the guy I started dealing with. Eugene, uh, the Wizard, he said that he liked to work alone."

"And you went for that? For a kidnapping?" Skip exploded.

Sonny glanced at Skip as if he expected him to say something else. When Skip remained silent, Sonny said, "He told me he'd need help. I just—"

Skip lowered his voice, "The Wizard's a hands-on manager, friend. He doesn't leave things to chance. And as you probably know, two of the 'team' have met an untimely demise." Skip made quotation marks in the air with his fingers when he said the word "team."

"The news said the girl died. It didn't say anything about a second person."

Skip had already decided that he'd approach this as though the Wizard had killed Dane. If he was wrong, Panaman would bolt. Skip worked his jaw back and forth as if he were contemplating telling a major secret. "The other was the girl's boyfriend." Skip saw the color rise in Sonny's cheeks, his breathing quickened and he shifted position. "Oh, you thought you were her boyfriend. Sorry, pal, but Stella liked sharing. Um, in fact, you may want to get yourself tested, if you know what I mean."

Sonny's anger drained from his face, good old fear replaced it. "Tested?"

"You two did, um—" Skip nodded.

Sonny muttered. "Shit."

Skip smiled. "Whatever. They got drugs to deal with all that these days. Anyway, the boyfriend, or, the other boyfriend, he got a little greedy and tried to rabbit. That's when the Wizard asked me to, um, assist. Made the *LA Times* the other day. He took himself a last walk on the beach." Skip twitched his cheeks for effect. "I got no more time for you. You either want the ransom money or you don't. Decide, now."

In Skip's mind, it wasn't much of a decision. Sonny had gone to the extent to seduce Stella, investigate a business, hire a kidnapper, and show up for his money. Skip had no doubts that Sonny's greed would make him accept the deal.

"I have the money," Sonny said.

Skip stared into Sonny's eyes for a moment. He waited, silently counting to three. "Good. You want to see what you're buying?"

The other man's eyes got wide, a sly smile crept onto his face. Then, a sudden wariness appeared. He sat straighter. "Let me get some coffee first."

"Suit yourself. Order one for me, too."

As Sonny turned away and went into the store, Skip felt helpless. Had Roxy gotten the message? Had they heard? He glanced over at the robot. The robot saluted, then did something that resembled a dance. He seemed to hop from foot to foot and then returned to attention.

A few minutes later, Sonny returned with two cups. He set his briefcase on the ground.

"No. Money first—let me see it," Skip said.

Sonny picked up the briefcase and opened it. Inside were bundles of cash. It was the most cash Skip had ever seen in one place in his life. He fought back a desire to ogle the money. Instead, he nodded. "Good. My turn."

He opened the laptop and waited while it booted up. He clicked the icon labeled "AWB" and waited again. He glanced sideways at Sonny, who sat on the edge of his chair, practically drooling into his coffee. The screen opened Internet Explorer and there was a pause for a few seconds. Skip said, "Slow connection here."

A page that perfectly resembled the AWB home page filled the screen. Skip turned the computer so that it faced Sonny.

Sonny blinked at Skip. "What?"

He handed Sonny the disk. "Put this in the drive. It's got the account number and the login credentials. If you want, you can change the password when you give me the money."

Sonny's fingers quivered as he placed the CD into the drive on the side of the laptop. He mumbled, "This'll show my old man."

"What's that mean?"

"He always said I'd never amount to anything. Well, I'm five million dollars richer. At my age, he was still selling used cars to jerk offs for peanuts. I don't need his rules anymore. The old fart can die any day for all I care."

Skip put both elbows on the table. "You want him to have an accident?"

Sonny waved the suggestion away. "He's got all that covered in the will. Once he's gone, I get shit. I've needed him till now, I don't need him anymore."

Skip pointed to the information from the disk that now appeared on the screen. "You should copy that so you don't make a mistake."

Sonny worked the mouse and copied the account number, then switched windows and pasted the copied text into the account number field. He clicked the login button.

Skip watched as the login field dropped down just as it had on the real site. Damn, Baldorf was good. "Before you go any further, hand me that briefcase."

Sonny reached down and grabbed the case. He handed it across the table to Skip. Then he switched back to the login information from the CD. He copied and pasted the user name, then repeated the process for the password. After that, he clicked the submit button.

They waited in silence while the screen displayed a little "processing" message. After a few seconds, the account information displayed. "Holy shit," said Sonny.

"Yeah, holy shit."

Skip's head snapped to the left. Sonny's did too. There stood Roxy.

CHAPTER FIFTY-FIVE

She said, "You sold me out!"

As Baldorf and I watched Skip in action, I had to admit that I felt a sense of pride in watching how easily he manipulated Sonny. This was my team getting payback; it was our turn to make the bad guys pay. I also felt a sense of professional jealousy.

Skip would have made a helluva con man. His timing was impeccable and the lies flowed like beer at a frat party. I desperately wanted him to succeed, but I didn't want to be shown up at my own game, either.

And it was letting my emotions into the game that made it impossible for me to sit on the sidelines as a spectator. Skip had already gotten enough to put the worm away for a very long time when I realized that seeing him in jail just wouldn't be enough. I owed him something else.

"Be right back," I said to Baldorf.

Baldorf grunted some sort of male acknowledgement, but his focus was on playing with the robot. He'd maneuvered the little guy to within a few feet of Skip's table. That's where I wanted to be. Up close. Within striking distance. I slipped away and strode out the front door. After I nailed Sonny, I'd run. If I could get lost in the mall's crowds, I might have a chance at escape.

I watched over his shoulder as Sonny copied and pasted the fake login codes into the laptop. He was so focused on his newfound wealth that he never even saw me. It was the look he'd had on his face when he told me about the Maserati. This jerk had messed with me one too many times.

Sonny gave Skip a sideways glance. "Holy shit," he said.

I moved to within two feet of Sonny and stood. "Yeah, holy shit."

It was like everything went into slow motion. Sonny freaked when he saw me. As did Skip. The look on Skip's face was priceless. If possible, the look on Sonny's was worth even more. Sonny stumbled to his feet, but as soon as he had his footing, I hit him. It was a sucker punch. It was a bad move on my part because I wasn't thinking about the hit. It was pure revenge and it felt great.

My knuckles landed squarely on Sonny's nose and sent him sprawling. Coffee and blood splattered in all directions as Sonny slammed into the table. He fell sideways and landed on Skip. The two men, the table, chairs, and the laptop all hit the ground in a mad crashing that sent everyone into shock-and-awe mode. Skip and Sonny were entangled like snakes in a basket. How perfect, I thought.

Chaos broke out around me, but I didn't care. I'd nailed that bastard. My hand hurt like hell because I hadn't paid attention to my form, but it still felt great. That's when I saw Skip staring past me.

Had I been paying attention to anything other than enjoying the possibility that I might have broken Sonny's nose, I wouldn't have been surprised when two hands seized my arms and locked them behind me in handcuffs.

Over my shoulder, I heard, "Roxanne Tanner, you're under arrest for—"

I reeled with astonishment as the woman who had cuffed me grabbed my arm. In that second, I realized just what Skip had done. Ahead of me, I saw another man pulling handcuffs from behind his waist as he ran toward Skip. The blood pounded in my head. I wanted to crumble to the ground and cry like a child. He'd turned me in. He really had turned me in. All I could think of was that I hated Skip Cosgrove almost as much as Sonny Panaman.

The female cop led me away from the scene. What had I been charged with? I hadn't heard. Everyone stared at the spectacle I'd created and, for once in my life, I wasn't pleased to be the center of attention. I'd been betrayed by the one man I thought I could almost trust.

I saw Baldorf in the doorway watching the cop haul me away. I glared at Skip and yelled, "Bastard! You bastard! You sold me out!"

The female officer shoved me into the back of a patrol car and slammed the door. I sat, isolated from the scene around me, for the second time this week. This time, I didn't expect my release to come so quickly. The cop with Skip shook his hand and pointed in my di-

232 ~ Terry Ambrose

rection. I could only imagine what he was saying, but I think I knew. No doubt, the cop was thanking him for his hard work in taking me as well as Sonny down in one operation.

I closed my eyes and waited until I heard the front door open and shut. I opened my eyes to find the world a blur. My cheeks were hot with my tears, but there was nothing I could do. I didn't know what hurt more, the fact that I was about to go to jail for years—or that Skip had abandoned me when I needed him most.

CHAPTER FIFTY-SIX

He said, "I had to. It was the only way."

Skip heard Roxy's accusation. At first, he thought she was referring to Sonny, but then realized she was looking straight at him when she said those words. "You sold me out."

Her accusation was like a red-hot poker searing his flesh. He watched the tears flow down her cheeks and felt her anguish. Anger surged through him and, when Sonny tried to move, Skip jabbed him into unconsciousness with his elbow.

He stood, unsteady, then took two steps in the direction of the patrol car where the female officer had placed Roxy. He stopped and leaned against the table, unsure of what to do next, when he felt a hand on his shoulder. To his right, he heard the male undercover officer.

"Are you okay?"

"Hell, no, I'm not okay! Why'd you take her away?"

"You mean, in addition to the assault?"

"What would you do if he kidnapped your father?"

The undercover cop said, "Maybe worse than she did. Look, we're holding her on the assault charge for now. We also believe Miss Tanner may have embezzled the ransom from her clients. If she did that, there will be more charges."

Skip saw Baldorf out of the corner of his eye. He was collecting the robot, which had been kicked to one side in the chaos. Skip felt like the robot, kicked aside by forces he couldn't control. He'd had a deal with the cops—they got the evidence to prosecute Sonny in exchange for dropping the firearms charges against Roxy. He hadn't wanted to disclose the embezzlement, so he hadn't bargained for immunity on

234 ~ Terry Ambrose

that. He stopped himself from speaking, knowing that he needed to be thinking clearly to avoid making things worse for Roxy. A few seconds later, he formulated a question. "What makes you think she embezzled? Who made that leap?"

"Grimes. He asked me to thank you for the tip." The officer reached out and took Skip's hand.

Skip recalled the phone call with Grimes. How Grimes kept asking questions about where Roxy got the money. He suddenly realized what his shaking hands with the officer must look like to Roxy and jerked his hand away. The officer pointed at the patrol car where they held Roxy.

"There's nothing concrete yet, but Grimes expects to get to the bottom of this within a day or two. Good work, Cosgrove, this ought to put you back in good standing with Carlsbad PD."

Skip's knees felt weak. He collapsed into the nearest chair and watched as the undercover officer read Sonny Panaman his rights. He stared, slack-jawed, at Baldorf, who returned his gaze with sympathetic eyes. In the parking lot, an officer got into the patrol car with Roxy and pulled away. In the backseat, Roxy cried. Seeing her like that was more than he could bear and nearly drove him into a blind rage.

Skip ground out the words, "Grimes lied to me."

The officer said, "No. Miss Tanner assaulted the suspect. Your deal with Grimes was to drop previous charges, not to grant her immunity for future criminal acts. And there was no discussion of embezzlement."

Skip felt a massive headache beginning in his temples and working its way to the back of his head. He glanced at Baldorf. "Get me out of here before I do any more damage."

"I don't think we can leave yet," Baldorf said.

"Why's that?"

"They'll want a statement."

"Screw their statement."

Baldorf stepped to one side. "Too late, dude."

Skip glanced up and saw the undercover officer still standing next to him.

"You want a statement, right?"

The man nodded and pulled out a small pad. "Since we didn't have time to wire you, we need to know what happened."

Skip pointed at Baldorf. "Give them the CD."

Baldorf handed the disk to the officer.

"You videoed this?"

Baldorf nodded. "I know, I'll need to be a witness." He handed a card to the officer. "Now, can I get him out of here? I think he's about to get sick."

The officer eyed Skip, then said, "Thanks for setting this up."

It was all Skip could do to not take a swing at the cop. He ground his teeth. "I had to. It was the only way."

The officer nodded. "We can catch up later." He handed Skip a card. "Either Sergeant Grimes or I will be in touch to do the interview. Eventually, the DA will want to talk to you."

Skip heard the words, but he wasn't paying attention. His mind reeled with what to do next. How to get Roxy out of jail. The problem was as old as the law itself. It was one he'd debated in school and fought against his entire life. How did you make the guilty look innocent?

CHAPTER FIFTY-SEVEN

She said, "Just leave me alone!"

It was late afternoon when an officer came to my cell and told me that I could leave. At first, I thought someone in the system had decided to play a cruel joke on me. I was taken to a holding room, where Skip's attorney friend, Wally, waited.

As the officer guided me to a chair, Wally approached. "Are you okay?" he said.

"What are you doing here?"

"I've been retained as your attorney." He nodded at the officer, who left the room.

"I—I can't afford you. Get me a public defender."

"The fee has been taken care of. Right now, the charge is only assault. The police also think that they can put together a case for embezzlement."

I groaned. It was my worst nightmare coming true. "What the hell do you want? Why are you here? Just leave me—"

"These are potentially serious charges, Roxy. You'll need the best defense you can get, so listen up. The police are starting an investigation into your business. They're still putting together evidence, but they expect to have enough for a warrant tomorrow. Your bail's been posted for the assault charge, but the police will be keeping your cell phone and what you had on you as evidence—at least for now. Unfortunately, the embezzlement charges will be much harder to defend."

"Don't worry, Skip will give them everything they need."

"You don't understand."

"Screw it. Do whatever you're going to do. Just leave me alone! I understand exactly what's happened."

"You're also prohibited from going within 100 yards of your business until the police have searched the premises."

I glanced up, "Anything else? Can it get any worse?"

"Obviously, you can't leave town, either."

I glared at him. "That's so cliché."

"We'll work it out." Wally looked at me. "You ready to go?" He took my hand and squeezed it. Still bewildered, I nodded. What the hell, it was better than the cell.

He stood and started for the door. He knocked.

I asked, "Did my Dad hire you?"

"Not here," he said. "Later."

Mom and Dad must have gotten his name from Skip, who probably felt guilty for distancing himself. The cops would probably give *him* a reward for what he'd done. Once I'd been released, we walked out of the jail and to the parking lot, where he opened the door to a black Lexus. I sank down into the seat.

He leaned over me and said, "Seat belt. No need to tempt fate."

I shook my head. Whatever. I took the seat belt from his grasp and secured it. He closed the door. That was the last thing I remember until we got to my condo.

CHAPTER FIFTY-EIGHT

He said, "You'll pay."

Skip parked Wally's motorcycle three blocks from Roxy's office building in a side alley. What he was about to do made no sense—even to him. But if he didn't do it, Roxy would spend years in prison, and that was a thought he couldn't bear.

He wore a black sweatshirt, faded jeans, and a baseball cap with the bill pulled down in front. Over his shoulder, he'd slung a shoulder bag. He gripped the strap tightly and kept his head down while he walked along the streets and avoided all eye contact. In the bag, he also had a ski mask that he could use during what would be an all-too-obvious escape.

It was 4:20 p.m. and passersby were busy heading home or thinking about the weekend. Not so for Skip. He had work to do. He had two very different roles to play, but both were necessary to free Roxy. He walked through the front door of the office building and went up the stairs. He pulled on a pair of latex gloves as he climbed and was thankful that he encountered no one. In the hallway outside Roxy's office, he checked both directions. There were still a couple of businesses open. He hoped they would be here until he was done. That had to be less than twenty minutes.

The door to Tanner Investments was locked, as Skip had expected. He extracted his picks from his pocket and inserted two long, thin strips of metal into the lock. He heard voices, then footsteps coming up the stairs. He spotted an emergency exit sign at the end of the hallway and walked quickly to the door. He opened it, praying that it wasn't alarmed. When no bells rang, he let out a sigh of relief and hid in the emergency stairwell, hoping against the odds that the voices weren't those of cops coming to search Roxy's office.

The voices, those of two men, became clearer. The first said, "I'm telling you, the Padres are going to kick butt this season."

"You are so wrong. They've lost all their drive. This is going to be their worst season ever."

"Okay, wise guy, I've got twenty that says ..."

The voices went silent as a door shut. Skip checked the hallway again. No traffic. He went back to Roxy's office and began working the lock again. He'd lost another minute and a half thanks to those two. He felt the tumblers click into place and twisted the knob. He slipped into Tanner Investments and locked the door behind him.

A quick look around told Skip that she'd done what he feared she might. She'd tried to clean up after herself. He checked his watch, 4:28. He had twelve minutes left. Skip pulled Stella's hard drive from his bag along with a screwdriver and the instructions that Baldorf had given him. Baldorf had explained how the cops wouldn't spend their budget on a forensic expert if the drive appeared to be in normal condition. All Skip had to do was restore the drive to an unaltered appearance and Roxy's tampering would go unnoticed.

Baldorf had worked his magic on the drive and added back Stella's address book, which he'd moved over from her phone. They'd even restored marketing-material files from Roxy's laptop. If Baldorf was correct, the computer wouldn't be analyzed by a forensic expert and they'd be fine. Baldorf had even taken apart an old machine of his and shown Skip how to remove and replace the hard drive—an operation that he completed in three minutes—it took Skip twice that long.

Six minutes to go. Skip put the computer back where it belonged, remembering what Baldorf had told him. Most people dust around their computers, make sure you get it positioned precisely.

Four minutes. He pulled the charger for Stella's phone and stuffed it into his shoulder bag. He pulled a can of spray paint from the bag and began spraying the walls of Roxy's office.

"Bitch."

"You'll pay."

"Rot in hell."

He stood back and admired his handiwork. Perfect revenge, he thought.

He checked his watch. Shit, he was out of time and he still had more to do.

He stuffed the baseball cap into the bag and pulled out the ski mask, which he put on, but left rolled up for the moment. Skip slung the bag over his shoulder and did a final check. He'd left nothing behind. He went to Roxy's file cabinet and grabbed the back. He pulled as hard as he could until it tumbled forward and crashed on the floor. He flipped Roxy's chair over, then the two opposite her desk. He pulled an extendable wand from the bag and smashed the desk lamp and the picture of her parents on the credenza. He swept everything from the credenza onto the floor and pulled down the mask.

He ran to the front door and stepped into the hallway. He locked the door, closed it behind him, then kicked with all his might. The door lock broke free and the door flew inward. He ran down the stairs and out the front door as shouts filled the hallway behind him.

"Call the police!"

Another voice, "Dan, call the cops!"

He hesitated at the base of the stairs. A third voice, this time a woman's, cut through the chaos. "There he goes!"

He hopped onto a bicycle that leaned against the building next to the front door and sped away. Behind him, he heard the third voice. It was the woman shouting. He looked over his shoulder as he rounded a corner and saw three people pointing in his direction. One had a cell phone to his ear. With any luck, they were calling the cops. With any luck, in all the chaos they'd never even realize that the damage had been done *before* the door had been kicked in.

Skip peddled as fast as he could to where he'd parked the motorcycle. When he came to a stop, he pulled the mask off and stuffed it into the bag, then tossed in his black sweatshirt. He walked the bicycle across a short span of sidewalk to a bench.

The young man on the bench said, "Everything go okay?"

"Just about perfect."

In the distance, Skip heard sirens approaching.

"Think she'll come through for you?"

Skip hadn't allowed himself to have any doubts to this point, but now, fear that Roxy might not do the right thing scared him to death. With what he'd just done, he might have thrown away his life as well as hers.

"It's all up to her. I don't know what she'll do."

"You've got one thing going for you," said the young man.

"What's that?"

"People make lousy witnesses."

The sirens wailed a couple of blocks away. They stopped in the vicinity of Roxy' office.

The young man smiled at Skip. "Dude, you are my hero. You better move. You got TV cameras waiting."

Skip smiled. "Thanks, Baldorf. I don't know how I'll ever repay you."

"You already did, man, you gave me a new idea for Baldorf's Revenge."

CHAPTER FIFTY-NINE

She said, "Who would do this?"

All I wanted to do was go back to sleep, but Wally insisted on ac-
companying me to my condo. It was almost five when we walked
through the door and I noticed the message light blinking.

He pointed at the machine. "You'd better check messages."

"Whatever." In this case, it was true. I'd do whatever I needed to
do in order to get rid of this guy. He was my attorney—one I didn't
even want—not my dad. That's why I was reluctant to check messages—I wasn't sure I could ever face my mom or dad again.

I listened to the first message, "Roxy, this is Mom. Your dad and I
want to talk to you. Please, we don't care what you've done. Call us.
Please."

I grimaced. "She sounds worried."

Wally nodded. The second message started.

"Miss Tanner? Officer Wilcox with the Carlsbad Police Department. There's been a break-in at your office and we need you to come
down here right away."

The message had been left just ten minutes ago. I stared at Wally,
"A break-in? Now what?"

His phone rang. "Wally Price."

He tapped his foot while he listened for a few seconds. "I agree.
We'll be there in a few minutes." He looked at me. "Wilcox called me.
He must have heard that you might still be with me. Let's go."

"To the office? I thought I was supposed to stay away from there?"

"They'll make an exception in this case."

Fifteen minutes later, Wally parked the black Lexus on the street
in front of my office building. The street traffic was heavy, but park-

ing easily available. In another hour, that would change as the restaurant crowd started to spill over to a larger area. For now, there were open spaces.

Two police cars were parked in front of the building. People walking by gawked in typical peeper-mode. As Wally took my arm and guided me toward the steps, I said, "I never want to see another cop in my life."

Under his breath he muttered, "It's just beginning."

We climbed the stairs in silence. At the top of the stairwell, I stopped and stared. Outside my door, which was now missing, two officers were talking to the other tenants. One of the women with whom I occasionally had coffee saw me and rushed in my direction.

"Roxy! This is awful. I'm so sorry."

One of the officers intervened. "Ma'am. Please."

She glared at him, but his resolve didn't wilt. "Fine," she said and walked back to her previous location.

"Miss Tanner?"

"What happened? Uh, yes, I'm Roxy Tanner."

"A short while ago a man dressed in black and wearing a ski mask broke into your place. We suspect it may have something to do with the arrest of Mr. Panaman earlier today."

I felt Wally's hand on my arm, reassuring me. I shook it away. "I'm okay." But my bravado was gone, I was dead tired and now someone had broken into my office? "Why would you say it's got anything to do with Sonny Panaman?"

The officer stepped to one side and gestured toward the open door. "You should take a look."

I walked through the door, my legs stiff as tree limbs. There was nothing wrong with Stella's area. It looked perfectly normal. "There's nothing wrong," I said.

"Your office, please."

I glanced through the door to my office and saw red lettering on the wall. I rushed forward and nearly knocked over a man coming out the opposite direction.

He apologized. "Sorry, Miss. I didn't see you."

I barely heard him through the roar in my head. The walls had been spray-painted, the filing cabinet turned over, and chairs upended. My credenza contents lay in a pile on the floor. I ran to it and found the photo of Mom and Dad.

As I reached for it, a woman stopped me. "Sorry, not yet. We haven't dusted those for prints."

I spotted Wally speaking with a uniformed officer across the room. Behind them, I saw the spray painted message, "Bitch."

The room began to blur. Tears ran hot down my cheeks. A voice intruded on my space. "Miss Tanner? I'm Sergeant Grimes. Do you have any idea who might want to do this?"

This had been my second home. Even though I'd eventually planned to abandon it, I'd been proud of this office and everything I'd picked out for it. Just because everything was rented, didn't mean I hadn't grown attached. The thought of someone violating it like this appalled me. I shook my head and wiped at my cheek.

"The messages on the walls, they make it look like revenge," he said.

I put a hand to my throat and croaked, "I can't read—too blurry."

He handed me a tissue, which I pressed against my cheek. "Of course," he said.

"Who would do this?"

Grimes looked at Wally. "You didn't tell her?"

"I told her there had been a break-in. Give her a break, Grimes, she's upset. You know how hard it is to focus under circumstances like this."

"What's that mean?" I snapped.

Grimes ignored me as he spoke to Wally. "I'm satisfied."

"It means we're done here." Wally took my arm and guided me out the door.

CHAPTER SIXTY

He said, "We just want to see justice prevail."

Skip took Grand Avenue to South Coast Highway and then turned left. He drove until he was in Oceanside and reached Cassidy St. He took a left and headed for the beach. When he got to Pacific, he took a right. When he reached Oceanside Blvd., he found what he was looking for, a trash can. He dropped the can of spray paint and the gloves into the trash and headed home.

An hour later, he'd been home, showered, and prepared himself mentally for the next task. The first news crew showed up right on time. After a brief round of introductions, the interview began.

The on-scene reporter was Emily Lim, a short, Eurasian woman with big, brown eyes and a sharp tongue. Her speech was short and clipped and put Skip on edge, but he needed her to broadcast this story. He knew that they were working each other equally—she wanted a story, he wanted publicity.

Skip asked, "When will this air?"

"You're timing was perfect, station manager wants to broadcast ASAP. Eddie will upload the interview as soon as we're done. Okay, let's go." Eddie turned on a spotlight and Emily smiled. "This is Emily Lim. I'm here with Skip Cosgrove, a local criminologist/ consultant who has news about the capture of a kidnapper earlier this afternoon in Carlsbad. Tell me what happened, Skip."

Skip put on his most professional tone. Believability and sympathy were the reactions he needed. "Earlier this week, Richard Tanner was kidnapped and held for five million dollars ransom."

"Five million dollars? Is Mr. Tanner rich?"

"No. Mr. Tanner is retired from the title business and he's just a normal guy who doesn't have a lot of money. The kidnappers went after Mr. Tanner because his daughter, Roxy Tanner, recently started up a venture capital firm."

"So why didn't we get more on this story prior to today?"

"We didn't want the kidnappers' demands broadcast while Mr. Tanner was held hostage by them. Today, the man we believe masterminded the kidnapping was arrested."

"So there's a happy ending to the story?"

"Almost. The reason I contacted you is that now the Carlsbad Police are alleging that Miss Tanner embezzled the ransom money from her company. I want to set the record straight. I loaned Miss Tanner that money. She did not embezzle it."

"That's quite a loan! Why would you loan a stranger that much money? And where did you get that much?"

"My reasons as to why I loaned the money are private. The how is from my trust fund. If we hadn't gotten the money back, I'd be broke. The thing is, I had faith we'd prevail."

"You were involved in the high-profile child-runaway case of Paul Nordoff earlier this week, weren't you?"

"I can't comment on that case other than to say that it turned out well."

"I'd say that you're on quite a roll, Skip."

Skip did his best to look embarrassed, which wasn't hard given what he'd just done.

As Emily and her cameraman were packing up their gear and heading out, she said, "You're going to a lot of trouble to make this case high profile. What's in it for you?"

"I'm not expecting to get anything from this, Emily. We just want to see justice prevail. And if that means raising the profile of the case, so be it."

He closed the door behind the news team as they left and glanced at the clock. Hell, he only had thirty minutes before the next one would be here.

CHAPTER SIXTY-ONE

She said, "What am I going to do now?"

I expected Wally to dump me at my condo. Instead, he took me to Keller's for dinner. The waitress seated us, handed us a couple of menus, then left us to read and decide on what we wanted.

Given that I might never see this place again, I had a desire for just one thing. "I already know what I want—a cheeseburger with fries."

Wally raised an eyebrow. "They've got salmon, chicken. Don't worry about the cost, this one's on me."

"Since when do attorneys buy their broke clients dinner?" Mom and Dad couldn't afford this guy. They certainly couldn't afford his markup for dinner.

Wally ignored the question. "I'm about to give you the best advice you'll ever get—and I won't charge you a cent for it."

I planted my elbows on the table. "Free advice from an attorney? Oh, please."

"Go to the bar, have the bartender turn up the sound, shut up, and listen. Now."

His tone was so insistent that I turned to see what was so important on the TV. It was Skip, being interviewed *again*. I glanced at Wally. He shooed me away. I rushed to the bar and said, "Tommy, turn that up for me? Okay?"

He nodded and turned up the sound. I only caught what must have been the last of the interview, but sat stunned. Tommy handed me a glass of Chardonnay. "Looks like you need this."

I stared, dumbfounded, at the glass.

Tommy grinned at me, "I'd say he's a keeper."

"He doesn't even like me."

"He loaned you five mil and he doesn't like you? Hot Rox, you're out of your freaking mind."

I shot a glance at Wally over my shoulder. Shut up, he'd said. He knew what was going on. I picked up my glass. "Thanks for the wine, Tommy. Put it on our dinner tab, would you?"

Back at the table, Wally must have seen the stunned look on my face. "You've had a helluva day. Almost no sleep. Airports. Punching out bad guys. In jail, out of jail. Break-ins, breakouts. Man, if I had a day like that, I'd be a basket case. I ordered your burger and fries, by the way."

"What's going on, Wally?"

"I just told you. It's been a big day."

"What was Skip doing on the news? Why'd he say he loaned me that money?"

"Smart girl like you, I'm surprised you need someone to spell it out."

I waited while the waitress refilled his water glass. "Bring me a Guinness, would you? I can't let her drink alone."

The waitress smiled and waltzed away.

I stared into my wine glass, trying to make sense of what I'd just heard. "I want to know what's going on."

Wally sat back as the waitress set down his beer. He took a sip and leaned forward. "I'm sure you're familiar with the adage, 'the best defense is a good offense.'"

I held his gaze. "So? You're going to tell me I need to go on the offense?"

"Not at all. What you need to do is to be quiet and let events unfold. My guess is that by Monday, the police will have forgotten all about you and your case will be closed. Except for that little assault thing, of course. That one might cost you—probably probation."

Wally's phone rang. He glanced at the display, smiled, and answered. "Wally Price." A few seconds later, "Oh, Sergeant Grimes. Yeah, I just saw that myself. Can you believe it? I didn't think he wanted anyone to know he had that much money."

He took a sip of his beer.

"You know, I didn't handle the estate of his uncle, but from what I understand, it was very large. I mean, very large." He seemed to listen for a few seconds, then spoke again. "Okay, I'll let you know if I hear anything."

Our food arrived and I stared at my burger, not sure if I was hungry or not. I didn't like having people manipulate my life. Skip had no money, but had just told the world he had millions. Had he lied about his background, too? He could pick locks. He had a condo on the beach. Nothing added up, including my feelings for the man who'd betrayed me. "Why's he doing this?"

Wally chuckled as he picked up his burger. "Isn't that just the five-million-dollar question? Eat your food before it gets cold. Oh, and by the way, you can see the next interview on the ten o'clock news. KFMB, if I'm not mistaken."

I sat up straight in my chair. It was my turn to be stern. "What else did he do?"

"He kind of put together a game plan. He did say he had to make a stop downtown. I'm not sure what that was all about."

"*He's* the one who trashed my office?"

"I'm an officer of the court. I could never condone someone breaking in, let alone vandalizing a place like that. Besides, the police are theorizing that this Sonny Panaman had some friends pay you a visit. They said something about him using a Gmail account for all this. I hear they're going to check that out. Anyway, they broke in. They only ransacked *your* office. That sure smacks of revenge to me."

"I need to see him."

Wally stuffed a French fry into his mouth and moaned. "These are *so* good."

"I need to see him. Now!"

"That can't happen. As your attorney, I'm advising you to keep your distance from Skip Cosgrove for a while. We wouldn't want to give any perception of impropriety."

"What am I going to do now?"

"Like I said, sit back and wait. Keep quiet and let events unfold. Oh, and go online tonight. There's a little money issue you need to deal with."

"What if I don't?"

Wally's eyebrows went up. He licked his lips and held my gaze. "I'm a lawyer, my concern is the law. But personal favors? Those are gold, lady. I'm going to give you one other piece of free advice. When someone throws you a lifeline, don't drag them down with you. But if you want to throw everything away, that's your choice."

I nibbled on a fry and thought about Wally's message. Nobody, not even my mom and dad, had ever put their life on the line to save me. Skip had done that. Twice. "It's really over?"

"Most of it. Except for that assault thing."

I swallowed hard, the pressure of tears blurring my vision. "I thought he didn't like me."

Wally smiled. "Lady, I'd think about that one. If this guy *doesn't* like you, just imagine what he'd do if he *did*."

I drained the last of my wine and motioned to the waitress. I needed another. When this was all over, Skip Cosgrove was in for a helluva payback.

About the Author

Terry Ambrose has written and enjoyed writing since he created his first short story as a child, which was inspired by a painting of three mountains titled "The Three Sisters." He has written an Examiner.com "Fiction in San Diego" column since June 2010 and interviewed bestselling authors such as Sue Grafton, T. Jefferson Parker, and Jan Burke for his "National Crime Fiction" column.

A writer at heart, Terry started out skip tracing and repossessing cars. Those early days of dealing with people who couldn't, or wouldn't, pay their bills provided him with insight into what makes people tick and created fertile ground for his own mystery/suspense writing.

Terry is a member of Arizona Mystery Writers, Sisters in Crime, and Publishers and Writers San Diego.